# PRIDE

A SINFUL EMPIRE DUET
BOOK 1

EVA CHARLES

QUARRY ROAD PUBLISHING

Murphy Rae, Cover Design

Dawn Alexander, Evident Ink, Content Editor

James Gallagher, Castle Walls Editing, Copy and Line Editor

Faith Williams, The Atwater Group, Proofreader

Virginia Tesi Carey, Proofreader

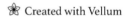 Created with Vellum

*To the girls who talked too much in class and the women who refuse to sit quietly.*

The moment we begin to fear the opinions of others, hesitate to tell the truth that is in us, and are silent when we should speak, the divine floods of light and life no longer flow into our souls.

— ELIZABETH CADY STANTON

# AUTHOR'S NOTE

Dear Readers,

Welcome back to Porto, and thank you for taking this twisted journey with me!

In Pride, Rafael is all grown up, and on the threshold of taking over the entire Huntsman empire. For those who are wondering, he is not Antonio, rather, he's the man Antonio raised him to be.

Rafael and Lexie's chemistry leaps off the page as they blaze a modern trail through a dangerous universe with old-world customs. Their journey is fraught with challenges and peril—and not just from outside forces. The demons inside them, and even their better angels, don't play nicely. I love these two together, and I hope you do too!

The story takes place approximately eight months after Valentina's wedding (Envy Epilogue II). While it's not *absolutely* necessary to read Greed, Lust, and Envy before Pride, your enjoyment and knowledge of the setting and characters will be greatly enhanced if you read the trilogy first.

For those of you who have read the trilogy, you'll be reacquainted with some familiar characters. Along with Will,

Valentina, Cristiano, Lucas, and Lexie, of course, you'll be treated to an older, perhaps more mellow Antonio, much like he was in the second Envy Epilogue. You will also meet some new characters you'll love, and a few you won't like at all. (We'll see Daniela in Wrath).

Please know that the Pride prologue chronicles the events of the day Rafael's mother disappeared. He was eight. It's painful to read, and I caution anyone who has experienced childhood trauma to proceed cautiously.

If you're still with me, pour yourself a cold drink, grab a fan, and settle in while I take you on a steamy, heart-stopping journey, with twists and turns around every dangerous bend!

xoxo

Eva

# PROLOGUE

## RAFAEL

I RACE toward the empty net, with the soccer ball well under control. I'm seconds from getting my boys a win when my brother, Tomas, shouts from across the field. "He wants to see you in his office."

I skid to a stop, tearing up the grass before my butt hits the ground.

*He* is my father, who never wants to see me in the middle of the day unless I'm in trouble. *Big trouble.* The kind of trouble that calls for the strap. Tomas knows it, too. That's why he gives me a cruel little smirk when I catch his eye.

The soccer ball rests near my feet, but I don't move to secure it. No one's going to steal the ball. The game's over.

My friends are frozen like statues on the field, gawking at me. They know the deal, and tomorrow they'll see the evidence.

*Papai* will be careful to hide most of the marks, but he always leaves one nasty welt for *Mamā* to see every time she looks at me. My broken skin makes her so sad she cries. *He loves to make her cry.*

"Get out of here, or I'll sic the dogs on you," Tomas sneers at my friends.

The boys take off running. Except Zé. He scowls at my brother, then jogs over to where I'm sprawled on the field. Most of my friends are eight, and I'm eight, too, but Zé is already nine. He's tall for his age and smart, and he's not afraid of anything. Not even of Tomas, who's twenty and lifts weights every morning before breakfast.

"We can make a run for it," Zé whispers. "Tomas is too lazy to chase us. You can hide in the fort behind my house until your father stops being mad."

I pull my knees up and rest my cheek against the hard ridges. Zé's right about Tomas. He won't bother to chase us. But it won't end there, because there's no plan that can help me if I did something to make *Papai* mad.

Zé bumps my cleats with his to let me know he means business. "I'll bring you a sleeping bag and some food. My mother is making *cozido* tonight. You like that, right?"

I glance up at my friend. My stomach hurts thinking about the guards dragging me out of the fort while Zé's family watches. "His men will find me. It'll just make things worse."

He nods, and his forehead gets crinkly, like he's trying to come up with another plan. "Do you want me to go with you to see him?"

I pull up a handful of grass and toss it over my shoulder. "Nah. It'll be okay."

I sound brave. My mother calls it putting on a good face, but my friend knows it won't be okay.

"You should go," I tell him, getting up. "I don't think Tomas is joking about sending the dogs."

There's only one person in the family meaner than my

brother, and that's my father. Neither of them would hesitate to send the dogs after a kid.

"Tomas is a coward," Zé mumbles. He looks me in the eye, then nudges me gently with his shoulder as he walks away. It's how boys show support and respect for their friends.

"You coming, asshole?" my brother jeers.

I keep an eye on Tomas while I cross the field. He's not smiling—not exactly. But his dark-brown eyes are glittery, and his chest is puffed out, like he beat me in a race and won first prize.

*Maybe my father doesn't want to see me.* Maybe Tomas lied to scare me, or maybe he wanted to ruin my chance to win the game. He would do something like that.

"Why does *Papai* want to see me?"

"Why do you think, you dumb piece of shit? Instead of running around with those idiots, you should be practicing your reading. You deserve what you get."

*He's not lying about my father.* My skin feels sweaty and hot, like I'm going to throw up.

"I practice reading every night before bed. You know I do." *But it doesn't matter how much I practice. I still suck at it.*

Tomas scoffs.

*Mamã* sits with me for an hour every night. We take turns reading, and she gives me a piece of chocolate, or some other treat, when we're finished. Last night she gave me a miniature racing car with orange and yellow flames painted on the sides. It's really cool.

"I'm getting better. *Mamã* said so." *Maybe she was just being nice.*

It doesn't matter how bad I read. My mother always tells me she's so proud of how hard I work. She's patient. Not just with me, but with Tomas too. She's never mean. Not even when we make a mess in the family room, or spill grape juice on her favorite rug. She doesn't yell, and she never hits us. Not even with her hand.

"Then why did the teacher call to say you still can't read?" Tomas taunts. "You're an embarrassment to the family."

The butterflies in my stomach are twirling faster and faster. It's making me dizzy.

*Papai* will be so mad the teacher called. I shamed our family. I'm going to get it, unless Tomas helps me. I glance at my big brother. He doesn't care what happens to me. He's not going to help me. *But I have to try.*

"Tell him you couldn't find me," I beg. "He's going to give me a beating, Tomas. He'll listen to you."

"Probably." He shrugs. "But I'm not using my pull with him to save your sorry ass."

I know it's a big sin to hate anyone, especially your brother. But sometimes I hate Tomas. Even when I don't hate him, I don't like him. He doesn't like me either.

On the way to the office, I look for my mother, but she must be upstairs. I'm kind of happy she's not here. She would be so worried—and sad. Besides, there's nothing she can do to protect me. My father is too tough. *Mamã's* afraid of him. I can tell. She never relaxes when he's around.

When we get to *Papai's* office, the leather strap is laid out on the desk, waiting for me. My heart thumps so hard, it feels like it's going to jump out of my chest and onto *Papai's* nice rug.

The strap has a handle with three long leather legs that whoosh when they fly through the air. It's the devil. *Thump, thump, thump.*

"*Bom dia, Papai,*" I say respectfully. *Can he hear my heart pounding? Do I smell like fear?* He would hate that.

"What did I tell you would happen the next time your teacher called? You shamed our family, again. What do you have to say for yourself?"

My father is big, so much bigger than me, and his face is scrunched up and red, and his voice is angry. *Really angry.*

I don't say anything, not because I'm being cheeky, but because I'm too afraid to talk. I might start to cry if I do. *Everyone hates a crybaby.*

Tomas stands with Costa, my father's second-in-command, near the closed door. My brother gives me a small, evil smile when *Papai* grabs the strap and comes around the desk.

I shake, inside and out, when he stops near me.

"You're the worst thing that's ever happened to this family," he barks. "A huge disappointment. Nothing but a fuckup." My father flicks his wrist, and I cover my face and head with my arms.

I'm wearing thin shorts, and the leather stings my thighs so bad. I want to scream, but I don't because he'll call me a coward and hit me harder.

I close my eyes, as the whoosh happens again, and again. The sounds come so quickly I don't have time to brace myself. After a few more lashes, I lose my balance and fall to the floor.

*"Maldito,"* my father spits in a disgusted voice, cursing me while he yanks me up by the arm to reach better.

I try to think about happy things, like my teacher taught us when we were sad that Luis's dog died. I think about the beach at Nazaré. I pretend I'm jumping over the big waves with my friends. If I concentrate really hard, I can smell the salt water.

After a little while, I'm hot and sleepy, and I can't hear my father's voice, or even feel the strap so much. I still hear the whoosh, but it's soft and far away.

When *Papai*'s done, he tosses the leather strap on his desk and shoves me at Costa. "Take the little bastard to the attic."

*No! No! Not the attic.* But I don't beg, because I need to show I'm brave. My father hates cowards.

Costa is big, like my father, and mean, too, and he doesn't

talk, even when he pulls me up the stairs and shoves me into the dark attic.

My stomach does a big somersault when the door slams. The lock clicks before my eyes adjust to the dark.

The attic is scary. *So scary.* It's hard to be brave when I'm up here. Even if I concentrate hard, I can never smell the beach.

Tomas told me that bats and ghosts live in the eaves. I've never seen the bats, but I once saw a ghost. *Mamā* said it was only a shadow. But I don't think so.

*Mamā* cries when my father's guards bring me to the attic. My chest hurts when I think about her crying—for me. *It's not right.* Women aren't supposed to protect men. Men are supposed to protect women. *My cousin Antonio told me.*

Soon I'll be a man, and I'll be able to protect myself. I'll protect *Mamā*, too. *Then she won't have to worry.*

My father's men won't let my mother come up to the attic to check on me, so she sends Ruiz, her personal guard. He's a big boss, so the other guards have to let him upstairs. He sneaks me food and a chamber pot. It's embarrassing to pee in a pot, but Ruiz shines a flashlight, and he doesn't watch as I go into the corner to do my business.

"There's no shame in it, Rafael," he says in a kind voice. "Men do what they have to do to survive."

I'm not really a man—not yet. But *Mamā* says it's his way of showing me respect.

Ruiz always helps me the best he can. He does it for my mother. He's loyal to her. But Ruiz has to be careful. He can't go against my father. *Papai* would kill him. *Then who will protect* Mamā *until I grow up?*

Even if my mother finds out I'm in the attic, Ruiz can't help me today. His daughter is getting married, and he's not at work. *No one's coming to help me today.*

My chest shakes and tears fall. *Don't be a baby.* I can't stop them.

I sniff and sit on the floor, in the middle of the room, away from the shadows and the eaves. When I feel brave, I look into every corner for trouble. There's nothing, but it's dark and ghosts are sneaky.

My skin feels like it's on fire. I'm tired. *So tired.* Too tired to stay awake so the ghosts and the bats can't get me.

Monsters are chasing me through the vineyards when a guard wakes me.

I open my eyes, and he looks like a monster. A little pee trickles out.

"Go into the bathroom and wash your face," the guard says when we get downstairs. "And put on some long pants. Your father has company."

*Company?* That makes me feel better. He won't hit me in front of guests—or call me bad names. He likes to pretend he's a nice *papai* when people are visiting.

After I change into clothes to greet guests, the guard walks me to the parlor. The pants aren't soft like the shorts, and every time I move, they rub against my sore skin, but I don't complain to the soldier. That's what a baby would do.

It's dark out, and I don't see my mother anywhere. *Maybe she's visiting Tia Lydia, her sister, or maybe she's with the company.* Usually she waits for me near the attic stairs and brings supper to my room. I'm always starving when I leave the attic. I'm hungry today, too, but I can't keep *Papai* waiting.

When we get to the parlor, my father is with some of his friends, and the police captain. He sends them away the minute I walk into the room. I want to beg them to stay so *Papai* doesn't hit me again, but I don't want to be a coward.

The men seem sad as they pass by me. *Maybe they know I'm going to get another beating. No,* Papai *would never let that slip, not even to his friends. Maybe the men came to tell him I did something bad. Maybe that's why the policeman is here. Maybe Senhora Soares told the police we stole apples from her tree. We were hungry, but we only took one each.*

The police captain puts his big hand on my shoulder as he leaves. *He doesn't look mad.* "It's going to be okay, Rafael. May God bless you."

*I must be in a lot of trouble.*

*Papai* gives me a bad look, but I don't see the strap anywhere.

"Your mother is gone," he says, like he ate rotten soup. "The whore left us and ran off with a man. Do you know why that is, Rafael?"

There's so much noise in my head that I can't hear anything.

*No! My mother would never run away without me.*

Everything is moving slow, even sounds, like when we change the speed on a video game.

"Do you know why the whore left, Rafael?" he asks, louder this time. *Meaner.*

I shake my head.

"Because you are a stupid boy. That *puta* was so embarrassed to have a son who can't read, a son that is such a disappointment, that she ran away."

My stomach hurts, real bad, and not because it's hungry. I'm scared. And mad. Ashamed. It feels like my head is going to pop off. I'm going to cry. *I can't, because he'll punish me.* But it's no use. No matter how hard I concentrate, I can't stop the tears.

"Get out of my sight, you sniveling fool," *Papai* growls.

I leave the parlor quickly, before he changes his mind, and run through the house, looking everywhere for *Mamã.*

When I find her, I'm going to promise her that I'll try harder. That I won't play after school. I'll just practice my reading until I'm the best reader in the whole class. Maybe even the whole school.

I tear through every room. I look in every closet. I search under every bed. I even peek in the bathtubs.

My heart is banging like crazy, again. I hope I don't have a heart attack, like our painter did, before I find her.

She's not in the house, but her suitcases are in the upstairs storage closet. She didn't take her clothes, or the heart-shaped picture of Tomas and me on her nightstand. She always takes it when she goes on vacation so that she doesn't miss us too much.

I ask the upstairs maids, and everyone else I see, but it's late, and not many people are around. No one has seen *Mamá* since this morning.

*Where did she go?*

I get the flashlight from the kitchen pantry and go out to the stable. Her horse is going to foal soon, and *Mamá* always checks on her before she goes to bed.

She's not in the stable. Or the barn.

My chest hurts more than the time Pedro kicked the ball and I didn't jump out of the way fast enough. *I am stupid.*

I jog through her garden, calling her name, until the guards send me inside. They're not as mean as usual, but I know they'll drag me to *Papai* if I don't obey. It doesn't matter, anyway. I've looked everywhere *Mamá* would be. She isn't out here.

After I go inside, I search the whole house again, everywhere except *Papai's* office. No one's allowed in there, not even *Mamá*.

This time I don't race around. I go from room to room, looking carefully for clues, but I don't find any.

When I'm too tired to search anymore, I go back to her sewing room and curl up behind the love seat, with the blanket my grandmother crocheted for *Mamá* when she was a little girl. *It smells like her.*

When I start to miss her too much, I cover my head with the blanket so no one can hear me cry.

*Please come back,* Mamá. *I love you.*

But she doesn't come back. Not that night, or the next. Not even at Christmas.

We're not allowed to talk about her anymore.

Sometimes I see her in my dreams, or in the vineyards, but when I get too close, she disappears.

Maybe she fell and hit her head and can't remember where she lives. She'd come back for me, if she wasn't hurt. I know she would.

When I'm a man, I'll have nice guards who'll help me find *Mamā*.

I'll never stop looking for her.

*Never.*

# 1

## RAFAEL

*Twenty-three years later*

THE PROMISE of sin pulses through the crowded club, creating a vibe rivaled only by white powder and a tightly rolled bill.

From the VIP section, I have an unobstructed view of the main room below.

Both bars are humming, and the dance floor is packed with sweaty bodies writhing to the punishing beat. Every inch of real estate is taken up by socialites spending trust fund money, and college boys out to get laid.

Just another Thursday night at Sirena—only it's not.

We're minutes from taking down two fuckers who are part of a ring that's been abducting young women all over Europe. They've eluded capture for the better part of two years, and my blood runs cold every time I learn about a new victim.

"Everything's in place," Zé, my right-hand man, assures me when he gets off a call.

I turn over my phone and pull up the feed from one of the security cameras out front, while he fills me in. "They're

Czechoslovakian nationals and have been part of the ring for at least six months. Their photos are in the updated packet we received a few weeks ago from Interpol. They were caught on film in Paris and Barcelona, both times with the same brunette, but she's not with them tonight."

"We're absolutely sure it's them?"

I plan on taking a piece from those assholes before we turn them over to the authorities, and the last thing I need is an ugly lawsuit because we got ahead of ourselves. It would be a PR nightmare not only for Sirena, but for Premier Port and all of Huntsman Industries.

While Sirena is mine alone, I own Premier with my niece Valentina. It's under the Huntsman umbrella, which is managed by my cousin Antonio. If I screw this up, he'll never let me hear the end of it, and worse, he'll be breathing down my neck, micromanaging every decision that involves Premier. *And rightfully so.*

"It's them." Zé's tone is unequivocal. "After examining the photos side by side with stills from our feed, I personally verified every bit of intel we have."

*That's good enough for me.* "What's happening in the neighborhood?"

"Nothing out of the ordinary. The perimeter we set up is still loose so as not to alarm anyone, but the moment you say the word, it'll tighten right up. Your soldiers have trained for this moment. Those bastards are not slipping through our fingers."

I draw a breath and scan the crowded floor one more time. The significance of the directive I'm about to issue weighs heavily on me. *Too many innocents in the club.* But there's no choice. Those sons of bitches are going down today.

"Let them in," I order, my voice not betraying my concerns. The command is directed at Davi, my man outside, but there are dozens of other trusted employees, not all soldiers, hearing it too. It's their cue that the operation is beginning. "Stay alert. These are bad men."

"Give me a few minutes to move the line along," Davi responds from outside. "I don't want to spook them."

Not only does Davi manage crowd control outside the club, but he's in charge of sizing up every person as they wait to enter. Even under normal conditions, no one gets inside this place with anything besides a small purse—checked thoroughly—and everyone walks through a metal detector. *Everyone.* Unlike some other clubs, there are no exceptions for short skirts or nice tits.

"Keep us apprised," I reply.

"Are you sure you want them inside?" Stella, the club manager, asks, wringing her hands. "It's hopping down there. I vote for taking them on the sidewalk. Less chance of collateral damage."

"This isn't a democracy," I quip.

Stella's shoulders hunch, but I don't regret the flippant remark. I want her—all my people—to feel comfortable speaking up, but I've made a final decision, and now I expect her to keep her opinions to herself and carry it out. I expect that of everyone on my payroll—except Zé. We've been friends since we were toddlers, and I depend on him to question me, to push me, to keep me honest. While I don't always listen to his advice, I always hear him.

I glance at her tight expression. She knows better than to question me at this stage—especially in public. But this takedown has enormous ramifications, and we're all wound tight. Stella's loyal, and she gets a pass for her insubordination —*today*.

In truth, I don't want those bastards dirtying up the club any more than she does. And I certainly don't want to put our guests or the people who work here at risk. But we need to catch them in the act. Otherwise there will be extradition issues, bureaucracy, and a whirlwind of kiss-ass diplomacy before those sons of bitches get justice. It could take years, if it ever happens. But if they break the law here, they belong to us. *And the reprisal will be swift and meaningful.*

"If you don't support this decision," I say with a deceptive calmness that's become my calling card, "I'll have someone show you out."

Stella pales and shakes her head. "I'm terribly sorry. I don't know what got into me. I'm one hundred percent behind you. Always." She continues to shrink under my glare. "I-I-I should go to the command center to see if they need an extra set of eyes."

After Stella leaves, I turn to Zé. "She needs to be circumspect, but she's right to be concerned about collateral damage. I want them taken down without casualties, or a major scene."

"That's the plan," he assures me patiently, as though it's not the fourth time I've said it in the past hour. "We might have been caught by surprise, but our people are crawling all over the club. Xavier's on top of the logistics inside."

Xavier manages security at the club, and ordinarily he'd be in charge of any problem that arises here. I'd trust him with my life, and I have, but this is its own kind of beast. We don't know its magnitude or how far the tentacles reach, and Xavier doesn't have the breadth of experience to run this type of operation.

"Rafael," Zé continues carefully. "You can watch this in real time from the command center. We've taken every precaution time affords, but we don't know how it's going to play out."

*Fuck that. I'm a highly trained soldier, and I don't hide or shirk my responsibilities. That's for men without honor.*

"We have a problem," Davi says in my ear. "They have company. Check out the feed."

My mouth is bone-dry as the screen refreshes.

Three women have joined the flesh traders. Two I've never laid eyes on, but the third I haven't stopped thinking about since Valentina's wedding.

*Fuck.*

# 2

## RAFAEL

"Ah, Christ," Zé growls.

Two brunettes, one with her hair twisted into a ponytail on top of her head, and a leggy blonde are greeting the men. No one in the group looks to be older than their mid-twenties. But it's hard to know for certain from the feed.

"Slow the line while we regroup," I order Davi. *This is a total clusterfuck.* "The blonde is a close family friend. Don't take your eyes off her for a single second," I add, because as much as I want to, I'm not prepared to go out there and drag her out of that queue. "She's an innocent."

*An innocent. There's nothing innocent about Alexis Clarke. Not a goddamn thing.*

Zé holds his phone up so I can see the screen. The brunette with her hair up is the same woman in the photos from Barcelona and Paris.

"What about the other woman?"

"Her ID says her name is Chiara Amato, a twenty-two-year-old Italian national. The ID looks legit, but it's probably a fake. Xavier is running facial recognition."

"Is Alexis using real identification?"

"Her ID says her name is Alexis Taft. Probably for security reasons."

*Definitely for security reasons.* Taft is her mother's maiden name, and it draws less attention than using her father's surname—although it doesn't open as many doors.

*What the fuck is Lexie doing with those bastards?* She couldn't possibly be involved in the ring. She's Valentina's best friend. *Her maid of honor.* The woman who whimpered so sweetly while I licked her pussy. "Alexis isn't a predator."

*That means she's prey. There are only two real choices here.*

He shakes his head. "I don't see it, either. We need to figure out how to get her away from them and to safety before we move."

In a perfect world, that's exactly what we'd do. But tonight, we're not in a perfect world—not even close.

"Even if we can come up with a ruse to pull her away from the group, they're likely to shut down their plans for the night. They've been successful because they haven't taken unnecessary risks. Put a couple of our best people on her. They should be ready to swoop in immediately if things start to go sideways. Otherwise, Alexis being here changes nothing."

The bullshit tumbles from my mouth easily. The truth is, Lexie being here changes everything. I've known her since she was a kid. And I got to *know* her in a very grown-up way the night of Valentina's wedding. *I can't let those feelings cloud my judgment. There's too much at stake tonight.*

I fully trust the plan and the people we have in place. I wouldn't have signed off on it otherwise. That's the bottom line. *It has to be.*

"The club is filled with innocents," I explain soberly. "We were already operating in a way that minimizes risk. Unless there's something you've kept from me, we shouldn't change course. It would be unconscionable to allow this to fall apart. We're so close."

"I don't keep you in the dark about anything."

I can almost feel the relief from Zé. He wants these fuckers as much as I do.

"Even in the middle of an operation," he says coolly, "she's safer in here than she is out there with those monsters."

*No question about it.*

Alexis's father, Will, is an overprotective bastard, and one of the most dangerous men roaming the earth. He's going to rip me a new one when he hears we conducted a takedown with his daughter in the middle of it. *I'll deal with the fallout when it comes.*

I switch on my earbud to communicate with the team. "Along with the two men, the taller brunette, with the ponytail, is a target. We don't know anything about the other brunette." I glance at the feed. Lexie's smiling at one of the women. Her vulnerability hits me squarely in the chest. "Remember, the blonde is a close Huntsman family friend."

The stakes were high before, but they're enormous now—at least for me.

"Let them in," I order, putting my people on notice for the second time tonight. "No mistakes."

———

"THEY'RE PASSING through the metal detector," Davi reports, and I suck in a long breath. "Nothing suspicious," he adds.

"Not a care in the world," Zé mutters, as we watch them laughing while they make their way inside.

*What the fuck, Lexie? What are you doing with these scumbags?*

Zé holds out his screen for me. A message from Xavier. "Carlos, Sabio, and Giana are on Ms. Clarke. There should be nothing to worry about."

*Nothing to worry about. Right.* Despite the security precautions, it's possible those bastards sneaked in something that the metal detectors can't pick up. Or worse, they might have someone on the inside who stashed weapons for them—or explosives. Our employees and contractors are thoroughly vetted, but all it takes is one lapse for things to go south.

The list of unknowns has me on edge as I wait for them to enter the club. *For Lexie to enter the club.*

We watch the feed as they hand over their belongings to the coat check downstairs. Nothing they've done, so far, would raise any suspicion. Just a group of friends out for a good time. *Fuckers.*

Finally, the two Czech males accompany the three women onto the club floor. My blood simmers as they sidle up to a high-top table near the back bar.

*Why Sirena?* They've been all over the European Union and the UK, but they generally stay away from places like Sirena, where the clientele is monied and the security tight. Either they've changed course and are going after wealthy marks, or this is a one-off, which means we're being specifically targeted. *But why?*

The men casually scope out the scene, while a waitress takes drink orders.

They're pros. But it doesn't matter how proficient they are at subterfuge, because it's unlikely that they're anything more than foot soldiers. They work for someone—and men who trade in human flesh are capable of anything. Including blowing up a club filled with innocent people—*and a gorgeous blonde.*

My grip on the rail tightens as I survey the sea of unsuspecting partiers. If we had more time to plan, every person in this room would be a trained guard. There would be no innocents. But time is our enemy tonight.

"Rafa," Zé nudges quietly from beside me. "You need to get out of here before they notice us up here."

"You think I'm going to leave Alexis in the middle of a shit-storm while I hide in my office?" I glower at him, and he's lucky that's all he gets.

"If Alexis sees you, she might unknowingly tip her hand and blow up the whole operation. All she has to do is wave, and it could spook them. You need to watch this go down from the command center."

He's right. *Goddamn it.* Clever angles and lighting obscure the VIP section from the club floor. People lay out a lot of cash for the privacy. But it's not entirely blacked out. Even if the traffickers aren't concerned about the shadowy figures, Alexis will likely be curious. *She's always curious. And she'll wonder if I'm up here.*

"Let's go." I drop the tumbler on the table, never looking back at the crowd below.

# 3

## RAFAEL

SIRENA'S COMMAND center is modeled after those found in casinos. Security personnel scour the floor for any sign of drug use, sexual assault, or other unacceptable behavior. Some scan the club through two-way mirrors, while others study live feeds. They act first and ask questions later. Consequently, Sirena is a safe club, even for women who come here alone.

After we arrive, I go directly to Xavier, who's at the glass, his suit jacket discarded and his sleeves rolled up the moment he learned there was trouble. "Have you identified the woman?"

"Francesca Russo, seventeen."

*I hope to hell that name is nothing more than a coincidence.* "Please tell me that she isn't related to Bruno Russo."

"Her father," he grits out through a clenched jaw. "She's on holiday, traveling alone, as far as we can tell."

*The seventeen-year-old daughter of the Italian prime minister. Just what I need. Christ.* "You've got to be kidding."

He shakes his head. "I wish. Just adds another layer of complexity. We're trying to figure out why she doesn't have security with her."

*What the hell is she doing traveling alone? I've met her father.*

*There's no way he allowed his* principessa *to traipse around without bodyguards.* I pound the edge of my fist against the wall. "Whatever the reason, it's not good."

"Do you have any idea why Ms. Clarke would be with these bastards or why she's without security?" Xavier asks cautiously.

*Not a fucking clue why she's with them, but I guarantee she ditched her guards.*

"No. But I assure you it's the first question I'm going to ask her." Right after, *What the hell were you thinking?*

"You're absolutely sure it's them?" I ask Xavier, jerking my head toward the two-way glass. I know he's going to confirm what Zé has already told me, but I need to hear it again. This is as close as anyone has gotten to the ring, and I'm eager for the opportunity to question them. *More than eager.* But with Lexie involved, a part of me wants us to be mistaken.

"Take a look for yourself." Xavier hands me several photos and a sheet of paper from a file Interpol sent.

"I can't believe they had the balls to bring their filthy enterprise here." Xavier shakes his head, disgusted. "We've been on the lookout, but I never expected them to actually show up. Not at a club like Sirena."

I skim through the short bios. The taller brunette is Romanian. Her name is Misha Albescu.

It's a common Romanian surname, if it's even her real name. There's not much information on her in the file. *Fucking Interpol. Knowing them, they have more than they shared. That's how it always is with those assholes.*

"Do we know if either the Italian or Ms. Clarke are involved?" It kills me to ask about Lexie, but I have to know, and the answer needs to come from an unbiased source, because I sure as hell am not that.

He shakes his head. "I can't imagine, but we shouldn't rule out anything until we talk to Interpol. Although as soon as we make the call, they'll be all over this place, barking orders with their usual flair for incompetence. Then it'll be a real nightmare."

*It's already a real nightmare.* Although losing these bastards to Interpol would be worse.

"Hold off on contacting the authorities. But until we learn otherwise, we need to proceed as though all five are associates." *Even Lexie.* It's such a gut-wrenching thought, I almost choke on the words. But the safety of everyone in the club is at risk. *There's no fucking choice.* "Handle the Italian and Ms. Clarke carefully. Despite how we're proceeding, it's a very low likelihood that they're involved."

"You don't need to say it twice. The last person I want to tangle with is Ms. Clarke's father."

*That makes two of us.*

Will is one of the most lethal men on the Continent, and when it concerns his daughter's safety? He doesn't ask questions before he lowers the boom.

"We put extra security on her," Xavier continues, "and I upped the number of personnel around the prime minister's daughter as well."

The room is quiet. Anyone not studying the feed has eyes glued to the club floor. We're taking some huge risks. I'm on edge, like everyone else. But I'm confident the men and women who work for me can pull this off without anyone getting hurt —*including the blonde in the dress that's too damn short.*

"Your people out front did a good job tonight," I murmur to Xavier. "Make sure they get something extra in this week's paycheck."

He nods. "They'll appreciate it."

After sipping her drink for a few minutes, Misha leaves the table and heads in the direction of the ladies' lounge. The blood vessels on the right side of my head begin to throb.

"Security is following," Xavier says, "and I just alerted the bathroom attendant."

"You've switched out the regular attendant for a guard in there, I hope?"

"Not just there. All the bathroom attendants have been replaced with guards."

The four left at the table are engaging in what looks like a lot of flirting. My blood pressure skyrockets every time Lexie gifts those fuckers a smile. It takes everything I have not to go down to the floor and drag her ass out of the club. *But I can't.* Too many women are missing, and too many families are searching for answers. *I can't blow this now. Not even for her.*

"The target has left the ladies' room. She looked about a bit, but that's it. The attendant checked the stall after she left and didn't find anything."

*I hope she's right.*

"Maybe she just had to take a piss," Zé grumbles.

Shortly after Misha returns to the table, Lexie leans over to say something to the Italian, who shakes her head.

"Is there a way to know what they're saying?"

Xavier shakes his head. "I thought about having the waitress slip a mic under the table or on the back of one of their chairs when she brought the drinks, but it's too loud in the club. We don't have anything sophisticated enough here that could get us anything useful. It's not worth the risk."

Lexie drains her drink, and the taller Czech puts his filthy hand on her lower back. Every muscle in my body tightens.

She grabs her purse and says something to the Italian, who shakes her head, before Lexie leaves the table, alone.

For a long moment, I contemplate having a guard intercept her, but in the end I'm back to the same thing. In two years, this is the closest anyone's ever gotten to them. I won't risk tipping them off—not now.

"Security's on her heels," Xavier explains, as she makes her way across the room to the ladies' lounge. "Giana will go in behind her. I've let the attendant know."

"We're sure nothing was left in that bathroom? Not even a powdered substance?"

Contact poison that could cause injury or death. The kind of powder the Eastern Europeans, the Russians in particular, are so fond of using. We've been careful, but if they believe they've been made—tipped off in some way—contact poison would make a nice distraction in a crowded club, affording them an opportunity to slip away.

"I'll double-check, but the guard in that lounge is highly experienced."

Seconds after Lexie disappears, one of the men, Misha, and the prime minister's daughter go off toward the dance floor. The Czech keeps an arm draped around each woman as they weave between tables.

"They closed the stall after the Romanian left the ladies' lounge and went over it with a fine-tooth comb. There was nothing."

The male target remaining at the table goes to the bar. The group is separated, which is never a good thing. "Hard to keep track of them when they're spread out," I mumble, mostly to myself.

"This is what we do every night, and we're damn good at it," Xavier assures me. "They're surrounded by our people. I don't care if they crawl under a floorboard. No one's taking a goddamn eye off them."

He sounds bitter. I'm sure his ego got bruised when I put Zé in charge of logistics. But I'm not in the business of soothing grown men's egos. *Not even my own.* I do what needs to be done.

"The shot is zoomed in, behind you." Xavier points to a large screen suspended from the ceiling near the back wall.

The Czech at the bar is talking to the bartender, who knows the score. I'd love to know what they're chatting about. If we had more time to prepare, everyone would be miked.

"Why didn't he just order from the waitress?" a young man

operating a feed asks. "It would have called less attention to him."

"Going to the bartender is the fastest way to get a drink," I mutter, eyes glued to the feed. "And if he returns to the table before she does, he'll have unfettered access to her cocktail." *I'm going to kill that bastard, and it's going to be a long, drawn-out celebration.*

"This could be what we're waiting for," Zé says, with an icy focus to his voice.

The screen on my left is homed in on the outer door to the ladies' lounge, and the one on the right shows the area of the dance floor where the seventeen-year-old is shaking her ass more than is wise. *She's too precocious for her own good.* When this is done, I'm handing over the tape of her *dancing* to her father. *The prime minister needs to keep a tighter rein on his teenage daughter.*

The asshole at the bar takes two drinks from the bartender and goes back to the table. He places his hand over one of the cocktails and inches the glass a bit to the side.

"Zoom in. More," Xavier instructs a woman to his far left.

It's only because we have the ability to rewind and freeze the frame that we know he used his thumb to push something into the cocktail while he moved the glass. *Son of a bitch.*

Lexie Clarke isn't a predator. She's prey.

# 4

## RAFAEL

"The male target, at the table, just dropped something into one of the drinks," Zé alerts our A team on the floor.

My outward demeanor is calm, but my stomach roils, much like it does whenever I'm anxious. A vestige of an *unpleasant* childhood.

Lexie comes out of the ladies' room, *finally*, and makes her way back to the table. She was in there for a long fucking time, or at least it felt that way to me. With the camera zoomed in, she looks younger than twenty-three, and hot as hell. Not in a loud, too-much-smoky-eye kind of way, but she's poised, and radiates fun and sass and natural beauty—right down to the freckles on her nose that she covers with makeup.

No surprise they targeted her. She would earn them a nice chunk of change when they sold her into the kind of life that sends terror through my veins. Those bastards need to be strung up and castrated.

*You're getting way ahead of yourself. Despite how it looks, you still don't know who the target is—it might be the prime minister's daughter.* I glance at the Italian swaying seductively on the dance floor. *She'd bring in a fat wad of cash too.*

Lexie eases her way through the club, stopping when a young man blocks her path.

The command center falls silent. He looks like a college boy with access to Daddy's credit cards, but he could be part of their game—a plant—and there could be others. *Too many damn unknowns.*

I'm seconds from aborting the operation when Lexie flashes him a cut-the-bullshit look and a smile as fake as Francesca Russo's ID. They exchange a few words, and he lays a hand over his heart in an exaggerated way, as though she wounded him, before stepping aside to let her pass. The entire room lets out a collective breath.

She's smiling as she walks away. A sassy, confident smile that reminds me of the one she gifted me right before I pinned her to the stone wall and kissed her.

*Focus, Rafael. Focus.*

"Either Ms. Clarke or Ms. Russo needs to accept the drink before our people move in," Zé mutters to no one in particular.

It's about to become real. *The moment of truth.* But the real truth is that I'm starting to feel a twinge of conscience for putting either the Russo girl or Lexie at risk—especially Lexie. All of a sudden, *the ends justify the means* feels like bullshit.

When Lexie reaches the table, she looks alarmed.

The man says something and points to the trio on the dance floor. She zeroes in on them and nods. The Czech inches the cocktail toward her. She smiles that phony, practiced one and shakes her head.

"Fuck," Zé grumbles.

The Czech picks up the drink and appears to be cajoling her.

"*Jesus Christ.* Take it already so we can end this." Xavier's clean out of patience. We're too damn close to drop the ball now, and it's making everyone prickly.

The Czech is insistent about her taking the drink. "Zoom in

on their mouths," I growl. "Let's see if we can figure out what the bastard is saying to her."

"It's hard to be sure, but I think he just said something like, 'Come on. Don't put a damper on the party,'" a woman behind me mutters.

*When I get my hands on him, I'm going to put a huge fucking damper on his party, right after I yank that asshole's tongue out of his mouth.*

He's wearing her down. I feel it. "Get prepared to move on my signal. We take all five at once. I don't need to remind you that the club is filled with guests. The petite brunette and the blonde are victims. Make it look easy."

I might be the guy with all the power, but standing here, watching that bastard play her, I've never felt more powerless. *Not since I was a young boy.*

Lexie hesitates for a long moment before reaching out her hand to take the drink from him. I watch her fingers unfurl with bated breath. If she changes her mind, we're back to square one. *But it's not the worst thing.* We don't know what he slipped in her drink, and the very worst thing is if she takes a sip before we reach her.

"Ms. Clarke is not to get that glass anywhere near her mouth," I growl into the earbuds.

As much as we need her to take that drink from him, I can't believe she's reckless enough to actually do it. I warned her and Valentina countless times when they were in college, and before, *and after*, to never take a drink from someone they didn't know well. *Actually, I warned them never to take a drink from any guy who wasn't me.*

"That's it," Zé murmurs. "Go ahead, Alexis. Take the fucking drink."

*This is making me sick.*

As soon as Lexie's fingers wrap around the glass, I bark into the microphone. "Go, go, go. Don't let your guard down. We don't know who else might be in the club that we haven't identified."

I don't watch the takedown unfold. The last words aren't out of my mouth when I bolt from the room and down the stairs like the place is engulfed in flames. Zé calls my name, but I don't stop, not until I get to Lexie, who is surrounded by security.

She stares into my face with a staggering fragility that makes my chest clench. It's not a look I've ever seen from her. *Not once.* The color is gone from her cheeks, and she's teetering on heels that are too damn high. I hold her arms to steady her.

For a moment, her hazel eyes are pale green. For a moment, her guard is down, and she's shaken. But it's merely a fleeting moment that passes before her irises darken and the sparks begin to form. After another moment, I see the spitfire emerge, and it won't be long before the artillery is aimed squarely at me. Honestly, it's a relief.

I was wrong about her. *So wrong.* Bought the bullshit she's always peddling about having the biggest balls in the room. An ice princess—completely untouchable. I wanted those fuckers so bad, I took a risk—with her—that I shouldn't have taken.

The tainted cocktail is in Sabio's hand. "Make sure they preserve that drink," I tell Zé, who followed me to the floor. "It needs to stay in camera range at all times so that there aren't chain-of-custody issues."

Lexie looks more like herself, but she's still too damn pale. And she hasn't said a word.

"Get me a bottle of water," I tell no one in particular.

"Everyone's been secured without incident," Xavier says from behind me.

I nod, but my gaze doesn't stray from the woman who's so close I can smell the amber in her perfume.

Carlos holds out a bottle of water, and I unscrew the cap and hand it to Lexie, who takes several gulps.

"You're safe, for now. But you have a fair amount of explaining to do."

"Where's Francesca?"

*That's the first thing you have to say?* It surprises me, although I'm not sure why. She's very protective of Valentina, who's always been a bit more naive, and whenever she's with Antonio's kids, she's like a camp counselor.

"We have her. She's safe too. What are you doing in Porto?"

She lifts her chin, and the defiance rumbles before she opens her mouth. "I don't answer to you."

"Like hell you don't."

Without another word, I drag her off the floor to an elevator that will bring us to a private garage, where a car is waiting to take her to my apartment at Huntsman Lodge.

Like it or not, tonight Alexis Clarke will be answering to me.

# 5

## RAFAEL

"WHERE THE HELL IS YOUR SECURITY?" I snarl before the elevator doors close.

"In London, I suppose," she quips, flipping her hair over one shoulder, like a diva.

I want to shake her but settle for a scowl. "You suppose? Have they informed your father that you're missing yet?"

"They won't. Me going missing reflects poorly on them. They like their job. It pays well." She shrugs, examining her deep-purple nails. "They also want to remain among the living. They won't breathe a word until it becomes necessary."

*What kind of fucked-up establishment is Will running?* The man has more enemies than anyone on the planet. Even more than we do. If what she claims is true, she essentially has no security. *There's no fucking way that's going to continue.*

"The guards might not tell your father, but it's the first phone call I'll be making." I don't give a damn what Will does with those guards. They'll get what they deserve.

Lexie marches closer to me, a hand on her hip. "I forbid you to call my father," she hisses.

I don't give a shit how sweet her mouth tastes—or her cunt,

for that matter—haughty princesses don't get to forbid me from acting in their best interest.

With too many emotions swirling inside, I flip the switch to stop our descent and inch toward her until she's backed into the far corner of the elevator, cornered but still daring me to defy her wishes. I'm not sure if I want to lift her dress and fuck her against the dirty carriage wall or take her over my knee and spank her ass until it's a lovely shade of red.

I pull in a long breath through my nose and let it filter through while I regain some modicum of control. "You forbid me? Really?"

She lifts her chin and stares me straight in the eye, not giving a damn that I'm towering over her and furious.

"Let's get something straight," I tell her with all the calm I can muster. "You ditched your guards. Hooked up with an underage *principessa* and some flesh traders, then showed up at my club. You don't get to forbid a damn thing."

"Fine. Be an unreasonable ass," she huffs, scrolling through her phone so she doesn't have to look at me. "But I'm an adult, and the least you can do is hear me out before you call my father." Her head pops up and she captures my gaze. "I think you owe me that. Don't you?"

It's a sharp barb from a woman who knows how to deliver a little pain. *And guilt.* I deserve it. I took off her clothes, buried my face in her pussy, and enjoyed her in ways that I shouldn't have. Then I ghosted her instead of facing her like a man and reminding her that she was too young for me, and there were too many threads that connected our families—we could *never* do that again.

It's not that I didn't have the balls to have the conversation, but I didn't fully buy into those excuses—although they were true.

There are almost eight years between us and long-standing family alliances that shouldn't be tested. A one-night stand, or even a stolen weekend, had the potential to create a lot of problems. Those were facts. Although there was something else too. Something I couldn't, or wouldn't, own up to then.

In addition to being sexy as fuck, Lexie is smart, and brave, and restless, *and too damn willing to take risks*—that characteristic alone has the potential to destroy me. I didn't trust myself to be around her after that night. *I still don't trust myself.*

The worst part is that, even knowing she could be my ruin, I want her. I wanted her then. And I want her now.

She lifts her brow triumphantly, like she's won. *I hope she doesn't think that a few pointed words will make me crumble.*

"I don't have time to listen to excuses about your reckless behavior," I grumble, "unless it's something pressing, or directly related to the traffickers."

Lexie shakes her head. "It can wait. But promise me you won't call him until we talk." She touches my arm, and her fingers sear my skin until all I can think about is owning her hot little body.

Her expression is soft. *Pleading.* The walls are closing in, and I'm having trouble remembering why I can't have her. Before I do something stupid, I pull my arm away to restart the elevator —and put some space between us.

"Rafa," she whispers in a throaty voice, and my traitorous dick remembers that's how she begged for it the night of the wedding. Sprawled on the desk, breathy little whimpers tumbling from her luscious lips. I grazed on her like she was a sumptuous feast, while she whispered my name into the sultry air.

*Don't go there, Rafael. You can't.*

"I'm so pissed at you, Lexie. Give me a few minutes to think about it, because if you force me to give you an answer now, you won't like it."

The elevator doors open, and two armored SUVs pull up.

"Where are you taking me?" she asks, suspicion curling around every syllable.

"You had no problem palling around with flesh traders, but you're concerned about where I might take you?"

"Pfft," she scoffs.

"I'm not taking you anywhere. I have work to do here." *Serious work, and as much as I'd like to keep an eye on you myself, you're too damn distracting.* "You're going to my apartment at Huntsman Lodge. A doctor will meet you there."

"I don't need a doctor. I'm fine. When I wake up tomorrow, if I'm not well, I'll see a doctor." She side-eyes me, lips pulled into a tight line. "But given the circumstances, I'm okay with staying in your guest room. Huntsman Lodge is more secure than my parents' house," she continues, "but my things are at the hotel."

*In my guest room. She couldn't resist.* "I'm going to say this once. The people you were with are part of an international trafficking ring, and your drink was spiked. You will allow a doctor to examine you. It's a precaution," I add, "but nonnegotiable. If you need to be sedated for that to happen, I'll be happy to order it." She rolls her eyes, like somehow that wounds me. "When I can spare someone, I'll send them to get your things."

While I'm leading her to a vehicle, the elevator dings, and the young Italian, a female guard, and Zé step out.

"Francesca," Lexie cries softly, rushing to the kid, who can easily pass for twenty-two. Although I suspect she looks younger with the layer of face paint scrubbed off.

"You have one minute to say goodbye. I want you both off the premises before the police show up, or worse, the Portuguese Intelligence Service and Interpol. They're each going to want statements."

"I'm happy to give them a statement," Lexie tosses over her shoulder.

"Neither of you are giving the authorities *any* statement tonight."

They're tired, and the authorities will twist their words in ways that suit them. I won't allow an interview tonight, but it's easier to have them off the premises before the authorities arrive. Getting into a pissing match with the Intelligence Service or Interpol is a last resort.

Francesca cries as she removes a gold bangle and hands it to Lexie. The two hug, and Lexie smooths hair off the girl's face. "My father is going to kill me," the Italian whimpers.

"Does he beat you?" Alexis asks, tipping up the girl's chin to peer into her eyes.

She shakes her head. "He'll take everything away, and he won't let me see Paolo."

I assume Paolo is her boyfriend, and she's worried about her access to dick being restricted. *Too damn bad.* She was minutes away from a journey where lack of dick would never be a concern. She's damn lucky my people were alert. I glance at Lexie. *We all are.*

Quietly pleading, Lexie gazes at me, her arms around Francesca. "There's got to be another way, Rafael."

*There's not a chance in hell that I'll smooth things over for the* principessa. *She's getting delivered straight to her father.*

"Not for someone her age."

She shoots me a poison dart and goes back to soothing the girl. "I know it's scary, but the most important thing is that you're safe. Your parents will feel that way, even if they're angry. I'm sure of it. It's going to be okay."

I nod at the female guard, who ushers Francesca into one of the vehicles. Zé's going along for the ride to question her, and then they'll leave the little darling in the custody of the Italian embassy before this becomes a diplomatic nightmare. After that, we're done. Her father can decide if and when she's talking to the authorities, if Paolo is finished, or if she's grounded for life. None of it's my problem.

"Where is she being taken?" Lexie demands, as Zé slides into the car across from the *principessa*.

"To the Italian embassy."

"Why are you sending Zé? Why not a more junior guard?"

If I had any sense, I'd think she's too clever for her own good, but in truth, I admire her savvy.

I'm not sure Lexie was ever naive. She's an only child who spent a lot of time around adults—adults involved in some shady shit. I always felt she grew up quicker than necessary. She wasn't sheltered from the ugly part of our world the way Valentina was sheltered. *It's a shame.*

I snatch her wrist and tighten my fingers so she can't pull away. "Careful with your tone," I warn, my mouth hovering just above her ear. "I decide which soldiers to send where. And I won't be questioned about it, especially in public. The *principessa* is in good hands. You don't need to worry about her."

When I let go of her wrist, Lexie steps up into the vehicle, and I reach out to help her. She turns awkwardly to avoid me, and my fingers graze her breast. It's quick and innocent, but it jolts us both. *I don't know what part of "she's off-limits" my dick doesn't understand.*

I wait for a sarcastic remark or some other sass, but she gazes at my hand and doesn't say a word as she engages her seat belt.

Desperate to change the vibe, I turn to Sabio and Giana. "Ms. Clarke is a pro at slipping her security." I say it loud enough for Lexie to hear every word. "I won't tell you how to do your job, but personally, I wouldn't even allow her to use the bathroom with the door shut."

Her jaw falls open. "You're—"
*Distraction successful.*

I lean into the car and hold two fingers to her mouth to shush her. "If you don't want me to place the call to London, then I strongly suggest you keep your opinions to yourself."

She wants to say more, because she always wants to say more, but she's not a stranger to this life, and she knows better than to push me too far.

"When will you be home?"

"When I'm done here. I expect it will take awhile."

"I'll wait up so we can talk about calling my father."

My dick twitches when it hears *I'll wait up.*

I don't know what I'd been thinking, but she can't stay at my apartment—it's a bad idea. A *very* bad idea.

"On your way up to the residences," I tell the guards, "stop at the security office and get the key to Valentina Cruz's apartment. Ms. Clarke will spend the night there."

"Valentina doesn't know I'm in Porto," she murmurs, looking almost sheepish.

There have been times when I was sure Valentina and Alexis didn't piss without consulting each other. That's how close they are. But Lexie is in Porto and Valentina doesn't know? *It's either bullshit, or she's hiding something bigger than that she skipped out on her security.*

"Valentina rarely uses that apartment anymore, and I know for a fact she's not there tonight. Also, I need your phone."

"My phone? I don't think so."

If she were anyone else, I'd walk away and let the guards deal with it. But I won't embarrass her that way, as much as she deserves to be taught a lesson. I also don't want anyone's hands on her. "Don't make me take it from you," I say, just for her ears.

"Am I your prisoner?" she huffs in response.

Not my prisoner, but she's not free to leave, at least not until I figure out how she got involved with these animals, and until I know she's safe.

"My prisoner? Don't be ridiculous. We need to be sure that

your friends didn't put anything on the phone that would allow you or your communications to be tracked."

"They didn't," she replies testily, without giving it a thought.

"That's what Francesca said too. But my people found a tracking device on her phone."

Lexie's hands tremble slightly as she fishes her phone from the purse and hands it to me. "Will you stop by later?" Her voice is a strained whisper.

"Much later. You don't need to wait up. We can talk in the morning." *When my head is clear and you don't have that uncharacteristic vulnerability about you that I can't resist.*

"Let me know when you arrive at the apartment," I tell Sabio and Giana. "Dr. Arruda will be up. That's it. No one else in or out." With that I turn away, and my attention shifts to the bastards who are waiting for me in the storage shack. *I want some answers before I turn those fuckers over.*

"Rafael?"

I stop and turn to the beautiful woman who captured my attention when she was nineteen, with her smart mouth and the promise of sin, rousing something inside that I'd never felt before—or since. I didn't act on it then. That didn't happen until much later, after a long celebratory day and enough booze to make me stupid. Under a moonlit sky in a vineyard awash in fairy lights, I surrendered to the siren's call. *I've been paying ever since.*

Lexie's makeup has faded, and those adorable freckles on her nose make her seem younger. She looks tired—maybe even a bit fragile. My chest tightens.

"Thank you for showing up for me tonight."

I lean into the SUV and sweep my thumb across her cheek. "Always. Now be a good girl and obey the guards."

# 6

## ALEXIS

I'VE SPENT the night so many times, Valentina's apartment is like a familiar friend. I know which cabinet holds the drinking glasses and where to find a spatula, and I know where the laundry machines are stowed and how to work the finicky gas fireplace.

Sometimes I sleep in the guest room, but more often we fall asleep in Valentina's big, comfy bed after gorging on junk food, wine, and Netflix. But I've stayed here only once since she married Marco, and I miss our sleepovers almost as much as I miss her.

"I'm going to take a shower," I inform Giana and Sabio, who are several years older than me, and serious, but not stern like the guards my father normally assigns to my detail. "There are no windows in the bathroom, and the vent is too small to squeeze these hips through. You don't need to worry."

"It's our job to worry," Giana reminds me gently, following me through the living area to where the guest room is located.

Valentina might not use the apartment much now that she's married, but the place smells like her. *I wish she was here. I could use a friend right now, and I can already tell Giana's not going to cut it.*

"You're not actually going to watch me shower?" It comes off flippantly, like, *you can't be serious,* but she's following so close on my heels I'm afraid she might actually join me in the bathroom.

"I'd prefer to wait in the bedroom."

"I'd prefer you wait in the living room, but the bedroom works."

"You'll need to keep the bathroom door open, but this is a large room, and I'll give you plenty of privacy."

"Rafael was joking about keeping the bathroom door open, Giana."

"He doesn't joke about security."

*Oh, for fuck's sake.*

There was a time when I'd have tortured the guards. Put on a little show for them, covering my embarrassment by making them feel embarrassed too. But I don't do that anymore.

Guards who work for men like my father and the Huntsmans aren't like the bodyguards who protect celebrities and CEOs. They're lethal soldiers. *Soldado* in Portuguese. *Soldato* in Italian. *Soldat* in Russian. It doesn't matter where they're from or what they're called—it's all the same. These men, with a few women sprinkled about, swear loyalty and follow orders. If they fail to do either, they pay with their lives. When I realized this, I stopped fucking with them.

Do I slip my detail? *Yes.* More in the last year than I ever have. But I'm careful to concoct schemes that won't reflect badly on them—at least not too badly.

My father might demote the guards and pull them off my detail, but despite what I told Rafael, he'd never order their death over my shenanigans. Although if he believes they should have been able to stop me—that's a different matter entirely. That's why I'm so careful not to implicate them in any way.

"Would you like me to see if Senhora Cruz has a robe you can borrow?"

*Senhora Cruz.* Valentina would cringe if she heard Giana call her by that name. "No. Thank you. I keep a few things here."

I pull open the bottom dresser drawer and dig out a pair of underwear, yoga pants, and a tank top. "I'm just going to wash my face and change. I'll shower later."

I won't toy with Giana and Sabio, but I have some measure of pride. I'll deal directly with their boss on this matter. But it can wait until he cleans up the mess from tonight.

Despite all the research I've done, the trafficking ring isn't something I can handle alone. Not that I ever really believed that I could handle the bastards at all—I just hoped to expose them enough that the authorities would take me seriously.

I'm on the right trail, but now that I'm getting close, I see how far over my head I am. There's no way to infiltrate them. *I don't know what I was thinking.* But once I saw the patterns emerge, I had to do something. It's what my grandmother Lydia would have done, and Rafael's mother, and Valentina's grandmother Maria Rosa. *The three amigas.* When I was younger, I wished that I could have been born sooner and been part of their badass posse. *Not that it turned out so well for them.*

I'm not giving up, but it's late and my brain is too fried to plan the next step. The important thing is that Francesca wasn't abducted. The rest can wait until tomorrow.

I wash my face, brush my teeth, and use the bathroom, all with the door open. Giana waits across the room to make it as easy as possible on me, and I appreciate her kindness.

The doorbell rings as we're leaving the bedroom. "It's just the doctor," she murmurs.

I almost tell her that I won't be examined tonight, but before I can throw down the gauntlet, she continues.

"Dr. Arruda works at the clinic downstairs. She's very nice. I don't expect any problems, but," she adds, "if anything makes you uncomfortable, I'll be nearby to help."

My father has few female guards, and while there was always one in my detail when I was growing up, she was more of a chaperone. I rarely saw her make any decision without consulting the male guards, and she never intervened on my behalf. It wasn't her job to be my advocate.

I don't need a damn exam, but I'm not going to argue with Giana—not over this. "Thank you," I tell her, sincerely.

# 7

## RAFAEL

WHEN I GET BACK UPSTAIRS, it's like nothing happened. Drinks are flowing and the dance floor is jam-packed. As I skim over the crowd, their naivety or lack of concern, whichever, is almost unsettling.

"Even corralling flesh traders among them didn't spoil the party," I mutter to Xavier, who's been hovering around me since Zé left.

"Fortunately for our coffers, nothing spoils a party."

"Are our friends ready?" I ask, right after the bartender places a bourbon in front of me.

"They will be soon. I understand they might try to escape."

"Pity," I drawl, excitement skittering through my veins. It never ends well for men who attempt escape.

He nods, fidgeting, like he has something to say that he knows he probably shouldn't. Fidgeting is a hot look on a woman who's naked and needy, but on a burly man in a suit? Not so much. It's making me edgy.

"Say it, Xavier. Whatever it is, just spit it out."

"Rafael, we all want a piece of them. But—"

"Don't worry. The bastards will be breathing when we hand them over to the authorities."

I'd prefer to mete out justice myself, but the Portuguese Intelligence Service will be able to get the most comprehensive list of victims from Interpol, and they'll be relentless until these fuckers talk. I want the families to at least have some measure of closure—even if their loved ones are gone forever.

No one knows better than me the horror it is to wake up every day wondering if someone you love is alive or dead. *Or if they're living a tortured existence in the clutches of the worst kind of evil.* We owe it to those families.

"You don't need to get your hands dirty with that scum," Zé says from behind me.

Their concern is starting to get old. They both know me well enough, especially Zé, that there's no fucking way I'm taking a pass on this.

"You're back already?"

He nods. "No traffic at this time of night. The ambassador was waiting at the curb for her, and he didn't invite me in for a nightcap."

I glance at Xavier, who's scanning the room impatiently. Now that Zé's back, I'm sure he wants to be doing something besides guarding me. "Why don't you check on our friends? Let us know when you're ready for me."

"Did you get anything from her?" I ask Zé even before Xavier has time to move.

"She was in Porto to meet her boyfriend. He didn't show up —or at least he hadn't. She told her bodyguard she had cramps and sent him to get some feminine hygiene products and a hot-water bottle, which apparently isn't easy to find. That's how she was able to sneak out of the hotel alone."

*Jesus Christ.*

"They must be teaching courses at Saint Philomena's on how to ditch your security," Zé mutters.

"She went to Saint Phil's?"

He nods.

Saint Philomena's is an exclusive girls' school outside of London, where Lexie was a student too. The security is unparalleled, and it's a favorite of uber-wealthy parents, from all over the world, who have formidable enemies. Valentina spent a few years there as well, but Francesca is significantly younger.

"Did she say anything of any importance?"

"She said it was Alexis's idea to come to Sirena."

"What?" My head's throbbing, again.

"She said it was—"

"I heard what you said," I snap. Zé's not a huge fan of Lexie. He thinks she's trouble—and she is—but he wouldn't throw her under the bus if he didn't think it was important. "Did she say why Alexis wanted to party here?"

"It's a fun place."

*Bullshit.* "Is the *principessa* involved with the traffickers?"

He shakes his head. "Only if they promised her a lifetime supply of Armani or Chanel. Otherwise, it would take too much effort."

"Those bastards in the storage shack better have some useful information," I snarl through gritted teeth.

This has all the hallmarks of a psychological thriller. Pretty rich girls who ditch their bodyguards to go clubbing with flesh traders masquerading as good-looking college boys. By the time the girls figure it out, they're on a ship to be auctioned like chattel.

Before this, the authorities were struggling to find any real connection between the women who had been abducted. Now both Lexie and Francesca have ties to Saint Phil's.

"I don't like the Saint Phil's connection. Increase Valentina's security."

"You do remember that we're not in charge of Valentina's security."

"I might have heard that once or twice." Didn't give a shit then, don't give a shit now. "I don't care about hurting Marco's little feelings. Just do it."

He nods and pulls out his phone.

"Xavier says they're about ready to be questioned."

"Good." I down the bourbon.

"I don't know if you heard me earlier," Zé says cautiously, "but you don't need to get your hands dirty."

He knows this is going to be a high-profile case with the ugly details splashed all over the media, and he doesn't want any of the scandal to blow back on me.

"We have a lot of men eager to teach them a lesson," he continues. "I'd be happy to do it myself."

"My club. The women who walk in here are my responsibility. This is exactly the kind of thing I should dirty my hands with."

"Rafael," he pleads, brow furrowed.

"I don't pay you to be my babysitter."

"No. You pay me to be honest with you, and to speak up when I think you're making a mistake. That's what I'm trying to do." He pauses as though weighing his words. "Antonio's on his way out, and everything will be yours. You're going to be the face of the region. The leader. This has the potential to dirty you."

No one who works for me, besides Zé, would ever speak so plainly—even privately. He's right—it's what I pay him to do, among other things. But his reasoning is misguided—just plain wrong.

"I'll never be an effective leader if I'm afraid of a little dirt. You can come with me and watch my back, or you can stay here. But either way, I don't want to hear another damn word about it."

# 8

---

## RAFAEL

WHEN WE GET to the shack, the state-of-the-art storage facility behind Sirena, I hear the pathetic wails of the man who's hanging from a hook on the ceiling, like the animal he is. He's been roughed up a bit, but nowhere near as much as he deserves.

"He tried to escape," Xavier sneers, his knuckles bloodied. "His buddy too."

"Is that so?" I tut, slamming my fist into the bastard's gut, hard enough to silence any cries while he gasps for breath.

There was never any risk of escape. Xavier's men kept the bindings loose so that the prisoners would try to run. If they run, we pursue, of course, and bad things happen during pursuit—like cracked ribs and slashes made with a sharp blade. Everyone knows that.

Ordinarily we don't need to provide explanations for anything that happens to assholes before we turn them over, and if it was just the Porto police involved, we wouldn't have bothered creating the ruse. They would have ignored the broken bones and deep gashes, happy that we did their dirty work for them. The Intelligence Service is more by the book and prefers to do its own dirty work. Interpol is always the wild card.

My fists itch to hit him again, maybe catch a rib this time. But if I expect any information, I can't assuage my lust for revenge.

Interrogations have a rhythm. I have to be methodical. "Who do you work for?"

"We work for ourselves," he mumbles.

I want the truth, but right now I'll take the lie.

"Is that so?" Without a second's hesitation, I send my fist into his face, and the blood spurts from his nose, spattering my white shirt.

"You couldn't plan your way out of a fucking paper bag, and your ugly-ass shoes don't belong to someone who sells flesh. How much do you get for every woman you bring them?"

He doesn't utter a peep until I unsheathe my knife, and the whimpering begins. They all whimper when the knife comes out to play. Sometimes it's a silent cry that you see only in their eyes. Other times it's a wailed plea.

This bastard is afraid. *But not as afraid as he's going to be.* The rage surges as I think about the unsuspecting women he's ushered into a life of hell, and how frightened they must be. *Women like Lexie. Francesca. And my mother.*

My worst fear is not that they killed my mother immediately, but that they turned her over to monsters who were worse than them. I have no evidence of that, just nightmares that dog me. *This isn't the time to ruminate about a past you can't change. You have these fuckers to question.*

"I doubt you're the mastermind behind anything," I say with all the calm I can muster, while sliding the knifepoint over the thin fabric covering his balls.

"When's the last time this knife was sharpened?" I ask Zé, who is off to my right.

"It's been a few months," he replies. "You use it a lot. If you expect to make a clean cut, it should be done."

I flick my wrist so he can appreciate the knifepoint a bit better. "If you tell me what I want to know, I'll sharpen my knife before I slice off your balls. Otherwise, there's no telling how long it's going to take to saw through them."

"Do you think we know anything?" he snarls.

"I thought you were the big guy? Worked for yourself."

"Kill me," he grunts. "Go ahead."

*I'd love nothing more than to watch you take your final breath, at my hand.*

He's goading me, although in my state of mind, it's a fool's game.

The bottom line is that we can't rough him up too much more than he already is before we turn him over—and he knows it. But this bastard is not leaving here scot-free. I turn and walk away, as though I'm done. When I'm behind him, several feet away, I swivel and fling my knife into his calf.

I flick my wrist several times as I retrieve the weapon embedded in the muscle. The screeching is so loud it hurts my ears.

"It's lucky my knife skills are so sharp," I say to Zé. "Otherwise, he'd have gotten away from us."

Zé snickers and mutters something about how we should dig a hole and bury them alive. Be done with it. It's the best idea I've heard in a long time, and as tempting as it is, I won't do it. Not when there's a chance that we could save even one woman.

We approach the second prisoner, who's strung up far enough away from his friend that he didn't see my knife trick. But he heard it—especially the screams.

"Your buddy's an idiot. Didn't get him too far," I explain, wiping my bloody knife on his shirt. He doesn't flinch, and I know this is going to be a wasted effort.

Successful interrogations can take days, especially in cases where the scariest motherfuckers are not us, or the authorities, but the guy the prisoner works for. We don't have that kind of time.

In the end, I'm right. He doesn't have anything to say that's particularly useful. Although he did confirm one thing. They hadn't planned to come to Sirena tonight.

"What made you change your mind?" I ask, gauging every move, every breath the asshole takes.

"Stupid British bitch."

*He's talking about Lexie.* I take a step back so I don't cut out his tongue.

"She insisted on it, and we couldn't get the Russo girl away from her."

"Why did she want to come to Sirena?" I brace myself for information I don't want to hear.

"I don't know. Getting the girls to go out was Misha's job."

*Misha.* The Romanian who's confined at the back of the building.

"What were you planning to do with the Brit after you had Francesca Russo?"

When he doesn't reply, I stick my knife into the back of his thigh. He shrieks and pisses himself.

"There's a lot of room for my blade to sink deeper," I coo. "You might not know much about how the ring operates, but you do know what you were going to do with the British woman." I slide the knife a bit deeper.

"No more," he begs. "I'll tell you."

"I haven't got all fucking night."

"They would have taken the extra girl," he squeals. "We could have sold them both."

My blood runs cold at the admission—although it's not a surprise. *Son of a bitch.*

"Where were you planning to take them?"

"The docks. Someone was going to find us."

*No surprise there either.* I don't need to ask, *Then what?* because I know what happens to women in the clutches of flesh traders.

"See what else our friend can be encouraged to remember," I mumble to Zé, before going to find Misha.

*Lexie brought them to Sirena. Maybe Misha can shed some light on why.*

# 9

## ALEXIS

AFTER I'M EXAMINED by Dr. Arruda, who is indeed *very nice*, and given a clean bill of health, I pour myself some water and curl up on the sofa with a book I found on Valentina's desk.

Giana and Sabio are in the kitchen, but they have a clear view of me—or at least Giana does. Aside from the bedrooms, the apartment has an open floor plan, perfect for invading my privacy. I don't mean to grouse. They shared their meat pies with me and a slice of pound cake Sabio's mother made. They're not pushovers, but they're good people.

I try to read, but I'm too distracted with the smoking-hot guy who saved my ass tonight—and Francesca's. *I knew he would.*

Sure, he saved me, but it means nothing. Once he's had a chance to pick my brain, he'll vanish—like before. At least this time I won't have just begged him to fuck me.

I feel the book drop from my hands as I drift off, wrapped in the erotic haze of *that* evening, with its vibrant scent of lush grapes. There's a slow, jazzy song playing. The melody wafts in the sultry breeze.

*I'd watched Rafael all day—for years, really—and now, after too many toasts celebrating Valentina and Marco, a long cocktail hour, and dinner with wine and Port, I couldn't even be bothered to pretend that I didn't want to climb all over him.*

*After he disappeared into the vineyard, I slipped off my heels and followed him. I had no idea where he was going, because this had been Valentina's grandparents' home, and I hadn't spent much time here.*

*I stayed a good distance behind him, being as quiet as a tipsy woman can be. I was confident that he hadn't noticed me—until he turned the corner and lay in wait. I didn't see him, but I felt his presence as he covered my mouth to muffle the scream.*

*"Are you following me, Lexie?"*

*When Rafael dropped his hand, he was smirking, and I wasn't anywhere near as embarrassed as I should have been.*

*He'd lost his tie, jacket, and cuff links hours before, but he looked delicious, with his dark hair combed back and his startling blue eyes flickering with something that felt—forbidden. Tempting me beyond anything I could resist.*

*But I didn't want to resist. I wanted to surrender.*

*"I thought maybe you were going somewhere fun," I teased. "Are you?"*

*His eyes darkened, and for a moment the air sparked with something dangerous. "I was going to the office because the cell service is better there, but I'm always up for some fun. What did you have in mind?"*

*I needed no more encouragement, as I stood on tiptoe and pressed a kiss to his mouth. It was all the encouragement he needed, too.*

*His lips were surprisingly soft and warm, insistent, but his tongue was magic, coaxing my mouth open with little effort. I brushed against his cock as he explored my mouth. It was an accident—not the kiss but the cock thing. Although his rough groan was so damn sexy that my pussy fluttered. I wanted to hear that groan again, so I rubbed up against him once more. Harder this time. Brazen. Like I wasn't playing with fire—or at least I didn't care.*

"Lexie," he murmured. "You should go back to the party. You're *too young for me and too precious*," he whispered, cradling my face with his large hands. "And too damn tempting. If we start, I'm not going to be able to stop."

"I don't want you to stop. I think about you all the time," I blurted like a fool. "Your mouth on my skin. Your cock in my pussy. You're my favorite fantasy."

Rafael groaned again, a deep rumble from his chest. His hands were everywhere. He devoured my mouth, the kiss deepening until I couldn't breathe.

"Let's go inside," he murmured above my ear as he pulled away. "Somewhere I can enjoy you without a care."

I shivered as he took my hand and led me inside the small building. I wasn't going to fuck him. I was going to let him fuck me. Because men like Rafael were always in charge. It was a sobering moment but filled with the kind of bottomless joy that children feel on Christmas morning. I had dreamed about this forever—or at least it felt that way.

When we got inside, the windows were cracked, and the music from the party waltzed in the thick air.

The door wasn't even closed before we were all over each other, our hands burning trails of pleasure as we explored. I was so intoxicated I could barely stand—not from alcohol, but from him. His possessive touch. His woodsy cologne, with the spicy, musky notes crackling as I breathed it in.

Rafael unzipped my dress, and it slid to my feet in a silky lavender pool. "You're gorgeous," he said, his eyes flitting over my skin.

"So are you," I croaked, burning for him.

I wasn't wearing a bra, and he lowered his mouth to my nipple, and I felt the sensations—everywhere.

When he dipped his hand into my thong, I whimpered and kneaded his shoulders as he stroked between my legs. Every nerve ending lit, the flames swaying seductively for him.

"I've thought about you too," Rafael confessed, sliding two fingers into my grateful pussy. "When you came back from college, you weren't a little girl anymore, and I thought about you more than was wise. I fantasized about you. Filthy fantasies that made my balls ache."

It was bliss. All of it, and I was out of my mind with the raw carnality of his confession. I couldn't think. I could only feel as a giant wave took hold. I clung to him, lowering my forehead to his shoulder as my belly coiled tight.

"Let go, Lexie," he cajoled. "Come for me, meu anjo."

There was nothing I wanted more than to be his angel—especially in that moment.

When he curled his fingers inside me, I clenched around them and shook, the gasps of pleasure finding their way into the night air.

"Good girl," he murmured, his warm breath grazing my temple. "Do you want more? Should I slide my cock inside your sweet pussy?"

I nodded. I wanted this. I wanted him.

He moved his fingers deeper, and I moaned. "You're tight, baby."

"And you're big," I teased, sliding my hand over his hard cock. It was true. Even through his trousers, I could feel he was long and thick. It was going to hurt. And I didn't care.

"Let's make you a little wetter," he whispered, "a little needier."

He eased me back on the antique desk and lowered his head between my legs, tonguing my sensitive pussy, licking and sucking while I writhed on Valentina's grandfather's desk.

I'd never experienced anything like him. The boys I had been with—were boys, not all that more experienced than me.

"I'm going to fuck you," he said, kissing my belly, "until you scream."

I don't know what it was, but he must have sensed something, because he hesitated before he stood, hovering inches from my face.

"Have you had lovers?" he asked softly, peering into my eyes.

I knew he didn't mean lovers I'd kissed or let play with me, or whom I played with. He meant, *Are you a virgin?* I wasn't going to answer that, not unless he forced my hand. If I told him the truth, he'd stop. I knew it. I wasn't sure how or why, but I was certain he wouldn't take my virginity—even if I begged.

The door creaked open. Before I could figure out what was happening, Rafael was standing in front of me, pointing a gun at the doorway.

"Are you out of your fucking mind?" Lucas snarled.

Lucas worked for Antonio, and they often collaborated with my father, who was at the party too. For a moment, I panicked. But my father wouldn't have sent Lucas. He would have come himself, and the consequences would be staggering.

"Get out," Rafael roared, putting away his gun while still blocking my naked form from the intruder.

"I saw you slip away with her. I'm not the only one who noticed. You need to get her back to the party. And you need to be smart about how you do it. Do you want my help?"

"Get the fuck out of here," Rafael barked.

After the door closed, Rafa turned to face me. "He's right," he admitted, the regret weighing down his words. He pressed a small kiss to my head. "I shouldn't have brought you here. And I certainly shouldn't have touched you the way I did."

There was a finality to his words, and my heart shattered into a million jagged pieces as he spoke.

I was embarrassed, still aroused, and on the verge of tears as he used the bottom of his shirt to clean my thighs and helped me dress. "I'm sorry," he apologized again, humiliating me further. "I should have taken better care of you."

No man I'd ever been with had taken better care of me.

As awful as the moment was, it became more painful. Much more painful.

Rafael didn't spare me a glance for the rest of the night, or during brunch the next morning, and he never contacted me. In the beginning, I showed up in places I thought he'd be, but our paths never *crossed. At Valentina's birthday dinner earlier this year, he smiled and nodded from across the room, but otherwise he avoided me like a mistake he didn't want to repeat.*

*But what made it impossible for my heart to fully heal was that he wanted me. He did. He called me his angel. It wasn't simply the fanciful thoughts of a woman who believed in fairy tales and hung on to words carelessly spoken in a moment of passion.*

*Rafael Huntsman told me he wanted me. He told me I was his filthy fantasy.*

*

# 10

## RAFAEL

MISHA IS FULLY CLOTHED, tied spread-eagle to a rack that hangs on the wall. It looks awfully uncomfortable. She wasn't beaten and she won't be, but that doesn't mean we're not going to make her life miserable.

The petite Romanian blinks several times when she sees me, but she doesn't whimper or shed a tear, not even crocodile ones.

"Comfortable?" I ask, sarcasm dripping from my voice.

She doesn't reply, and I move to within inches of her.

"I asked you a question, Misha, and I expect an answer."

She shakes her head.

"Good. I hope your arms and legs burn like a son of a bitch. It still won't be as bad as the life you lured innocent women into."

"I didn't have a choice," she whispers.

"Everyone has a choice," I reply, but I know it's not true. Women often find themselves in our crosshairs because they didn't have a choice. Misha could be one of them. But I'm in no mood to show her mercy.

I hold my knife against her throat. The blood drains from her face, and she lowers her eyes.

"Who do you work for?" I demand roughly.

"I-I don't know," she says softly, staring at my wrist, like she could will it to drop the knife. "I've never seen him. But he has a lot of power."

I don't make too much of the information, but file it away. A man who has power over her is not necessarily a powerful man. It's unlikely she's rubbed elbows with the man at the top.

"How do you get your instructions?"

"A man. I once heard someone call him Hughes. He usually sends a message with some random person."

"How did you meet him?"

"They drugged me and a few other girls. We were at a club celebrating my friend's birthday. We were kept in a cell for a few days, and they did stuff to us—dirty things. Then one day Hughes pulled me out and said they wouldn't sell me if I helped them."

The story she tells is familiar. The bastards need women to assist them, and they normally choose docile women who won't garner them much cash. So far, I have no reason to believe she's lying about that, or anything else. In many ways, she's a victim, and I might have let her go, if she hadn't caught Lexie in her trap. I can't forgive that so easily, but I move the knife from her throat and sheathe it.

"What did they ask you to do?"

"Make friends with women and bring them to the bar." Her voice belongs to a hollow shell. "That's all."

"That's all," I repeat, my words laced with venom.

"I have a sister," she says, and for the first time I see the fight in her eyes. "Once I didn't bring the girl to the club, like they asked. Hughes visited my sister. She's fourteen. He put his hands on her. I can't let them sell her."

Family is family, and it's hard not to feel great empathy for her situation. "How old are you?"

"Eighteen."

She looks older, haggard, too used up for someone who's just a kid.

"Why did you come to Sirena?"

"I was supposed to take Francesca to Club Azul. But then Alexis saw us in the hotel lobby. They knew each other from school. Alexis convinced Francesca that Azul was a terrible club and that we'd have more fun at Sirena. I don't know who chooses the clubs, but I didn't think I'd get into trouble if we went to a different place. The important thing was that I had to get Francesca someplace where we could meet up with the guys."

Azul isn't a terrible place, but they're lax about who they let in, and the bouncers are easily distracted by an attractive woman, or a buddy who stops in for a drink. It's not a particularly safe club.

"Why Francesca?"

"That's what I was ordered to do," she replies with some exasperation, like she's answered the question already. "Make friends with her and take her to meet the men."

"Did you know she's the Italian prime minister's daughter?"

Her eyes bug out, and she shakes her head.

*I didn't think you did.*

"Have they started targeting wealthier girls?"

"I don't know," she replies after a moment. "But I was given expensive clothes to wear this time and a designer purse. Usually I just wear my own clothes. When I asked what I should do with the fancy things after, they told me to keep them for next time."

*Next time.* "Zé," I shout. "Over here."

"Yeah," he says, glancing at Misha.

"Misha wants to help her situation."

I turn to the kid who has been through hell herself. "You tell this man everything you know, and you answer every question the authorities have for you, and I will make sure your sister is safe." I can't let her go, but I can take some of the burden off her. "You have my word."

"My mother too?" she pleads.

I nod. "Give the information to this man." I point to Zé, who looks almost as lethal as he is. "He won't hurt you."

I move out of Misha's hearing range and motion for Zé to join me. "Cut her down and be careful with her. She's one of their victims and has likely been sexually assaulted."

His expression is grim.

"I don't think she's lying, but don't let your guard down."

He nods.

"Also, have Tamar poke around to see if any students from Saint Philomena's have gone missing recently. Not just current students, but former students as well. Have her look back at the student body, ten years." After that, it's a waste of time. The former students will be too old. Flesh traders target young women.

"A list of Saint Philomena's students, past or present, is going to be a bitch to get our hands on," Zé replies. "It could take awhile. Even for Tamar."

Tamar is former Mossad, and my head of IT. Although she's not really mine. She belongs to Zé. He met her on holiday, and they fell hard, but her job was in Tel Aviv, and his was in Porto. I didn't want to lose him, but I was concerned about having a trained spy working in our organization. Eventually I got tired of Zé looking like someone stole his dog every time they were apart, and I offered her a job, praying it wasn't a mistake. Hiring Tamar is one of the best things I've ever done for my business —and for Zé.

He gauges me carefully. "Is there something you're not telling me?"

"Misha said something that made me wonder if they've started going after women from prominent families. It's probably a red herring. Even if it's not, it might be impossible to get any info from Saint Philomena's in a useful time frame. But if anyone can pull it off, it's Tamar."

"*Senhor?*" Misha calls softly. "Please don't wait too long to find my family."

When I glance at her, all I see is a victim—although she's not without culpability. I stride over to where she's hanging and pull out my knife and slice through her bindings, because I can't stand to see her hanging like that any longer.

"You're going to tell this man where your family lives, and we'll get to them within hours. But if you don't give us and the authorities everything you know about the ring, I'll turn your sister over to the traffickers myself."

If Misha turns out to be a victim, as she claims, we'll reunite her with her family when she's released. Somewhere far away from Romania where they'll be safe, and I'll make sure she gets whatever help she needs. If she's lying, she's going to prison for the rest of her life—or until someone on the inside slits her throat. Misha will get what's coming to her, if that's the case. But turn her sister over to traffickers? I would never do that— not in a million years.

I text Giana as I leave the shack.

Rafael: *How's your charge?*

Giana: *No trouble. She's asleep.*

Rafael: *I'll be there within the hour. Don't wake her.*

# 11

## ALEXIS

SOMETHING TICKLES MY ARM, and I jump, but it's just a soft blanket.

"Go back to sleep. I didn't mean to wake you."

*Rafael?*

It takes me a moment to snap out of the malaise. One minute I'm dreaming about him, and the next he's standing over me—with swollen knuckles and a shirt splattered with what looks like blood.

He looks exhausted, like he needs a hot shower, a whiskey, and a long holiday away from traffickers and everything else that eats at him.

"Did you just get back?"

He nods.

I don't see Giana and Sabio in the kitchen, but I want to know where they are before I ask too many questions. "Where are the guards?"

"Downstairs, on a break. You can speak freely."

"What happened with the traffickers?" I glance at his knuckles. "Did you kill them?"

He shakes his head. "They deserve a painful death, but we questioned them, then turned them over to the authorities."

"It looks like you talked with your fists."

He draws a breath and lowers himself to his haunches. "It's late. Why don't we do this tomorrow?"

*I know you're tired, and it's selfish, but I don't want to wait.*

I've waited a long time to know why he ghosted me. Earlier, he promised to tell me *later*. But he's not going to want to start with that. He's going to want to know why I was with the traffickers at Sirena. I can be patient through that conversation, but I won't wait until tomorrow to learn what happened after the wedding. How I went from being his *anjo* to someone covered with plague germs.

I prop myself up, my back against the rolled arm of the sofa. "Let's get it over with, while everything's fresh."

Rafael doesn't respond, but he goes over to the bar cart and pours a bourbon, and I assume we're going to talk. I pull my knees up to make room for him on the sofa, but he takes the chair across from me. It feels almost like a slight.

"If you want to talk, let's talk. We'll discuss your father after you tell me why you're in Porto and how you got mixed up with those assholes."

"I'm writing a piece for *Eve* about a young Portuguese designer who creates beautiful purses out of cork." It's not the main reason I'm here, although I have been assigned that piece and planned on popping in her shop to look around. It's no secret that I do a lot of freelance writing for the magazine. If he doesn't believe me, he can look it up.

He sips his drink, and his wary blue eyes narrow. "What's her name?"

"Judite Furtado."

He nods, and his expression becomes less severe. It appears I've passed the first test, although I suspect there will be many more.

"Valentina doesn't know you're here?"

He asked me about Valentina earlier, and I could tell he was suspicious that I hadn't told her.

"I was planning on going to Judite Furtado's shop tomorrow, then swinging by to surprise Valentina."

"Did you have an appointment with Judite?" He says *Judite* with some familiarity, as though he knows her. I better parse my words carefully.

*No, I didn't have an appointment.* "Why are you so interested in my schedule? Am I being interrogated?"

"You're being prodded so we can get to the important details and then get some sleep. It's been a long fucking night, Lexie." He throws back the rest of his drink and places the empty tumbler on the accent table beside him. "Did you have an appointment with Judite?"

"Not for a set time. I spoke with someone from the shop, who told me she'd be in all day. They assured me that she would give me a few minutes of her time."

"You ditched your guards, hopped on a plane, and came to Porto on a promise from a shop girl?" He leans back in the chair and raises his brow, waiting for a response.

"I had no reason to doubt the woman I spoke with. Any up-and-coming designer would love to see her name splashed on the glossy pages of *Eve*." I never spoke to anyone from the shop, but it will be harder to track down that lie than if I told him I had an appointment.

"Valentina is out of the country," he says, stretching out his legs in front of him. "How were you going to surprise her?"

"She's getting back tomorrow night." The truth is, I'm not sure when Valentina will be back—she wasn't sure herself.

Rafael leans forward with his elbows on his thighs and buries his face in his hands.

*I don't think he's buying a single word. Maybe I should have waited until tomorrow, when I was sharper, but then he would have been sharper too.* If he doesn't believe me, he's likely to call my father and send me back to London to languish in a posh cell. My father's guards won't be so easily fooled next time.

Rafael gets up and pours himself another bourbon. "Do you want something?"

I do, but I can't afford to relax while we're having this conversation. "I have water."

"All right." He sighs, sitting back down. "How did you meet the traffickers and the *principessa*?"

"Stop calling her that. She's not an Italian princess. She's a person with a brain and feelings and blood running through her veins."

"You'll pardon me if I'm not completely sold on the brain. But fine. Tell me about how you met Francesca."

"When I walked into the bar in the hotel lobby, I recognized Francesca from Saint Philomena's. She was sitting at a table with Misha."

Prime ministers' daughters are heavily guarded, but I didn't see a single one in the vicinity. *If I know anything, it's how to spot a guard.* Francesca had slipped her security too. There was no other explanation. Misha had all the trappings of an uber-rich girl—couture clothes, shoes, and purse—but even from a distance, something was off.

"She's a little young to be your friend."

"Friends and allies come in all shapes and sizes. Saint Phil's has a big sister program—like a mentor program. I knew her from when we would go down to visit our little sisters. Given how many Saint Phil's girls you hooked up with when you were studying in London, I'm surprised you don't know more about the school."

He brings his hands up and laces them at his mouth to hide a smile—or maybe it's a smirk.

"What happened after you spotted your little friend?"

Why I'm in Porto isn't something I plan to share with him.

He'll blow an aneurysm. But I can tell him everything that happened once I arrived.

"I went over to say hello. Francesca introduced me to Misha and invited me to have lunch with them. Sometime before our salads came, Francesca told me they were going to Club Azul, and she invited me to come along. Her boyfriend, Paolo, was supposed to meet her in Porto, but he missed his flight and couldn't get here until the next day."

"What made you decide to go out with them?"

Ten minutes with Misha, and I knew she wasn't who she claimed to be. "Misha gave off a weird vibe. I was worried about Francesca. Women getting abducted from clubs all over Europe isn't exactly a secret."

He cocks his head. "What kind of weird vibe?"

"I don't know." I try to recall the moment when I decided she was a liar. "She pretended to be someone who came from money, but the things she said didn't add up. I don't care how much money her clothes cost or what kind of vacations her family takes—people lie all the time about money. But there was something off about her. I didn't trust her."

"The idea that she might have something to do with a trafficking ring occurred to you, but yet you agreed to meet up with her friends."

*Initially, I felt like I won the damn lottery—until a healthy fear of being sold at auction took hold.*

"It occurred to me, because like most other young European women, the traffickers are always in the back of my mind when I'm out. But Misha could have simply been a thief or a social climber. Either way, Francesca was adamant about going with them. She was bummed Paolo didn't show up, and she wanted to blow off some steam. I wasn't taking any chances."

"Why didn't you contact the police, or your father, or your security?"

"You said we'd talk about my father after we finished with

this. Not calling security is tied to that—besides, they were in London."

"And the police?"

"The police? Really? You're asking me why I didn't call the police? That's rich. Do you call the police when there's a problem? Because my family doesn't. My father takes care of all problems in-house."

"Fair enough," he says, and for a few seconds, I relax.

"Why did you want to go to Sirena, instead of Club Azul?"

*Because I knew you'd be there and wouldn't let anything bad happen.* It sounds like the kind of foolishness children cling to, and I'd never say it out loud, but I believed it with all my heart.

"I've been to Sirena many times with Valentina." *Hoping you'd come out of your office and join us.* "The security is tight, and dozens of people are watching the floor from the command center."

"You took an unfathomable risk. Things could have so easily gone bad. They almost did. Why didn't you call me?"

He seems put out. Almost hurt. I want to shake him.

*Why? You can't possibly be* that *dense.* "I think you made it pretty clear after we shared a few kisses that you didn't want to have anything to do with me." I'm careful to keep my tone controlled so that I don't sound pathetic.

His expression falls, and I see regret in his eyes, but the mask is back in place before I take a single breath.

"When it seemed clear that all three of them were bad news, I tried to get Francesca to come to the bathroom with me, but she wouldn't. No one at the club looked familiar. I didn't see Zé or Xavier or even a waitress I recognized. By that time, I was certain they were part of the ring. But I didn't know who I could trust." My insides tremble as the details come crashing back.

"I went into the bathroom and activated the GPS in the bracelet I lent Francesca. Then I swallowed my pride and texted you."

# 12

## RAFAEL

*Texted me?*

I pull out my phone without letting on that I didn't see the text. There are dozens of unread messages. I stopped reading them while we were in the command center, focused on what was happening on the club floor.

"Are you sure you don't want something to drink?" I ask, getting another refill.

"A splash of bourbon would be great," she replies, most of the color gone from her cheeks.

Lexie: *I need your help. Please. I'm at Sirena. I think the sex traffickers are here. With me. I'm worried about a girl that's with us. We're at a table near the back bar. Please, Rafa.*

My chest tightens as I read the words and imagine how frightened she must have been when she sent the text *begging for my help.*

*I didn't get your message, Lexie.* I was so focused on taking down those fuckers that I never saw it.

I don't tell her that I never saw the text. I don't tell her that I knew they were flesh traders, and that instead of aborting the operation, we went full steam ahead, risking her life. I don't tell her any of it, because I'm a goddamn coward.

I hand her the tumbler of bourbon, and our fingers graze. A spark flies like it always does when we touch. But instead of making my cock jerk, it jolts my conscience—and my heart.

I want to fling my glass at the window and watch it splinter into a million pieces. She risked her life because she couldn't trust me enough to place a call this afternoon. She waited until it was almost too late.

The rage and self-loathing take over every inch of me. I'm angry at her, at those fucking traffickers, at everything and everyone, but mostly I'm furious with myself. If I hadn't ignored her after the wedding, she would have called me from the hotel as soon as she realized Misha was bad news.

If I had an ounce of sense, I would have pulled her away from those fuckers immediately and turned them over to the authorities. But I wanted to catch them in the act so they couldn't squirm free. I was willing to allow her to become collateral damage. It doesn't matter how many safeguards we put in place. The bottom line is I was willing to take a chance with her safety.

Yes, she takes too many fucking risks, but this was my fault, and if anything had happened to her—I can't bear to think about it.

I gulp down the bourbon and drop the tumbler on the cart so hard it cracks the glass top. *Is she afraid to tell me why she's in Porto? Is that another risk that she's willing to take because I'm an untrustworthy fucker?*

I glance at her, remorse eating at me. *And shame.*

"I need to go, and you need to sleep. When you wake up in the morning, I want you to think long and hard about the pieces that were missing from your story. Like why you're in Porto. I'm not some chump in a bar that you can feed a line."

"I told you the truth," she says indignantly, but her heart's not in it.

*I won't allow her to keep this secret.*

"You slipped your bodyguards to come here to write a story and surprise Valentina? Save the bullshit for some slob who wants in your panties so bad they'll buy anything."

She leaps off the sofa and stalks toward me, and some part of me hopes she'll scratch my eyes out or knee me in the balls for being a prick. "You have some goddamn nerve."

"Tomorrow you're going to tell me the truth." My voice is low and controlled, but it doesn't invite negotiation.

She doesn't fight me. She changes the subject. "You said we were going to discuss what happened the night of the wedding. Or was that just another manipulation to get what you wanted from me?"

The words are biting, but the hurt in her eyes betrays her.

"I'm sorry I never got in touch with you after that night." *Sorrier than you'll ever know.*

"Got in touch? You could barely stand to look at me."

*Because every time I looked at you, I wanted to tear every stitch of clothing from your succulent body and fuck you until we were both sore and panting.*

"We will have that discussion. But not tonight." *You deserve the truth, but I need some leverage until you tell me why you were really in Porto.*

"Get out," she hisses, gathering all the anger and hurt she can fit into two small words.

*It's okay, Angel. Your rage...your pain—give it all to me. I can take it.*

I hold her by the arms. "I'm leaving. But I won't allow you to rewrite history. I didn't manipulate you. You followed me into the vineyard." She tries to pull away, but I don't let her. "And that night was about more than just a few kisses, Angel. A hell of a lot more."

Every cell in my body wants to ravage her mouth, but that would be another mistake. *Nothing's changed since the wedding.* Instead, I drag her toward me and press a long kiss to her forehead, where it meets her hair. She whimpers as though it's torture.

I want to pull her closer, comfort her, tell her just how much that night meant to me, but I don't. I leave without another word.

# 13

## RAFAEL

THE PHONE RINGS BEFORE DAYBREAK, startling me from a fitful sleep. *Antonio.*

*Christ.*

Before we contacted the Porto police last night, I called Antonio. I didn't want him blindsided by the news. I have too much respect for him to allow that to happen. *I owe him too much.* I mentioned Francesca Russo, but not Alexis. I agreed not to call her father, but I couldn't be sure Antonio would grant her that grace.

I groan and answer the call. *"Bom dia,"* I mutter.

*"Bom dia,"* he says in a glib tone that tells me he knows he woke me.

Antonio's been a father to me since shortly after my mother disappeared. Not a father figure, but a father. He's the reason I'm still in one piece. *Alive.* But he's also a ballbuster who'd be easier to deal with after a shower and some caffeine.

"Don't you ever sleep?"

"I'll sleep when I'm dead," he replies dismissively. "I understand the men you captured last night were turned over to the authorities in rough shape."

*So much for the pleasantries.* "That's what happens when you try to escape."

"Tried to escape?" He chuckles. "Is that the story we're telling?"

"They got off easy."

"I'm proud of you, Rafael."

*I'm proud of you, Rafael.* It doesn't matter that I'm a grown man soon to take over an empire—those words, from Antonio, never get old.

"Those assholes have been terrorizing much of Europe for too long," he continues. "I'm also pleased you found the self-control to keep the bullets in your gun."

"They have information the authorities need to track down victims. The families deserve to know what happened to their loved ones. That's the only reason the bastards are still polluting the earth." I draw a breath. "But I wouldn't have wasted a single bullet on those animals. I would have stared into their eyes while choking the life out of them."

He pauses for a long moment. "I heard Alexis was with them and that she's now with you."

*Here we go.* There's nothing, *nothing*, that happens in Porto that Antonio doesn't know. He has eyes everywhere.

"She slipped her security, and she's in the country alone. We both know flesh peddlers are dangerous motherfuckers."

"Lexie needs your protection. *Ahh.* You're acting as a good Samaritan. Silly me. I thought you took her home for more selfish reasons."

*I didn't, but it crossed my mind more than once.*

"What was I supposed to do? Valentina's out of the country. She's practically family. I had to do something with her."

"Her father doesn't see it quite that way."

*Her father.* "He called?"

"About twenty minutes ago. He heard about what happened at Sirena last night and can't reach his daughter.

He knows she's at Huntsman Lodge. He's pissed. Really pissed."

*Can't really blame him, although I'd prefer not to be the target of his anger—especially when it comes to his daughter.* "Is he coming to Porto?"

"I talked him out of it. For now. I assured him that I'd get to the bottom of what was going on and get back to him. Among other things, he's concerned that Lexie is in your bed. That you might have taken advantage of the situation."

"So heartwarming that Will, and you, believe I'm that kind of opportunist." He hit a nerve, and my response is snarky and defensive. "She's staying at Valentina's apartment, and I'm staying at mine. If you'd like, feel free to interrogate Giana and Sabio about the sleeping arrangements. They've been with Lexie since Sirena."

He doesn't jump to take me up on the offer, but he doesn't shy away from asking a question that I know is difficult for him. "Are you sure she isn't involved?"

Antonio's known the Clarkes for longer than I have. His mother, my Aunt Lydia, married Lexie's grandfather after her husband died. She treated Lexie's mother, Samantha, like a daughter, and Lexie—along with Valentina, who came into the picture much later—were her greatest joys in life.

"We're not sure about much at this stage, but the traffickers admitted targeting the Russo girl and taking Lexie as a bonus."

The espresso maker hisses in the background, and I imagine him with his back pressed to the countertop, his features pulled tight.

"You know the difference between men and boys, Rafael?"

I roll my eyes, because it's too damn early for this shit.

"Well, do you?" he demands.

*How could I forget? You drilled it into my head for years.*

"A boy follows his dick, wherever it takes him. No peripheral vision. No questions asked." He pauses. "A man doesn't follow. He leads."

I feel like a teenager being lectured for sneaking a girl into my room. But the truth is, Antonio would say this very thing if he walked in on Lexie and me as adults. It's what he would have said the night of Valentina's wedding. *The stakes are too high. You have responsibilities to things bigger than yourself. Put your dick away.*

"I've been at this for too damn long," he mutters. "I'm tired. I want to begin stepping back, but I can't, until I'm certain you're ready."

"I'm not sure anyone is ever ready to take on the kind of responsibility that sitting in your chair demands. But I'm not a boy," I add firmly.

"You are not." Antonio sighs. "*Cuidado*, Rafael," he warns in a somber voice. *Be careful.*

"Will isn't the first irate father I've encountered."

"I'm not talking just about Will. You disrupted a human trafficking ring. Interfered in their business. It's a highly lucrative trade. Revenge is sure to follow. Keep your eyes open."

"I don't have a death wish," I murmur. "My team is on high alert. As am I."

"Don't be too proud to ask for help. All of Huntsman Industries is at your disposal, including me."

After we say goodbye, my head drops to the pillow.

My biological father was a monster, but when Antonio took me in, he gave me everything a boy needs to thrive and grow into the kind of man who can lead. Love, support, empathy, discipline, respect, time—the list is unending.

Antonio was in his twenties when I went to live with him. We had our share of struggles. He, as a young man rising to power, while learning to parent a kid who'd lost his mother and suffered years of abuse. Me, as a kid who had forgotten what it was like to be loved and cherished—to be anything other than a madman's punching bag.

Despite all he had on his plate, Antonio gave me everything he had, and more, even when I became a rebellious teenager testing my boundaries and his limits. He was never afraid to lower the boom, but punishment never involved fists or a leather strap. Unlike my father, Antonio never laid a hand on me, unless it was to pull me into an embrace.

He's right about the fallout. We disrupted the ring, and they'll seek revenge. It's likely to be big and splashy, a clear message to anyone even thinking about taking them down. It might not happen today, or tomorrow, but revenge will come.

# 14

## RAFAEL

AFTER I WORK out and grab a shower and coffee, I stop by Valentina's apartment. Carlos, who relieved Sabio, lets me in.

"Ms. Clarke's asleep," he says, following me into the kitchen, where they've set up shop.

"Any problems?" I ask Giana, who's in a chair at the center island, working on her laptop.

"None," she assures me. "Ms. Clarke was cooperative."

*I'm sure she's saving the arguments for me or trying to lull you into a false sense of security so she can bolt out the door when you turn your back.*

It's highly unusual to have two guards stationed inside an apartment on the residential floor of Huntsman Lodge. Normally we have guards stationed at each exit on the floor, and another outside the main elevator. When Valentina stays here without Marco, there's a guard outside her apartment door as well, but no one inside. *That's because Valentina isn't in the habit of ditching her security to meet up with traffickers.*

"I don't want to overstep," Giana continues, "but since she's not a suicide risk, would you consider allowing her to have the door closed—especially the bathroom door? She wanted to shower last night but changed her mind when I told her the door would need to remain open."

The three cups of coffee I gulped down earlier are sloshing around my gut, painting every inch with acid. Before they left the club last night, I told Giana and Sabio that if I were them, I wouldn't allow Lexie the privacy of closed doors. I said it so she would understand that skipping out was off the table—but mostly I said it to distract her from the awkwardness between us. Given the circumstances, I should have known the guards would take me literally.

"Ms. Clarke can't come and go as she pleases, not until we know more about what happened last night, but she's not a prisoner. She's free to go anywhere in the apartment. Give her as much privacy as she wants."

Giana nods.

"Did her things arrive?"

"Shortly after you left. Sabio placed an order for groceries like you asked. They'll be here by eight. Ms. Clarke also wondered about her phone."

Tamar downloaded the contents of the phone and checked for tracking devices—there was one that we traced back to Lexie's father, but it had been disabled. I'm sure it was Lexie's doing. We added a remote monitoring device of our own—it's state of the art, but I'm sure eventually she'll figure it out.

"I have it with me. I'll leave it for her."

I take a sheet of paper from Valentina's desk and scribble a note to leave with the phone. The authorities want to talk to Lexie, and I want to avoid her sitting for an interview. Once she speaks to them, the word will leak out that Will Clarke's daughter is involved, and every media outlet in the world will want a piece of her. *That is not happening. Not on my watch.*

The guest room door is ajar, and I slip inside quietly so as not to wake her.

As it happens, the woman who courts the devil sleeps like

an angel—a beautiful angel, seemingly at peace. Although it's hard to believe that after last night there could be any real peace for her, even in sleep.

She's on her side, legs tucked up and her golden hair a halo against the snow-white linen. There's nothing playful or defiant about her now, just an innocence that rouses every protective instinct I have.

*Whatever mess you've gotten yourself into, I will fix. Even if it means dragging you kicking and screaming to the solution.*

I place her phone and the note on the nightstand and shut the door behind me. A sense of relief washes over me as the latching mechanism catches. She's safe and where she's supposed to be—at least for now.

"Ms. Clarke shouldn't leave the apartment," I remind the guards, "and no one should come in who hasn't been cleared by either me or Zé. I'll be downstairs in my office for most of the day. Contact me if there's a problem of any kind."

# 15

## RAFAEL

WHILE THE OFFICE is still quiet, I force myself to stop fantasizing about the woman with the golden hair in bed upstairs, and tweak the plans for the project Valentina and I have been working on for more than two years. Although the idea has been kicking around since I interned here more than a decade ago.

We're launching a product that will transform the centuries-old Port wine industry into something youthful and energetic. Using the valley's prized grapes, Premier has created a line of lighter Port beverages and mixers that dovetail with tradition but are flirty and fun. They made a huge splash in Europe during the soft rollout, and we're going full steam ahead, including rolling out the new product in the US over the next year.

It's an exciting project, but not without vocal detractors. Modernizing Port has the old guard clutching their hearts. Not that they need to be worried.

I have no intention of shitting on Port's storied history— that's not what either Valentina or I want. We want Port and the valley to thrive and prosper for centuries to come. But beyond the holiday season, it's nearly impossible to get anyone under thirty interested in sipping fortified wine after dinner, or at any other time—not even in the Douro Valley, where Port is inextricably tied to our existence.

The data doesn't lie. The vintners and Port makers in the region can either begin a new chapter and flourish, or die a slow, painful death. Even Antonio, who was skeptical at first, has come around. He's even stopped calling it the bastardization of Port.

Although not everyone agrees. We've had a lot of pushback and nasty press. The worst of the opposition has quieted some, at least in Porto, but it's still here, waiting for us to screw up. People hate change, even when it's good for them.

Who it's not good for is Bancroft Spirits, who dominates the US market. At least they have up until now, but that's about to change.

"Henry Fausto is here," my assistant Noelia calls from inside the doorway. "And there are some agents from Interpol downstairs who want to see you. Security at the front desk tried to send them away, because they don't have an appointment, but they're refusing to go until they have a word with you."

Interpol is a pain in the ass, and I don't have the patience for their games. I told the authorities everything I knew last night. Much to their annoyance, I insisted on talking to the Porto police, the Intelligence Service, and Interpol all at the same time. There was no way I was sitting for three interviews, like they wanted. *I don't have time for that bullshit, and it wouldn't have made the case any stronger.*

The Intelligence Service wasn't happy, but they did their job. Interpol sat at the table, but they didn't have many questions, and the agents were cagey about the ones they did ask. They mostly listened. I'm sure they're here now to question me about information they didn't want to share with the Portuguese authorities. That's how they operate.

They had their opportunity. I won't be talking to them today. But I'm happy to have the agents park their asses in my conference room until I get good and ready to drop that little nugget on them. *That's how* I *operate.*

"Send them up and put them in the small conference room."

"The one off your office?" Noelia asks, brow raised.

"*No.* They're not setting foot in my office. Put them in the room just inside the suite where we put everyone who's peddling bullshit."

She nods and turns to leave.

"And Noelia? Tell them to get comfortable, because I'm in a meeting and can't be interrupted. Send Henry in."

When I interned at Huntsman Industries, more than a decade ago, Henry worked for Antonio, or more specifically, he worked for Antonio's bookkeeper. He walked me through balance sheets and every financial statement with the patience of Job. I learned more about financial accounting from him than I learned in graduate school. When I took over Premier, I convinced Antonio to let him come work for me, as Premier's bookkeeper, and he's been here ever since.

There's a knock on the open door, and I close my laptop.

"Henry." I stand to shake his hand. He's in his early forties. A proud man whose appearance is painstakingly exact, like his calculations. "It's nice to see you."

Henry doesn't pop in often. When he does, it's normally to verify some expenditure that he could as easily email me about. But he hates paper trails. I do, too, but I also hate meetings that don't need to happen.

"What's going on?" I ask, motioning for him to take a seat.

"I'm not sure." He clears his throat. "There are eight thousand and thirty-seven euros that seem to be unaccounted for in the main account. I . . . I was wondering if perhaps you made an off-the-books purchase that I didn't know about."

"From Premier?"

He nods.

"No. Have you ever known me to withdraw money like that?"

"I've never known you to do that. Ever." He sits up straighter, like he has something important to say and wants me to take notice. "But we're stretched a bit thin with the launch about to begin, and tracing small sums of money in a multimillion-dollar enterprise is sometimes more time-consuming than tracing larger amounts. Not that eight thousand and thirty-seven missing euros is a small thing." He waves his hand. "I thought it made sense to check with you before we headed down that rabbit hole."

Premier is my company—and Valentina's. I draw a generous salary, and investments and benefits are worked out through the CFO's office and human resources, but otherwise I don't dip into the coffers for anything. Not even petty cash if I left my wallet at home and I'm taking an investor to lunch. Not my style.

"Look into it, if you want, but don't sweat it. I appreciate that you like to account for every cent, but eight thousand euros is nothing for a company our size. Don't spend time that could be better spent elsewhere chasing chump change."

I don't mean to be flippant, because it's not exactly chump change, but I need Henry to focus on the launch. After that's over, he can spend days chasing eight euros, if that makes him happy.

"It's a matter of pride, Rafael. I don't sleep well unless my books reconcile."

He pauses and clears his throat again. Our conversations are always stilted. I'm a big-picture, think-outside-of-the-box kind of guy, and Henry loves the safety of the box.

"Would you mind if I checked with Valentina when she's back from her trip? Perhaps that's where the discrepancy lies."

"You don't need my permission to talk to Valentina, but I doubt she knows anything about the missing money." Valentina is as careful as I am, but let him ask so he can put the issue to bed.

"I agree. She's as meticulous as you are about keeping personal and business expenditures separate. Don't worry," he says, "I'll get to the bottom of it."

*Not worried. Just need you to leave so I can tell those fuckers in my conference room to get the hell out of my building so I can get back to work.*

I stand, signaling the end of the meeting. "Don't spend too much more time on it. There's a lot to do on the US launch. But let me know if you figure it out."

Not that I actually give a damn about a few thousand euros.

# 16

## ALEXIS

WHEN I WAKE, the bedroom door is closed and there's a note with my phone on the nightstand. As much as I've missed having my phone, I reach for the note first.

The floral stationery dotted with chicken scratch that's decidedly male makes me smile. But like everything else with Rafael, I'm sure the small pleasure will be short-lived.

*Good morning,*

*Your phone is clean and safe to use. Your father heard about what happened last night. He's worried. If you don't want to speak to him, call your mother. Also, draft a statement for the authorities, then email it to me so I can have my lawyer look it over before we send it off. They also need to see your passport. Give it to one of the guards, and we'll make copies. I'm not handing over the original. You need to hang out in the apartment until we have more information about the traffickers and any danger they might pose to you. Let's meet for dinner and finish our conversation from last night.*

*In the meantime, stay out of trouble.*

*RH*

In the meantime, stay out of trouble. RH. *Were you expecting a love letter?* No. Of course not, but that doesn't make me wish that there wasn't some—I don't know. Maybe one sentence that didn't seem so businesslike. This is something he might leave for his assistant before he went out of town.

I glance down at my to-do list for the day, from a man accustomed to issuing orders. He didn't even bother couching any of his demands in ways that might make me actually want to comply. A *please* or *if you're up to it* would have gone a long way. I reread the note, looking for a reason to forgive his bossiness, but it leaves me even more prickly, and I fire off a text.

Lexie: *Stay in the apartment? And exactly what am I supposed to do here all day?*

Rafael: *Did you not see the part about calling your parents and drafting a statement?*

I'm happy to give them a statement. More than happy. I've done everything but stand on my head to get someone in authority to listen to what I've discovered about the traffickers. But there's no way I'm contacting my father, although I don't mind calling my mother. I'm already starting to feel claustrophobic. I need to get out of here. And even more important, he needs to understand that I'm not his captive. I don't give a damn how good he kisses.

Lexie: *I have to run over to Judite Furtado's shop. I won't be long.*
Rafael: *No.*
Lexie: *I have a feature to write. Pesky deadline and all that.*

Ten minutes later, and I still haven't heard back. Surely he doesn't think I'll go away quietly.

Lexie: *Giana and Sabio are welcome to join me. You can come, too, if you'd like.*
Rafael: *You won't be going today. I won't be going ever.*
Lexie: *She won't be at the shop over the weekend.*
Rafael: *Pity.*
*What a prick.*
Lexie: *Where I come from, guards are able to protect a woman in a small boutique.*

It's childish, but it gives me a great sense of satisfaction to press Send.

Rafael: *Where you come from, guards are easily tricked, which means they're not protecting a damn thing.*

*Clever comeback. Annoying, but clever.*

Lexie: *This conversation isn't over.*

I toss the phone on the bed. The interview won't have the same flavor, but I probably don't need to go to Furtado's shop to write the piece I'm working on. *Ugh.* I can peruse the website and talk to her on the phone or via email. If the magazine needs pictures, they'll send a photographer anyway. I hate half-assing things—because that's what this feels like—but I know all about picking my battles.

Plus, he's right. It's too soon to have a sense of the fallout from last night. I might have left myself exposed—too exposed. I need to think through the next steps, but first I need some tea.

# 17

## RAFAEL

"I HOPE you're not calling to tell me my husband is missing," Valentina quips sarcastically before saying hello.

I smile at her insolence. "Isn't he with you?"

"No." She sighs. "He left at the crack of dawn."

"Trouble in paradise?"

"That would make your entire weekend extra special, wouldn't it?"

I'm not a huge fan of Marco, but I don't want her marriage to fall apart. She's too invested in a life with him, and it would destroy her dream.

"No, sweetheart. It wouldn't. Nothing will ever convince me that he's anywhere near good enough for you, but you love him, and I love seeing you happy." *But if any of that changes, and he's responsible for any of your unhappiness, "missing" will simply be a code word for brutally tortured before his bowel was ripped out.*

"Why are you calling so early?"

From her tone, she's noticed the extra security. I hope she doesn't expect a *mea culpa*, because she's not getting it.

"Not so early here. But I heard you had an appointment

with that asshole from Bancroft Spirits, and I want to know how it went."

"You heard? You mean you checked my schedule. Or maybe you asked one of the additional guards that's been shadowing me since the wee hours of the morning?"

"We'll get to that. But first talk to me about the meeting with Scott Bancroft." *Once I tell her about the traffickers and Lexie, that will be the end of any Bancroft discussion.*

"He cornered me at the reception last night and insisted we meet for breakfast."

"Cornered you?" *My blood pressure is rising. I don't like that fucker, even when he's not cornering women I care about.*

"That part wasn't a big deal. Breakfast was fine too. But I don't like that guy. Every time I see him, I feel like I need a shower."

*I feel like I need a shower. What the hell does that mean?* "Did he say something to make you uncomfortable? Did he touch you?"

"Jesus, Rafael. With the amount of security that's been added to my detail, you think anyone can get close enough to touch me? And we are going to talk about that. Don't think I'm going to forget," she huffs.

"It's just a feeling I get about him," she continues, seeming distracted. "He has that smarmy television preacher thing about him. Too pious. Too good. Too charming. Too slick with all that thick, shiny dark hair that's so perfectly coiffed you can't tell if it's fake or his own. He's creepy."

I've heard enough. "Don't meet with him alone again. Next time, he talks to me, or he doesn't talk to anyone."

When we launch in the US, we're going to cut into Bancroft's profits in a *big* way. He's focused on Valentina because he thinks she'll be easier to pry information out of than me. *Good luck with that, buddy. I've pried information out of seasoned Bratva soldiers, but Valentina has had me chasing my tail more than once. She's not spilling a goddamn thing by accident.*

"I don't plan on meeting with him again. Okay. Let's not start with, *You're not in charge of my security.* That's so yesterday," she taunts. "Instead, let's begin with, *What's with the extra security?*"

Working with Valentina on this project has made it the single best thing I've ever been involved in. If my mother were alive, she'd be thrilled that we not only run Premier together, but we share a special bond—*despite what the monsters wanted.* I do my best to treat her like a partner, but I won't compromise her safety, even if it means incurring her wrath.

"You're on Premier business. Premier decides when it's necessary to increase the security on employees or principals traveling abroad." Technically, I should have gone through Marco, but I'm not big on asking permission, especially from the likes of him.

"You might not be smarmy, but you're as full of shit as Bancroft."

I don't want to worry her, but I do want her to call Lexie, and I want her to come back to Porto, especially now that Marco's not with her. Not that I would ever trust that pussy to protect her.

"The traffickers were in Porto last night," I say quietly. "At Sirena."

"What? Oh my God. Was anyone hurt? Did they abduct another woman, Rafa?"

"No. Everyone's okay, and the assholes we caught were turned over to the authorities."

"You turned them over to the authorities?" she asks, like I just said the Douro River completely dried up last night while we slept. *It's just a huge hole in the earth now.*

"Sometimes there's no choice." I pause, trying to figure out the best way to tell her the rest without upsetting her more than necessary. "You should know that Lexie got snared in their net."

Valentina doesn't say anything for several seconds. I'm sure she's trying to wrap her head around it, much the same way I was when Lexie walked into Sirena with them.

"Lexie? My Lexie? Is this some kind of sick joke?"

There's fear and anguish in her voice, and for a moment I regret telling her.

"She's absolutely fine. You don't need to worry. But it's no joke."

"Rafael. That's so scary. How is she?"

*Gorgeous. Sassy. Sexy as hell.* "A little shaken up. She's staying at your apartment for the time being, so she doesn't have to deal with her father. I didn't think you'd mind."

"Of course I don't mind. I wouldn't want to deal with my father either if I skipped out on my security."

*Whoa, whoa, whoa.* "How do you know she skipped out on her security?"

"She was in a club in Porto and got snared by some traffickers. That doesn't happen with a cadre of guards surrounding you. It's Lexie. I'm surprised she didn't try to capture the bastards herself."

That would be funny if I hadn't seen the look on her face last night when security swooped in, or read the text where she begged for my help. "I don't think even Lexie, with all her self-confidence, would attempt that kind of stunt. What's the deal with her and her father?"

Valentina is quiet for a moment. "Do you know that Will has prostate cancer?"

*Jesus. Is that why Lexie didn't want me to contact him last night?* "No. I didn't know he was sick."

"He's not exactly sick. He has a very slow-moving kind that's common in men his age."

"Let me get this straight. Her father has a cancer diagnosis and Lexie decides to make his life more difficult?"

"*Nooo.* That is not what I'm saying. Since his diagnosis, he's become more and more protective. I mean like scary out of control, Rafael. He makes my father look like a lax parent. The way he's going, it's not going to shock me if he locks her away in a tower at some point."

*If he expects that to work, it better be a mighty tall tower surrounded by a moat filled with crocodiles. Even then, there are no guarantees.*

"Lexie's mother allows this?"

"Samantha doesn't *allow* it," she snaps. "But it's not so simple, because clearly there's more to Will's behavior than meets the eye."

Will has always been over the top when it comes to security for Lexie and Samantha. *Why not send a dozen guards when three would do? Although I'm probably not one to talk.*

"I'll call her as soon as we get off."

"She'll be happy to hear from you." *And maybe less annoyed at me for making her stay in the apartment.*

"Any chance you can cut your trip short and come back to Porto and hang out with her a bit? I realize you have a job and a husband, but she's alone, and I'm trying to get her to stay put until we have a better sense of whether the traffickers are going to retaliate. We caught foot soldiers, not the men in charge."

"Are you asking because you want me to keep Lexie company, or because you want me home where you think I'll be safer?"

*Not think. I know you'll be safer, and I know if you're here, your friend is more likely to stay, and that means she'll be safer too.*

"A little of both, sweetheart. A little of both."

There was a time in our world when a man's word was final. No questions asked. It might not have been fair or right, but it made it a hell of a lot easier for him to protect the women he cared about. As I sit here, waiting for her to decide, I miss those times.

If I push her too hard, she'll balk and stay away twice as long. Could I drag her back to Porto? In a heartbeat, and I'm not above it if the situation warrants, but it would come at a cost.

"I'll cut short my trip. Not because I'll be safer at home, but because I'm sure Lexie could use the company. She puts on a tough front, but inside she's not so tough. The thing with her father has taken a huge toll on her, and now this. I'm worried."

*She puts on a tough front, but inside she's not so tough.* I remember the fragility in her face last night, and the way she thanked me for being there for her. *No. Inside she's not so tough. And she shouldn't have to be either.*

"Rafa?"

"Hmm?"

"She's into you." Valentina pauses. "Really into you."

*We are not doing this. I'm not having this conversation with you.* "Did she tell you that, or are you reading tea leaves in your spare time?"

"No. She'd never admit it. But I don't need to be a *bruja* to know her feelings. It's so obvious, I bet her father has a bullet with your name on it."

One that he wouldn't think twice about using if he knew I had his daughter sprawled on a desk while I licked her pussy until she begged me to fuck her. "He wouldn't be the first."

"Or the last," she quips. "Seriously, though, be careful with her. Especially now."

*You mean don't almost fuck her and then walk away like a huge dick?*

In my experience, women who take enormous risks to wage war against monsters—women like my mother—are dead. They leave behind a trail of broken hearts, littering a river of tears and loved ones who never fully recover from the loss.

Lexie might not take the kind of risks that my mother, her sister, and their friends took, and she doesn't share a drop of blood with them, but she's cut from the same cloth. *The very same.*

"Don't worry. I don't get involved with reckless women."

"I've met some of the women you've taken home. Although I suppose too stupid to live isn't the same as reckless. But I do know this, Rafael. You can't resist a woman who needs to be rescued. My warning stands. Be careful. Be the good guy I know you are."

*Too late for that.* "Reading tea leaves isn't a very lucrative profession, *menina*. Given how much you like designer shoes, I'd stick to Port if I were you. Where's your husband, anyway?"

"Quimper."

"Quimper? What the hell's he doing in the north of France?" *While you're alone in the US.*

"Closing a deal for a client who's investing in pottery."

"When did pottery become art?"

"Don't take that tone with me. I'm not talking about the bowls you slurp your breakfast from," she scoffs. "They make some exquisite pieces in Quimper. Collector's items."

*Collector's items.* Maybe he can pick up a few heavy plates to toss at some bastard's head who gets too close to her. God knows a knife would make him squeamish.

My phone vibrates with a message from Zé.

*Molotov cocktail tossed at the front entrance of Sirena. No injuries. I'm here.*

*A Molotov cocktail? What the hell?* Retaliation came sooner than I expected.

"I've got to go, Valentina. Call Lexie, and then come home."

## 18

# RAFAEL

"What the fuck happened?" I snarl, while Zé's still grunting "yeah" into the phone.

"Some asshole threw a Molotov cocktail at the building. It bounced off a window in the area where guests will be waiting in line tonight."

"You sure no one was hurt?"

"The street was empty—except for whoever tossed the goddamn thing."

We were lucky. If it had happened in the evening, dozens of innocent people could have been injured—or worse. "How much damage?"

"Everything under the portico is gone. Security cameras—everything. The awning's gone too. But because the thing bounced off the bulletproof window, the brick front didn't sustain any damage. Maybe some soot. That's it. Xavier says the front will be patched up before the doors open."

"You agree?"

"The entrance won't be covered, but it's not supposed to rain tonight. Otherwise, I think it'll be fine. They're already working on it."

"Did the police show up?"

"I called the station before I texted you. Told them one of our heaters malfunctioned and there was an explosion. They asked if anyone was injured, and I told them no. They offered help if we needed it, and I thanked them."

"Good." The police don't really bother us, but it's always less of a hassle if they're not involved at all.

"The fire alarm went off, too, but Xavier took care of it."

"Someone was sending a message. If they wanted to incur maximum damage, they would have waited until eleven o'clock tonight when the line was snaked around the block." The thought of bodies piled up in front of the club—a place that's been a little oasis since I bought it—makes me sick.

"No doubt about it," Zé replies. "The only question is *who* was sending us a message. It seems a bit tame to be a warning from the upper echelon of a trafficking ring."

"It does. Although there are probably a dozen layers between the bastards we caught last night and the kingpin. We'll need extra security tonight. I want those streets cordoned off as soon as possible. Let the police know to expect it."

"What do you want me to tell them?"

"That we're taking extra precautions because of what happened last night. You know what? You focus on collecting evidence. Let Xavier get the place ready for tonight. I'll talk to the police." Zé has enough to do. Besides, I can call the captain directly, and he'll put his officers on notice. It's more efficient this way. "I'll be there within the hour."

"Last night was long and brutal. Why don't you stay home and relax tonight?"

"Why don't you do your job, and let me do mine?" I end the call before Zé can nag me like a fishwife. Before I speak to the police, I need to let Antonio know what happened. He can decide whether security should be tightened at Huntsman Lodge as well.

———

"RAFAEL," Arturo, the Porto police chief, says, "your ears must have been burning. I just told my deputy that I was going to call you."

"We have it under control. It might have been a faulty starter. My people are all over it."

"I'm sorry about the explosion, but that's not why I want to talk to you. The three suspects that were arrested at Sirena last night are dead."

A cold shiver runs up my spine. *Dead? All three, already?* Misha—just eighteen years old. What a waste. Fortunately, we got her sister and mother out of Romania last night. *Someone needs to tell them she's dead.*

"What happened?"

"Sometime this morning, while the Intelligence Service and Interpol were fighting in front of a judge about who should have custody of those assholes, they were murdered. Possibly before."

"How?"

"The woman was strangled, one of the men had a broken neck, and the other took a shiv to the kidney. All died in their cells. They didn't even bother to make any of it look like an accident."

*Ballsy as fuck.* "You're sure it's not just a rumor before moving them to a safe house location where they can assist in catching the bigger fish?"

"I can't speak to the woman. But I have a close friend who works at the men's prison. He saw the aftermath with his own eyes. Somebody didn't want them to talk."

*Somebody with a lot of power.* "By the time they were questioned and processed, it must have been daybreak before they got into a cell. Two separate facilities. It's not easy to pull off something like that without inside help."

"Someone tipped them off, and they were waiting for them to get there. And by *they*, I don't mean inmates. I mean guards. It's the only way it could have gone down so quickly. I'll let you know what else I hear."

"One more thing, Arturo. Given what happened last night, and now this news, I want to cordon off the streets around Sirena, starting this afternoon." We've done this before, although not during the day. "We'll make sure it's not a huge inconvenience for anyone who lives in the neighborhood. It's for their protection too."

"I think it's better to be safe than sorry, even if it aggravates some of the neighbors. I'll let my people know."

"Thanks, Arturo. Keep me apprised. I'll do the same."

I toss my phone aside and sit back in the chair, my heart pounding like a son of a bitch. There's no doubt that Lexie's in danger. Francesca Russo too. *I'll contact her father on the way to Sirena.*

I pick up my desk phone and buzz Noelia. "Make sure Valentina is en route to Porto. Keep me updated."

My plan to take Lexie out to dinner, someplace neutral where we could talk without emotion getting the best of the conversation, just became take-in. Even with tight security, I won't take her to a public place.

I glance at the time. *I need to get to Sirena.*

A Molotov cocktail that bounced off bulletproof glass to cause minimal damage doesn't seem like a message from the people who ordered a successful hit on three high-profile inmates in federal custody.

The truth is, there are a number of people who would want to cause trouble for anyone named Huntsman. While we enjoy the support of much of the valley, including Porto, we also have a lot of enemies. It might be a competitor who heard about last night and wants to kick us while we're down, or it could be someone who's angry about the new direction Premier is taking. *If only it were that simple.*

I send Giana, Sabio, and Carlos a message on my way out: *No mistakes.*

# 19

## ALEXIS

AFTER SHOWERING AND EATING LUNCH, I listen to my mother plead for nearly forty-five minutes. She wants me to come home. My father is out of his mind with worry, and me, sleeping in my childhood bed for a few nights, will help.

She lays on the guilt pretty thick, not that it's necessary. I love my parents dearly. Even though I refuse to take responsibility for his out-of-control behavior, I'm racked with guilt.

No one is in a worse position than my mother, caught between me and my father. Although I didn't point a finger, part of this mess was created because she placates him much too often. I'm sure it's exhausting to hold your own, over a lifetime, against a man like him. She's not a pushover, but over the years, she's lost some of her fight, especially after her father was killed.

"Life's too short," she told me when I asked about it. "I love your father with every cell of my being, and I refuse to spend any more time than absolutely necessary squabbling."

That might be true, but if I asked, she'd be willing to wage war with him—for me. But I would never ask her to do it—not anymore. It's different now anyway.

My father is in a particularly bad place. And he doesn't want help. *He can take care of it himself.* That means tightening his control over everything—especially me. When it started, I fell into line and did everything he asked, including moving home. It didn't help. If anything, it made him want even more control over me. I would be willing to sacrifice all my freedom if it would actually unburden him. *But that's not what he needs.*

He needs a goddamn intervention—but no one is willing to step in and do it. Will Clarke can do whatever he wants, whenever he wants, make a huge mess, and the sycophants will gush all over it as though it's a masterpiece. Anyone with a shred of sanity recedes into the shadows, leaving my mother and me to mop up after him.

There is one thing that would change things for him—for us—at least my mother believes it would.

Dad was eleven when he went out to get his father a pack of smokes and pick up the cake his mom ordered from the neighborhood bakery for his baby sister's fifth birthday. It was one of those standing doll cakes, with a poofy skirt made out of pink and white frosting. The doll had blonde hair, like the little girl. Some of the tragic details were in the yellowed newspaper clipping I found in a box in his office when I was snooping. My father stopped to kick a ball around with his friends, and when he got home, his entire family had been brutally murdered.

The culprits were caught several years later, and they had a grisly end at my father's hand, but he's never found the person who put out the hit. When things started to spin out of control and I was stuck at home, I dug deep into the past for information that might help. Like my father, I hit every dead end—at least where my family was concerned. But I did stumble across other devils, and their evil plans.

I take my laptop from the bag that was delivered last night and immerse myself in graphs and charts and lists that I've painstakingly created over the last couple of months.

Plotting where the traffickers have been, I add Porto to the graph and assign it a permanent color. Then I cross it off my alphabetical list of European cities. I study the patterns on the graph and stare at the list of cities, trying not to be lulled into any false premise. *Oslo has to be next.* Then Rimini or Riga.

But what if I'm wrong? What if they change their MO?

They've been caught on camera a couple of times— although the photographs have not been released publicly. But last night was a major slipup. What if that causes them to change course? *I can't let that thought alter my direction. Not without evidence that they're doing something different.*

If they stick with what they've done in the past, they'll make a move in exactly thirteen days. That gives me more than a week to plan, and to get there. I have to assume I'll be on their radar now. These bastards don't play around, and although the possibilities terrify me, I'm not quitting on this. *I'll just have to be more careful.*

I'll send the Oslo police a message, and Interpol too. Although it's probably a waste of time. I've given Interpol many warnings, but they have *never* responded to any information I've sent. Never returned a call. Refused to meet with me in their London office. I don't expect them to lift a fucking finger now either. I'm sure they think I'm some sort of crazy person, obsessed with the traffickers—*maybe I am.*

"Ms. Clarke," Sabio says, knocking on the door. "There's someone here to see you."

*Someone to see me?* There's no way that the Intelligence Service or Interpol would just show up. Well, they might, but there's no way they would be allowed on this floor. *My father?* That's a different story. He'd be allowed up, even if he had to call Antonio to make it happen. My mother would have told me if he was in Porto. *If she knew.* But who else would it be? No one knows I'm here.

I open the door quietly, but Sabio's already gone.

With a deep breath, I gather the strength to do battle with my father and slip on my shoes.

When I get to the living room, a petite woman with a scarf draped fashionably around her shoulders is waiting. I smile at her cheeky grin.

"I understand you want to interview me," Judite Furtado says with a conspiratorial wink.

My cheeks burn as I burst out laughing. "I don't think I need to ask how you know."

"We have a mutual acquaintance. Charming, but persistent." She lifts her brow. "He emailed me at five this morning and followed up with a call at seven thirty when I didn't respond promptly." She chuckles.

By the time we texted this morning, Rafael had already contacted Judite. It's too dangerous for me to go to her, so he brought her to me. *Oh, Rafa. Please don't do things like this. It makes it too hard to keep any emotional distance.*

"I'm thrilled you're here, but I'm so sorry about the early phone call."

"Don't be. Rafael's great. I was struggling to find my place in the design world when we met at a friend's wedding in Lisbon, about three years ago. We were seated next to each other during the formal dinner. By the time the bride and groom said their goodbyes, he'd convinced me to open a shop in Porto. He's very persuasive."

*Maybe he used that lethal tongue to persuade her.*

The taste in my mouth is so sour I have to force my lips from puckering—but not before Judite notices.

"Rafael's been a good friend to my company, but there was never anything between us."

*Would it be too much to ask for the floor to swallow me whole right now?*

"He wanted me to bring you something special from my collection." She holds out a shopping bag. "It's a one-of-a-kind prototype for a brand-new design that won't be available in the stores until next year."

I gaze at the bag, and although I'm tempted, I don't take it. "That is special." *And totally unethical for me to accept.* "It's very generous. But the magazine's policy is that we can't accept gifts from designers we feature. I'd love to peek at it, though."

"It's not a gift," she explains, while I loosen the drawstring from the protective cloth sack inside the shopping bag. "Not from me, anyway. Rafael paid retail price for it."

I've grown up with so many luxuries it's almost embarrassing. If money can buy it, I can have it. It's made me jaded about material things, and gifts in particular. The best present for me is one that takes some thought and effort. It doesn't need to cost a penny. *Although this one clearly did.*

"It's stunning," I gush, sliding my fingertips over the seam where the cork and the fabric meet.

"I think so too," she says with a small laugh.

I like her. And I can see why Rafael wanted to help develop her business.

"Please, make yourself at home," I tell Judite, after I admire the purse for far too long. "I'll grab my laptop and we can get started on the interview. That way I won't take up too much more of your time."

I'm swamped with emotion, but I don't let myself revel in it for too long.

*Don't make too much of this. He probably had his assistant email Judite Furtado under his signature. Maybe Noelia came up with the whole idea.* I repeat it to myself several times as I gather my things for the interview. My musings don't even make sense given what Judite told me, and the grand gesture has Rafael's signature all over it. But I need to believe it wasn't him. A woman's got to do something to protect her heart—especially from a man who's already been careless with it.

# 20

---

## RAFAEL

I JERK my chin in greeting when Sabio opens the door to
Valentina's apartment.

"No problems," he mutters, without being prompted.
"Alexis is in the shower."

I stride past him and into the kitchen before I rearrange his
face for saying the words *Alexis* and *shower* in the same
sentence.

Giana is at the espresso machine when I enter. "Do you
want a coffee?" she asks, as I place a bag of takeout on the
counter. I promised Lexie dinner, but thanks to dead suspects
and a Molotov cocktail, I don't have all night.

I shake my head. "Ms. Clarke," I say pointedly for Sabio's
benefit, "and I are going to have dinner. Why don't you both
take a break? I have to be at Sirena in an hour. I'll text you
when I'm ready to go."

"Do you want one of us to stay in the hall?" Giana asks,
downing her espresso like it's a shot of tequila.

"Not necessary."

I turn the oven on low and go find Lexie.

The bedroom door is ajar, and I hear water running when I

enter. The image of her standing under the spray, naked, her hair in ringlets, the water clinging to every curve, is visceral, and I shove it away before I do something I'll regret.

I take a breath, my eyes trained on the closed bathroom door. I need to let her know I'm here and we don't have all night. As I stare at the door, the image of a naked Lexie pops into my mind again, and it's more difficult to push away this time. *What are you, fifteen? Get a fucking grip.*

I right myself and knock, but she doesn't respond. Between the powerful exhaust fan and the running water, she probably can't hear me.

*I don't have time to wait around for her to take a leisurely shower.*

When I crack the door to tell her to move it along, it opens wider than I planned, and the words die in my throat.

My eyes are transfixed on the mirror across from the open shower.

*Oh, baby.* This is hotter than anything I imagined. *Much hotter.*

The naughty angel in the glass has my dick rock hard.

Round, firm tits, a graceful arch in her back, mouth open, head tipped as the warm water sluices over her flawless skin— it's tantalizing—all of it. But what steals my breath is the portable showerhead aimed straight at her pussy.

With one foot propped on the bench, she holds the spray arm inches from her cunt. An ethereal cloud wafts around her as the fan pulls the steam toward the ceiling vent. Her hand is braced on the marble tile while the jets beat on that sweet pink flesh. It's the closest thing I've ever come to a heavenly vision.

I'm the worst kind of bastard for watching, but I can't pull myself away.

She's naked and aroused—and no more than a few strides from me. I can't think of *anything* besides joining her in the shower and soothing that ache between her legs.

My dick throbs ruthlessly as I watch, demanding to be pulled out and stroked raw.

A decent man would leave her to find her pleasure alone. He'd shut the door quietly, back away, and never say a damn word about it.

*Be careful with her. Be the good guy I know you are.* The echoes of my conversation with Valentina don't do a thing to dissuade me. I never claimed to be a saint, and Lexie has always struck me as the kind of woman who prefers a sinner. There's no fucking way I'm retreating.

I tear off my clothes and step into the shower.

She drops the spray arm when she sees me, eyes like saucers. Her skin is stained pink. I don't know if it's arousal or shame. *And I don't care.*

"Thank you for the purse. It's beautiful," she blurts, as though we're not standing here, her naked, me with my cock sticking straight out.

"That purse didn't come with any strings. Not a single one. Tell me to leave," I murmur, my hands on her hips as I drag her toward me. "If that's what you want, I'll go."

Her eyes are dilated, and she's still recovering from the surprise when she shakes her head. It's an achingly slow movement, left to right, and again. *But it's enough for me.*

I close the gap between us and slam my mouth against hers, coaxing her full lips open and exploring every sensuous corner, until she's teetering on her feet and my balls are ready to explode.

I swivel her hips until she's facing the corner. "Hold on to the wall, *meu anjo.* It'll support you while I fuck you hard. *So hard,*" I whisper, before I bite into her shoulder to hear her whimper.

"*Ahh.*" She gasps and moans, and I do it again, just to hear that sweet sound that goes straight to my throbbing dick.

"Do you like to play rough, angel? Or do you prefer it more tame?"

She turns her head and sinks her teeth into my forearm, not hard enough to leave a mark, but enough so that I feel it at the base of my spine.

"That's not an answer. I want to hear your words, Lexie." I graze my mouth over her neck until she shivers. "Tell me what you like."

"Yes," she whimpers. "I like to play rough. Fuck me, Rafael. I don't want to wait anymore."

*I like to play rough. Fuck me, Rafael.* My cock weeps, and my self-control is in tatters. *Oh, baby, you don't need to ask twice.* I nudge her legs apart with mine and pinch her nipples. She jumps and gasps in a mouthful of air.

With my foot, I drag over the spray arm and grab the handle, pressing it into her hand.

"I'm going to fuck you while the water beats on your pussy. It's going to be merciless, and you're going to come so hard for me, Angel, that your guards will hear your screams from the security office."

She whimpers.

"You'll like that, won't you?"

"Do it, Rafa. Just do it. *Please.*"

"You're so sweet when you beg, Angel." I run my tongue around her ear, rimming the delicate shell until her head falls back. "You aim that nozzle at your pussy when I tell you. It's going to feel so good."

She wiggles her ass into my cock, and the little control I have evaporates.

I tug on her hair, tipping her head so I can see her face, and with one brutal thrust, I plunge balls deep into her. The slide is so vicious a growl escapes from my chest.

Her face contorts, with a muffled sob, and the spray arm hits the ground with a thud.

I still, my heart hammering like a son of a bitch.

A tear escapes from her closed eyes and trickles down her cheek.

For several seconds, while my dick twitches inside her tight walls, I'm not sure what to do. This isn't the reaction I'd expect from an experienced woman, even if I slid too deep or was too rough. *This is something else.*

She's a virgin. *Was a virgin. No. Can't be.*

*Fuck. Fuck. Fuck.*

*No condom, against a shower wall, with my cock shoved against her womb. Fuck. Fuck. Fuck.*

With a gentle hand on her hip, I pull out with the utmost care. She winces as I withdraw, and I feel it in my chest. "Are you okay?"

She nods.

I tug her closer, her back against my front, and wrap my arms around her. "You should have told me."

Her heart pounds, but she doesn't say anything.

"You were a virgin?" I ask the question, knowing the answer, but hoping like hell I'm wrong.

She shrugs, and it's so cavalier that anger begins to simmer inside, overtaking the stark regret I felt a moment ago.

"Jesus, Lexie. Why didn't you say something?" I reach over and turn off the water. "What the hell's wrong with you?"

She shivers, and I pull away and step out of the shower to get her a towel. My mind is numb, but my dick still hasn't gotten the message, and I grab a towel and hitch it around my waist.

"That's why I didn't tell you," she hisses. "Because even though I wanted to give it to you, and even though you wanted it, you wouldn't have taken it. You'd have walked away, like you're doing now, and I'd never hear a fucking thing from you again."

I might deserve every word she spewed at me, but I'm too

furious to see it—furious at her for being reckless with her body, and at myself for being such a goddamn prick.

"And tricking me into it was supposed to change things?" As soon as the words are out, I want them back, even before I see the hurt in her eyes.

I grab a couple of towels and step back into the shower. "You were shivering. I was just getting you a towel. I'm not going anywhere. But I'm not fucking you against the wall either," I tell her, rubbing the soft terry cloth over her skin until it's pink and dry, and then wrapping a fresh towel around her. She doesn't fight me, but she's tense and uncomfortable, like she doesn't know what to do with herself.

I tip her chin up and gaze into her eyes. They're washed out, laced with sorrow. I would have preferred them flickering with rage.

"You didn't trick me into anything. I wanted you badly. But it shouldn't have been like that. You deserve something better for your first time."

She reaches up and trails her fingers over my jaw.

I close my eyes as the emotion swirls between us, ballooning into a deadly beast. I want nothing more than to run before it has me in its clutches.

"What exactly is it that I deserve?" she asks, softly, and the beast is so close it swipes at me with its paw and draws blood.

"A conversation and some foreplay," I reply in a tone that's too dispassionate and clinical, even to my ears, and not at all how I'm feeling. But I can't take the rank emotion for a second longer. I don't want to hurt her, but it's a matter of self-preservation. Lexie proved, again, that she's an unpredictable risk-taker —that I can't resist. "A lot of foreplay," I tease, winking at her.

She pulls her hand from my face and narrows her eyes, readying them to shoot a dagger. "Don't forget a sprinkle of sweetness."

Her tone is so saccharine my teeth ache.

"I don't do sweet, Angel. Never cared for it. Not with coffee, or cocktails, or fucking. But I think you've probably figured that out by now."

She swallows hard.

"But after I've properly taken your cherry, I'm going to slap your ass, because you deserve that too." I bring her hand to my mouth and nip her fingertip. "I'm pissed you didn't tell me."

"It wasn't a big deal. You're making more out of it than necessary."

I secure the towel around her and set her cute little ass on the countertop before she can protest.

She's not going to like this conversation, but if I'm not running, she's not running either.

# 21

## ALEXIS

"Not a big deal," he says with that deceptive calmness I know to be wary of. "The twenty-first-century woman who clung to her cherry for twenty-three *years* claims it's not a big deal."

He cradles my face in his big hands and forces me to meet his gaze. "It's a fucking big deal. So unusual, I bet they'd love to do a Netflix special about it."

I swat his hands away. "Technically, you're incorrect. A sleek pink vibrator with a curved shaft popped it years ago. I hope Netflix isn't too disappointed."

He scowls at me. "It's not my business why you haven't had sex. But you're not doing this, Angel. You're not going to act like giving up your virginity is nothing. If it wasn't a big deal to you, why didn't you just hand it over to some bloke in a bar?"

I ball my hands tight so I don't slap him in the face like he deserves.

"Sex means many things. Just because I haven't had one kind doesn't mean I haven't enjoyed other kinds. Don't you worry. I did plenty of *things* with blokes in bars."

He grabs my arms. "You. Are. Not. Doing. This. I won't allow it."

I don't want to fight with him. It's bad enough the moment I fantasized about has turned out to be a nightmare. I sigh. "What do you want me to say, Rafael?"

"I don't believe for one second that it meant nothing to you. I already told you I don't care why. You don't owe anyone an explanation—certainly not me. But stop acting like a bratty teenager who got called out on her bullshit."

A giant wave of embarrassment washes over me. I feel too young, and ridiculously unsexy. Whatever mood there was when he stepped into the shower is gone. I've had sex before— just not peen-in-the-V sex, and the vibrator is real—although I much prefer it near my clit, so it's been inside only a few times. Still, I thought I could pull it off so that he would never be the wiser. But that giant cock of his is so much healthier than my delicate pink vibrator.

*I need to swallow my pride and own the decision I made. A bad decision, as it turns out.*

"I should have told you." *Because the truth couldn't have possibly been more embarrassing than this.*

Pride is a big dry turd that I choke on while I try to force it down, and my voice strains as I admit the mistake. It's the closest thing he's getting to an apology. *I'm not sorry.* Maybe I will be tomorrow, or next week, but not yet.

Rafael slides his hands into my wet hair and presses his forehead to mine. "If you trusted me, I could have made it good for you."

"I do trust you," I whisper, and it's largely true. *Just not about this.* Rafael *dates* women who are drop-dead gorgeous and sophisticated and sexy as hell. I didn't want to come off like a teenage girl, unworldly and inexperienced, but in the end that's exactly what happened.

Rafael pulls back, resting his fingers on my thighs. He's sober, and I know he's going to give me some bullshit line about how we can't do this—how it was a mistake. *He's sorry.* That's what he'll tell me, etching another crack in my soul.

His eyes are a muted blue, filled with concern. My mind begins to conjure all sorts of scenarios that might be going on in his head.

All of a sudden, he's too close—*and yet not close enough.*

My brain refuses to engage in a drawn-out war with my heart and fires a warning shot that jolts me. I respond in the way that people have come to expect. "If you can trust me, I'll make it good for you too."

His shoulders shake before he throws back his head and laughs. It's not a genuine laugh. There's a measure of exasperation in it. "You're killing me, Angel."

"But what a way to go." I slide my hands across his chest and down to where the towel meets his skin.

He places his hands over mine, rubbing his thumb across my fingers. "You still up for a little playtime?"

"You still want me?" It's a needy question, even though I don't allow desperation to color it. I hate myself for it, but I had to ask. I need an assurance that this isn't some pity fuck. *I'd never be able to face him again.*

He takes hold of a small section of my hair and lets his fingers slide to the ends. "Always, Lexie. After I had a taste at the wedding, I haven't stopped wanting you."

A great sense of relief rains over me. Still, I close my eyes, trying to understand why a man who couldn't stop wanting me avoided me like the plague. *I don't need the answer right now.* That's what I tell myself. I don't need answers now. *I need him.*

"I'm going to my apartment to get condoms. I'll just be a few minutes. Dry your hair while I'm gone."

*Not a condom, but condoms. Like he'll be here for a while.* That's what a pathetic woman does. She holds on to every little thing that supports her dreams—her fantasies—even when she knows, deep down, the fairy tale ends without a happily ever after.

"Valentina probably has some in her bathroom or in the nightstand," I tell him, because inside I'm still worried that he might not come back. *Just a little worried.*

He grimaces, and I squeeze my lips together so that I don't smile.

"I'm sure. But she probably also has some other shit in there that I'd never unsee."

*Not probably, definitely.* "I'll get them."

He shakes his head. "I need to grab something else too."

I sit on the counter, quietly, and watch him dress. His thighs are dense muscle that extends seamlessly into his fine ass. In some ways it feels natural to admire his sculpted body, like I've done it before, and I have, but not like this. He doesn't bother with underwear, just tucks his cock into the black trousers before zipping them up and reaching for his shirt.

"Your hair isn't going to dry while you sit there watching me get dressed. It's not that interesting."

*Oh, but it is.*

I'm mesmerized with his fingers as they navigate the shirt buttons—long and thick, but nimble. I remember how good they made me feel in the vineyard—and on my skin in the shower until—

"Be right back," he mutters, squeezing my thigh.

After he leaves, I get the hair dryer, wishing that we could go back to the shower, where we weren't discussing condoms and the future. We weren't *discussing* anything. We were driven by the most basic of instincts, and by lust. Maybe it's not practical, or smart, but it's simpler.

Before I've even turned the hair dryer on, he's back.

"Forget something?"

"This," he says, kissing me until my knees are wobbling so much, I clutch the counter to stay upright.

"I also want to tell you something, so you can have a few minutes to think about it."

Whatever he's going to say, I'm not going to like it. I see it in his expression. "You have herpes?" I tease, because humor deflects pain nicely.

He chuckles, but my attempt to lighten the mood is fleeting. "No. I'm clean." His throat ripples, and I hold my breath, waiting for what comes next. "This thing we have"—he shifts his finger back and forth between us—"no promises."

I knew it was coming, or something like it, when we stood with our foreheads touching earlier. It's not some stunning revelation. But still, it's hard to hear. The little girl inside me scurries to a corner to cry because her feelings are hurt. But the truth is, I'm not ready to make promises either. *Although the knowledge does little to ease the hurt feelings.*

"You're off the hook, Huntsman. One night is all I'm looking for too."

Rafael taps his fingers on the counter. "Oh, I want more than one night. You might be too tired for that spanking you deserve, and I want you fully sentient when I deliver it." He presses his mouth to the bridge of my nose. "But I don't want to mislead you, Lexie. I don't know about next week or next month. If that doesn't sit well with you, you're not obligated to finish what we started. You can change your mind."

*It sounds like maybe you've had a change of heart, and you're hoping I'll take the out. I won't change my mind. I've wanted you for too long. If you don't want me, you'll have to say it. In the meantime, I'm going to put on a little armor.*

"Did you not hear what I just said? Your cock might be impressive, but I'm only interested in taking it for a whirl, not buying it." I wave him off and turn on the blow-dryer, because if we continue this discussion, the little girl inside, who's sobbing again, might make an appearance and give me away.

But he doesn't leave, at least not before he studies me in the mirror, as if hoping to catch a glimpse behind the mask.

"I have a birth control insert," I say loudly enough to be heard over the whir of the dryer, "but we should still use a condom." It's my way of dismissing him before he sees too much. Although Rafael isn't that easily dismissed. He won't go until he's ready.

I don't turn around, but I can see him in the mirror. He doesn't respond, but he raps his knuckles against the door-frame and disappears.

The last fifteen minutes have been a major buzzkill, and I won't be surprised if he doesn't return. *I don't care whether he comes back.* I repeat this at least a half-dozen times in my head, hoping it'll take root, but it doesn't. It's a damn lie, invented to protect my heart, but my brain refuses to categorize it as anything else.

If he doesn't come back, I'll be crushed—again.

# 22

## RAFAEL

THE LAST TIME I had sex with a virgin? It was so long ago I can't remember.

But the last time I dipped my cock into a pussy without a condom? I remember it like it was yesterday—or rather, I remember the fallout like it was yesterday.

I was fifteen when Elena Dias had a pregnancy scare after we had unprotected sex. She was too worried that someone would see her buying a pregnancy test and tell her parents, so I went to the pharmacy, knowing that I could get busted as easily. But better me than her. *At least that's what I thought at the time.*

After some busybody squealed to Antonio, I was forced to spend the rest of my school vacation volunteering at the daycare center at our main vineyard, preparing diapers to be laundered and chasing cranky toddlers. When I complained, Antonio told me that at least I had some time to myself in the evening, but if Elena had been pregnant, I wouldn't have gotten a break from the responsibility until I was an old man. When I went off to college, he would periodically send me photos of snotty-faced kids at the daycare center.

It wasn't until much later that I understood that wearing a

condom is not only a way to protect myself, but a way of taking care of a partner too. *Something I failed at miserably today.*

Lexie is tough, and frankly, more trouble than I need. She's conflicted in some way that I haven't quite figured out, and talks a lot of trash to hide her feelings. But the mask slips from time to time, and all the sass and bravado disappears.

The woman with the mask makes my dick hard, but the one without it? She's so much more alluring, beguiling even. She reeled me in until I was so stupid that a condom didn't even register. I don't even mind the trash-talking—at least I wouldn't if I didn't believe it was a front for something raw and beautiful.

If I had any sense, I would text her that there's a problem at the club and Zé needs my help. *Given our history, I'm sure she half expects it.* But I have no sense—not when it comes to her. I proved that the night of Valentina's wedding, and again tonight. *I want her. I want her in the most primal way.*

If I'm being honest, there's some part of me—some leftover relic from when cavemen roamed the earth—that isn't at all unhappy she's never let another guy fuck her. I get to be first. *That fucking vibrator that I'm going to toss in the trash if I ever find it doesn't count.*

When I saw her getting off in the shower, nothing could have stopped me from going to her. *Nothing.* Not that she's Valentina's best friend. Not that Huntsman Industries regularly does business with her father, or that our family ties run too deep to poison with hot shower sex. Not even my own sense of self-preservation could have stopped me. *Nada.*

I change into athletic shorts and a T-shirt, then shove a few things into a small backpack and glance at the time. *I should be on my way to Sirena by now instead of getting my dick wet. But it's more than that—that's the problem.*

I text Zé on my way back to Valentina's place.

Rafael: *What's going on?*

Zé: *Quiet. I doubt anything will happen tonight.*

I don't think so either. We doubled security inside and out and put in a tight perimeter for a couple of blocks. They'll assume we're prepared for them tonight. If they strike, it'll be when we have our guard down. It's all true. But why, then, do I feel like such an irresponsible asshole for being here instead of there? It's a no-win situation. If I leave Lexie now, I'll feel like an asshole too. And I don't want to leave her. That's the bottom line. I don't want to leave her.

Rafael: *Something came up, and I'll be there later than I expected.*

Something came up. Like my dick.

Zé: *Don't sweat it. I'm here until the last employee leaves.*

The best part of having Zé on my team is that we've been tight for so long, it's like we share a brain. I trust him implicitly. Between him, Xavier, and Stella, Sirena is in good hands until I get there. But it still feels like I'm shirking my responsibilities. I have been with my share of women, but I never let the fun and games get in the way of my business. After tonight, I won't let it happen again.

Rafael: *My phone is on. Call me with any issues.*

# 23

## RAFAEL

WHEN I GET BACK to Valentina's, Lexie's in the kitchen, taking the food I brought out of the bag. She has on a casual terry-cloth dress that I'm pretty sure I've seen Valentina wear, although it wasn't so damn sexy on her.

"This looks great. Are you hungry?" she asks, not looking up.

*Only for what's hidden under that little dress.* "I can always eat." She's still messing with the food, and I'm beginning to think she's going to take the pass I offered her. It seemed like the right thing to do then, but now I'm sorry I opened my big mouth.

If she doesn't want it, she's going to have to use her words, because her nipples are pushing through that thin fabric, begging to be touched, and I'm not changing course unless she stops me.

I take the candle out of the backpack and light it while she wets her lips and pretends not to gawk. *She hasn't changed her mind. She's just playing it cool, in case I have. Not a chance, Angel. I'm planning to own your sexy little body all night.*

"*Mmm.* That smells nice. Didn't figure you for a scented candle kind of guy."

"We're having silver ice buckets with swag made up for our big launch." I gesture toward the flickering candlelight. "It's a massage candle. The company sent me some samples. This one's bergamot and citrus."

"What else is going in the bucket?" she asks, inching closer to where I'm standing.

"A bottle of the white citrus blend that we've been showcasing and a few other goodies."

She gazes into my eyes and gifts me a sultry smile that makes my dick throb. "Young and sexy, with a touch of class, like a fizzy pastel Port cocktail. It's a fabulous idea. But what does one do with a massage candle?"

Lexie could be bullshitting, but I choose to believe that she doesn't know about massage candles—or at least that she's never experienced them before now—and my mouth tugs at the corners. "I suppose we could just enjoy the scent, but I thought we'd burn it, and play with the oil."

She looks up at me, eyes twinkling with mischief, and I know she's all in, but first she's going to bust my balls. "You want me to drip hot wax on your chest?"

*That is never happening.* She's predictable in many ways. Turning the tables or dropping some outrageous comment is one of her tells when she's uncomfortable. I expect to see a lot of those tells tonight, because I plan on making her very uncomfortable.

"Not wax," I tell her matter-of-factly, peering into her eyes. "Oil. I'll control the drip."

"Ouch," she says, ignoring the last thing I said, but she heard it.

Her eyes are dark, and her nipples are tight little peaks that give her away. I don't know how long I can take this flirty banter before I tear that poor excuse for a dress off her body.

"Sounds like a lawsuit waiting to happen," she remarks, setting a baguette on the cutting board. "Do you actually think the new Port is strong enough to numb the pain of a third-degree burn?"

"I don't know. We could try it. Then you can tell me."

She breaks off a piece of bread and pops it into her mouth, chewing carefully. "I'm not really into pain."

*I doubt she knows what she's into. But she's curious by nature.*

"How do you know you're not into pain? Have you tried it?"

"No," she says, forming each letter carefully. "Unless stubbing my toe on that ugly chair Valentina put in the guest room counts."

"It doesn't." All I can think about is serving her up a little pain right before she comes. Just a bite, to magnify every sensation the orgasm brings.

She cocks her head, and the sparkle is gone from her face. "Is this a serious conversation?"

"It is." That reply did nothing to bring back the sparkle, but now that we've started down this road, I want to know more about how she feels.

"The thought of it, even with you," she adds softly, "doesn't make my lady parts flutter."

*Even with you.* I don't spend a second analyzing the remark, but I file it away for later.

"There's no pain involved with this activity. The oil isn't hot enough to cause a burn."

She raises an eyebrow.

"It's the truth. I'm not a liar, and I sure as hell wouldn't lie to you about something like this. There could be a small sting when we begin, I suppose, but that's the extent of it. Pain's not my thing either. Not real pain, anyway." *I might be into some kinky shit, but I'd never hurt you—and tonight it's vanilla, all the way.*

"Too bad," she adds flippantly. "I planned to flog you later."

*You don't want to play this game with me, sweetheart, not tonight, when you're still so inexperienced and I'm getting more and more turned on by the minute. You want me patient.*

I step closer to her until she's between my body and the kitchen island. "Floggers don't normally cause pain. They sting, some more than others. They're often used to play mind games or to raise the nerve endings to the skin surface to increase pleasure."

This shuts her mouth—for a moment. But her wheels are turning, and I keep my gaze heated and steady, until I can almost feel her squirm.

"Sounds like you enjoy being flogged." It's soft, and cheeky, but there's absolutely no tang.

"Not me. But I can wield one pretty well. Next time, I'll be happy to show you the finer points of flogging."

"Next time. Why not today?" She lists toward me, and it takes everything I have not to rush this along to the final course.

"I don't bring women here. My toys are in the apartment I keep at the Intercontinental." My apartment there isn't a secret, and I'd be surprised if she didn't know.

"I'm a woman. I'm here." She grazes my stomach with her fingers, and I suppress a groan.

"You are very much a woman," I reply as the faint scent of her perfume and the heat off her body consumes me. "But you're not a security risk." *Although maybe you should be.*

She licks her lips, and I've had enough conversation. *More than enough.*

"We'll eat later," I mutter, moving the food off the island before I sweep it onto the damn floor. She tracks me with her eyes, and I would give anything to know what's going on inside that pretty head.

When I'm done, I cage her feet between mine, towering over her.

She doesn't move a muscle. Or say a single word. She's going to let me lead, like she did in the vineyard, and in the shower. Not like a submissive, but like a bottom. I don't know if it's because I'm so much more experienced and she's nervous, or if she needs me to lead. Needs it with every cell of her being, even if she can't put it into words—she might not even know she needs it.

But none of it matters right now. Because I *need* her to follow. It's how I'm built. And tonight, we're going to see just how much control this angel is willing to relinquish to me.

I brush some of her silky hair behind her ear, my cock hardening, almost painfully. "Take off your pretty dress and hop up on the island."

# 24

## ALEXIS

THE COMMAND MAKES my pussy pulse.

My brain might be addled, but my body knows what it wants. *So does my heart.*

Although *take off your pretty dress and hop up on the island* is not at all what I expected. I don't know why, but somehow I thought *you deserve better for your first time* meant a bed. *I've been reading too many cheesy books.*

He studies me carefully as though waiting for a sign that I'll do as he says. There's a challenge in his eye, daring me to defy him. Normally I love a challenge, but this one leaves me unnerved.

I'm on uneven footing with Rafael when it comes to sex. Not simply because he's fucked half the women under thirty on the Continent—maybe under forty—and I haven't fucked anything with a pulse, but because he has a way about him that seizes control of the moment. It's effortless. A subtle swing that you don't see coming until it's too late. I remember it from the vineyard.

As he silently watches, the control slips through my fingers like fine grains of sand.

"In case you don't know," I tell him, trying to regain a sense of control, even with the relentless beat between my legs, "there are a couple comfortable beds in this apartment."

His eyes flare with something that looks an awful lot like amusement. "I plan on visiting at least one of those beds, maybe both, but oil is *very* messy and impossible to get out. Messier than anything you'll leave behind on the sheets."

I feel my cheeks pinken, even as my breasts tingle with arousal.

"Giana and Sabio work here all the time—they eat here." *Valentina eats here.*

He smirks—it's a tiny little thing, but I see it. "Are you worried you're going to like the oil play so much that your juices are going to soak into the counter?"

*Maybe,* but I don't respond.

"Quartz isn't porous, so you don't need to worry, Angel."

*Oh God.* I'm nervous. I don't even know why. I want him. I've wanted him for so long, but right now he's not asking just for my clothes. He wants *everything.* I'm not even sure what *everything* entails, but I feel it in every cell of my being.

Rafael runs his nose along my jaw. "I've seen you strut around in a bikini that was nothing more than a few scraps of fabric cobbled together, and I've already seen your gorgeous body naked. You don't need to be shy with me."

"I'm not shy."

He slips a finger between the halter strap and my collarbone. "Then take off your dress, so I can take care of you."

*So I can take care of you.* I shiver. The words are gentle, and the tone cajoling, but they're weighted with promises of sin from a man who looks like he's minutes from devouring me.

He runs a finger through the valley between my breasts, and something shifts inside me. Maybe I'm afraid of losing control, but I want to be devoured. I want him to devour me. That I'm sure of.

I gaze at him while I untie the halter top and let the straps dangle, exposing my breasts for him to admire. The room is cool, his gaze searing. My nipples pucker, beckoning him.

Rafael steps forward and takes the fabric between his fingers, rubbing small circles with his thumb, that I experience like gentle caresses on my breasts.

*So I can take care of you. Yes. Yes, I want that.*

"Soft," he murmurs, his eyes ablaze, searing my flesh more than any oil ever will. "But not velvety like your skin."

The timbre of his voice is low and gruff, silently threatening to do unspeakable things that I'm going to enjoy.

When he steps back, I shimmy the dress below my hips. Somewhere, deep in my consciousness, I remember I'm not wearing panties. But the thought is too far away to hold on to.

The dress puddles at my feet, and I step out of it.

He appraises my naked form. Unabashedly. *Like he owns me.* He doesn't say a word as his gaze skims every inch of my body, but I see the unfettered lust shining in his eyes, as I burn for him.

"Do you need help getting up on the counter?"

*So I can fuck you like a whore?* He doesn't actually say the words. They're unspoken, utter filth flitting in the charged air, making me ache for him.

I shake my head. "No."

My arms are strong enough to hoist myself up without too much trouble. *Although barely.* Rafael watches me squirm as I try to get comfortable on the cold countertop. It's nearly impossible. *I have never felt so naked.*

He moves closer, nudges my knees apart, and stands between my legs. The shorts he's wearing hide *nothing.* The fabric is so flimsy, his cock pushes it without effort until he's nearly grazing my swollen clit. But it's not quite enough to give me *any* relief. I need his mouth to soothe it like he did when I was sprawled on the desk in the vineyard.

Desperate for him, I wiggle my bottom to get a wee bit closer. When he catches me, he lifts my chin, forcing me to look into his eyes. The irises are black and blue swirls of depravity, sending a gush of arousal onto my thighs.

"I'm going to make you so needy, so wanton, you're going to hump me through my clothes, Angel."

*Too late. I'm already there.*

I'm not a woman who anyone would ever call *angel*. It feels almost sacrilegious as I sit naked on the island, my nipples hard, achy points and my pussy begging for his touch.

I run my fingers over his jaw, enjoying the rash of stubble. He shuts his eyes for a moment, letting me explore.

Something inside me is still unsettled. I don't know what it is, and every time I try to form words, they die in my throat.

He opens his eyes and inches closer until he's wedged against my pussy. "Whatever you're thinking about, Angel, put it away. There's no thinking now. Just feel."

He lowers his mouth to mine, and I return the kiss with all the passion and need I feel, squelching all the chatter misfiring in my brain. All I feel is him. His masculine scent filling me. His calloused fingers on my thighs. His mouth that tastes of bourbon and sin. The sensations beckon as they lull, luring me closer to a dangerous place, where I've always ached to go.

"Rafa, I want you," I pant, shamelessly.

My hands glide aimlessly over his broad chest, over hard ridges and canyons, eventually finding his waistband, where they begin to wander toward what I really want. *What I'm too afraid to want. What if this is one and done?*

"You're overthinking," Rafael tuts, taking hold of my wrists with one hand and pinning them at the base of my spine. My back arches and my breasts jut forward. I'm helpless, and what confuses me most is that I like it.

"You can stop this at any time. Just say the word. That's your prerogative. But what you may not do is control the script. That's *my* prerogative."

His voice is low and rough, and my pussy is throbbing with anticipation, even though I'm not sure I'm capable of giving up that kind of control.

"So it's all about you?" My voice is shaky, and I curse myself for sounding weak. "You get to decide what's good for you, and what's good for me too? That doesn't seem fair."

They're just words. I know this isn't all about him. But I don't know how to do what he's asking. I can't give up control, even to him. It's not in my nature. He'll have to take it if he wants it. *I'll let him.* But I can't hand it over.

He lets go of my wrists and cradles my face. "Tonight is all about you, Angel. I won't push you hard—just nudge you gently."

*Gently? I'm not sure you're capable. And I'm not sure I care—or if I even want gentle.*

"Trust me to lead you to pleasure—only pleasure. If following isn't for you, then you'll know, and you'll never have to follow again."

*But I'll never touch you again either.* He doesn't say that part out loud, but it dangles between us, with sharp, craggy points.

It's a risk, my head says, but my body is fully on board, and all my heart has ever wanted is him.

"I'll try to follow your lead. But I don't know if I can. I'm not a good follower."

"Following in life is different from following during sex. Maybe you're not cut out for either, or maybe it'll feel just right."

"You'll stop if it gets too weird for me?"

"Just say the word, and it's over."

His voice and his expression are earnest. I'm not worried about him hurting me. I'm worried about what comes after.

"Will I get to touch you?" I ask, my fingers itching to stroke his cock.

"We'll see," he replies, his lips brushing mine. "Where do you want to touch me?"

"Everywhere." I gasp as he holds my earlobe between his teeth.

"Does that include my cock, Angel? Will you dip your fingers between your legs and slather your arousal all over my cock?"

*Yes. Yes. Yes.*

"Are you wet enough to make it slippery?" He slides a finger inside me and brings it to his mouth, but not before he shows me how it glistens.

"You have a dirty mouth," I whisper.

"And you love it."

*I do.*

"You blush like a schoolgirl, but your breasts get heavier, and your nipples get harder with every filthy word." He lowers his mouth to my temple. "I bet a little gush coats your thighs every time, doesn't it, Angel?"

His voice is hypnotic, and although he's barely touched me, I'm so aroused I can't do anything but nod.

Rafael takes the candle and blows out the flame, but his eyes never leave mine. The emotion is so stark that I'm treading water helplessly, unable to keep up.

"Are you going to give me a massage?"

He shakes his head. "I'm going to paint your skin with the oil, swirl it around with my fingers until you're so aroused your sweetness floods the counter where Giana and Sabio have lunch."

I feel my cheeks warm as he spoons the dollop of shame onto my conscience. It's not bitter like one might expect, but shimmery and bright, enticing me deeper into his spell.

Rafael pours oil onto the inside of his wrist. It looks like ordinary oil, but it smells divine. He nods when it hits his skin. "Perfect," he murmurs, pressing a small kiss to my mouth, and all I think about are his fingers swirling the oil into my skin.

He lifts the candle and drips the scented oil onto my shoulders while I watch.

I flinch at the first sensation. It's quite warm, but there's no pain.

"Too hot?" Rafael asks, stilling.

I shake my head. "It just came as a surprise."

"Good." He nods. "Lie on your back, Angel. Let the cold stone be the yang to the warm oil."

As I lower myself, the quartz is an icy kiss to my overheated skin, almost dizzying, but I don't have long to contemplate the contrast. Before I've even adjusted, Rafael whips off his shirt and climbs on the island with me, straddling my thighs while he drizzles oil between my breasts, warming my skin until it tingles.

I gasp with each new drop, writhing as his fingers dip and swirl, tracing a circuitous route from my breasts to just below my navel, sparing no inch as he zigs and zags across my curves.

Rafael gazes at me without a word as he raises and lowers his arm so the warm liquid can rain on my skin from various heights. Some warmer, others cooler.

"Rafa," I moan when the oil drips across my breasts and onto my nipples, sending a jolt straight to my pussy.

"What is it, Angel? Do you want me to stop?"

I shake my head vigorously, but the curl of his mouth tells me he knows I would murder him if he stopped.

"Lie still," he demands, sliding farther back until he's almost at my feet.

He continues to rouse my flesh with the oil, his fingers playing my skin expertly. When his hand hovers over my belly, I feel liquid pool in my navel. It tickles, and I clench my buttocks to stop from writhing.

"Good girl," he murmurs, rewarding me with several warm drops on my bare pussy.

"Ahh." I gasp at the sensation, waiting for his fingers to draw the torturous swirls that have every nerve ending on edge.

"We're running out of oil."

*Oh no, not yet. We're at the best part. Don't stop. Please.*

"Let's just warm this up a bit."

I close my eyes while he places the candle on the counter and relights the wick. The bergamot-and-citrus scent comes alive again—it might be the best thing I've ever smelled.

While the candle is burning, Rafael whirls the droplets of oil around my mound with enough pressure to make my toes curl. But he doesn't dip his fingers through the outer lips—no matter how much I will him to do it.

When I find the strength, I open my eyes and gaze at him. *My tormentor. My beautiful tormentor.*

I smile softly, and he runs a thumb over my lips, and I draw it into my mouth and suck, the faint taste of oil teasing my tongue. He groans and pulls his hand away, his eyes black now, with no trace of blue. I spread my legs wider, but he makes no move to take what I'm offering, and I squeeze my eyes tight to stop from combusting right here, on this island.

"I'm not telling you what to do," I whimper, desperation curling around every syllable. "But I think you missed a spot."

He smirks. "What spot was that, sweetheart?"

When my hand grazes the pink flesh between my legs, he draws a noisy, ragged breath.

"The oil isn't lube," he grunts. "It has fragrance and other stuff that doesn't belong in your pussy. You'll need to be patient, Angel."

*I can't be patient for one second more.*

He lowers himself over me and draws a nipple into his mouth, sucking and nipping until it's tender. Then he blows out the candle, and I know what he's going to do, even before he lets the oil stream onto my nipples. Still, I practically levitate off the table when the *very* warm liquid caresses the sensitive nipple.

What I don't expect is for him to lower his mouth and blow cool air on the tight point until I'm thrashing against the polished quartz. When he's finished, he lavishes attention on the other breast.

"Rafael," I wail, bucking off the stone. "I don't care if it's not lube."

"Just a little more, Angel. Be patient. Good girls get special rewards."

I can't take any more. I can't. *But I want the special reward. I know it will be something wonderful—like a thigh-shaking orgasm.*

I curl my hands into fists and fill my lungs with breath, finding a wisp of patience somewhere deep inside. He drizzles the last of the oil over my inner thighs and sweeps his palms up and down, staying just short of the place where I need him most. It's torture. *Exquisite torture.*

Just when I'm about to tackle him and rub my pussy all over his hard muscle, he wipes his hands on a towel and brings them between my legs. His fingers graze lightly over my clit, so lightly it's like they're barely there.

"Look at me, Lexie. I want to watch your eyes change color when you come for me."

He leans forward, lowering his mouth to mine, and we engage in a ruthless battle, tongue against tongue until I can't breathe.

Rafael slides a finger inside me, and as his mouth continues to explore mine, he adds another finger, keeping the pressure on my clit.

My body welcomes his fingers, squeezing them until it's not enough, until I need to rock my hips to quicken the pace.

He pulls his face back from mine. "Are you ready to come for me, Angel? Open those eyes. Let me see your pleasure."

I buck into his hand, pressing my head and shoulders into the stone counter.

"That's it, sweetheart. Let go. You're safe. Let go."

His words. His face. It all begins to fade as I grind against his hand like a wild animal in a blistering heat.

"So beautiful. So raw," he murmurs as the orgasm crashes, battering my damp body against the unforgiving stone, until I'm shaking and gasping for air.

My eyes are closed when I feel his warm lips on my forehead. "You're magnificent when you come. A lioness. Clawing and wild while you tremble."

The praise is like a warm embrace in loving arms. I let every word seep into my soul.

When I open my eyes, he's inches from my face, his eyes hooded and heavy.

"I need you," he murmurs. "I don't think I've ever needed anything as much. But not here, Angel."

He shoves something into his pocket and tosses me over his shoulder like a Neanderthal, and I don't care. *I don't care.* I'm in such a daze I'm not sure I could walk.

# 25

# RAFAEL

SHE'S DRAPED over my shoulder like a rag doll when I yank down the duvet and lay her on the bed, being as gentle as I know how to be in this moment. It's not enough, but she has me so worked up it's the best I can do.

*She's never done this, Rafael.* Cuidado. *But she's not a complete innocent either. The way she fucked my fingers and that orgasm she had on the counter? It about killed me. Doesn't matter. She's never done this before. I need to keep reminding myself so I don't hurt her.*

I should ask if she's okay. If she needs anything. If she's sure. But I don't do any of that. I fish the condoms and lube out of my pocket, toss them on the nightstand, within easy reach, and climb on top of her like a big wild cat desperate for a meal.

I don't pull off my shorts—because I don't trust myself not to plunge into her at the first opportunity.

Hovering over her, propped up by my forearms, I still and take her face in my hands. Her eyes are bright and dilated, like she's drugged, and the freckles dot her flawless skin, reminding me of how fragile she is—how young.

*Be careful with her, Rafael. Be careful.*

She reaches for my cock through the fabric, but I jerk my

hips away from her grasp and shake my head. Not because I don't want her to touch me, but because until I can scrape together some self-control, it's a bad idea.

"You can touch me later—as much as you want. But not now."

Her face falls, and she looks hurt, or maybe confused. I could remind her that I lead and she follows—it's the truth. And it's what she agreed to try. But I tell her a different truth.

"I'm aroused—more aroused than I want to be right now. The base of my spine is prickling like a son of a bitch, like it does right before I come. The minute your sweet fingers slide over my cock, my control will be nonexistent."

I brush a tendril off her face. "I don't want to come on your belly. Or on your tits. Not tonight. I want to come inside you. I want you to know how wild you make me. I want you to feel my desperation. My struggle to hold back." The emotion welling inside my chest clings to every word. "I want you to know what kind of power you have over me. Following doesn't make you weak, Angel. It makes you powerful."

Her lips pull into a soft smile, and a tear trickles out of the corner of her eye. *That's it, sweetheart. Give me your tears. They're safe with me.* I catch the lone tear on my tongue as it rolls onto her cheek. It's sweet and salty—just like her.

"You okay?"

She nods, but I study her to be sure.

"I'm not used to you being so quiet."

"I'm not used to feeling . . ." She pauses. "I don't know. Overwhelmed? I'm scared, Rafa," she whispers.

"What are you afraid of, Angel?"

She doesn't say anything, even though I'm sure she knows what scares her. I bring her fingers to my mouth and press a small kiss to the tips. "Be brave, Lexie. Tell me what scares you. Once you say it out loud, it won't seem as scary."

"I'm—I'm—I'm afraid that I might end up with a broken heart."

My own heart clenches at her vulnerability—vulnerability that she is letting me see.

"You might." *Or I might.* "It's always a risk."

If I had a lick of decency, or common sense, or if my balls didn't ache, I would end this now. But instead, I rock my hips, wedging my hard cock between us, and hold her bottom lip between my teeth.

Her hands trace the contours of my face until all I can think about is owning her body.

"Fuck me, Rafael. Please. I've waited so long for this."

She begs so sweetly, and there is no way I'm denying her.

"I'm going to lick your pussy, Angel. I want you nice and wet for me."

She came hard earlier, and I know she's ready for me. But I want her more than ready. I want every cell in her body pleading for her release.

"You don't need to treat me like delicate glass. It's okay. I'm not a total newbie—"

I see red as the growl escapes from my chest. "Yes. I know. With blokes in bars. I don't want to hear about a fucking thing you've done with another man—not while you're under me. Not unless you want me to hunt them and put them down like dogs."

"You're out of control," she groans.

"Oh baby, you haven't seen out of control." I trail my tongue over her clavicle, between her breasts, lower, and lower, lapping up the remnants of oil, until my face is buried in her cunt. Only when her whimpers and moans reach a frenzy, only then do I reach for a condom and slide it onto my weeping cock.

*Slow, Rafael. Slow.*

Her eyes are closed, her cheek against the sheet. I pause to watch her before rubbing my cock over her clit and notching it at her entrance. "Open your eyes, Lexie. I need to see you."

She opens her eyes and gasps softly as I slide in, an inch at a time, letting her bloom around me. As I gaze at her and sink deeper into her tight little cunt, emotion that I don't recognize is beginning to weave its way in, competing with the intense physical sensations dragging me closer to the brink of insanity. It's too much. *Too much.* I shove it away.

"Hook your legs around my hips. That's it."

"More," she whimpers, and I fight not to give her what she thinks she wants but isn't quite ready for. I will not take any more chances with her tonight.

"You'll take what I give you, Angel. Don't be so greedy."

My hips rock slowly, inching deeper. She's tight. The pace is torture. The sweat trickles off my face as I struggle to keep my movements controlled.

She uses her legs to pull me closer. It's unexpected, and I slide deeper into her and curse. There's a flicker of defiance in her eyes that I'd like to fuck out of her. But instead, I still for a moment, to be sure she's okay, before sliding my hand between us to rub her clit. Her legs clench as I stroke her, and her back arches off the bed.

"Rafael," she whimpers.

My name is like heaven as it slips from her lips.

"I'm right here, baby."

Her walls tighten around my cock, and it almost ends here. *My Angel's close.* She clings to me as I roll my hips in a steady motion, swirling my fingers faster, and adding more and more pressure onto her little nub.

"Let go. Just like before. Come for me, Angel. Come all over my cock."

My touch is rough now, and she begins to buck, clawing at my back and grinding on my dick until she cries out, sinking her teeth into my shoulder to muffle the scream.

The bite of pain detonates every damn nerve. I lose control —*all control*—chasing my own release like a demon in search of salvation.

# 26

## ALEXIS

Rafael rolls onto his back, taking me with him. For a few moments, we lay quietly, my body molded to his, trying to catch our breath.

But it's not quiet inside my head. The thoughts are racing at warp speed as I try to make sense of them.

The sex was everything I imagined, despite what I'd been told about first times being a disappointment. It'll hurt. He'll be clumsy. You won't orgasm. *Wrong. Wrong. Wrong.*

Despite my own explorations with self-love, at first my pussy felt full—too full. It was uncomfortable, but there was no stabbing pain—not like in the shower. Rafael wasn't clumsy. He was careful, and even when he wasn't checking in with words, his watchful eyes rarely left my face. As foolish as it sounds, it made me feel cherished.

What I lacked in skill, I made up for in unfettered desire. I wanted him. Not just his mouth, or his hands, or his cock to satisfy my lust—I wanted *him*—every fiber of his being, with every fiber of mine.

When he admitted how aroused he was—how aroused I made him, and how much he wanted me—the emotion rolled over me like a tidal wave. In that moment, I couldn't remember a time when I didn't want him.

"Are you okay?" he whispers, hoarsely, like he's too spent to speak any louder.

"I'm more than okay," I reply, quickly realizing it was too honest of an answer. I showed too many cards. It's more than I want him to know.

His mouth is on my head with a warm, tender kiss that makes me feel safe and terrified all at once.

"You?" I ask, with a hint of sass that I can barely muster. "Do you need a heating pad or some ice for all those sore muscles? You're not as young as you used to be."

Rafael pinches my ass, and I yelp. "You're going to be the death of me, Angel."

He pulls away from me, and I feel a panic rise. "Where are you going?" I ask in a voice that sounds almost panicky. *What is wrong with me?*

"Hey," he says, tugging gently at my hair. "I'm just going to the bathroom. I'll be right back."

*God, I'm a pathetic, needy mess.* He's the only person who can make me feel this way, and I hate it.

Since the wedding, it's become an entrenched response. The embarrassment, the anger, and the hurt—*so much hurt*—mangled as they burrowed deep. Like heartless barnacles, they attached themselves to my soul and fed off my desperation as I waited for days, weeks, months for him to call, to text, something, *anything*. It's taken root, and I don't know how to make it stop.

Before I berate myself too much for being weak, Rafael comes into the bedroom with a warm cloth and a small towel. He kisses my nose and presses the compress between my legs, holding it there until it cools, while he peppers my shoulders and neck with small caresses. *Let me take care of you. I'm* completely undone by the time he dries me gently and tosses the linen on the floor.

We need to deal with this now, because I can't spend every moment we're together wondering when he's going to disappear. I can't spend one second more worrying. It turns me into someone I don't respect.

"Rafael," I murmur from my side. He glances at me as he climbs into bed, facing me. "Are you ever going to tell me what happened in the vineyard? Why you left?"

He takes my hand and presses a kiss to my open palm. "Once Lucas walked in, it became pretty obvious why we needed to leave."

I shake my head vehemently. *That is not good enough.*

"You don't get to do this, here, in the place where you fucked me. I deserve an honest answer, even if I'm not going to like it. Be brave, Rafael," I tell him in the same tone he used when he said the words to me.

He turns onto his back and throws an arm over his eyes.

I feel my heart crack. It's just a fissure, but that's how earthquakes start too.

"What I believed, that night, especially after Lucas called me out, is that you were too young for me, and that our families have too many important ties that could unravel if we got involved, and it got messy."

There's an eight-year age difference between us. A big spread for teenagers, nothing to write home about for adults. The family ties? Those are real, but we have full control over whether it gets messy. They're just excuses.

"Do you still believe that?" I ask in a voice that is so dispassionate it's almost robotic.

"I do." He turns onto his side and takes a tendril of my hair in his fingers. "But right now I don't care."

I'm buoyed by his response until I play it over in my head. *But right now I don't care. Right now. What about later tonight? Or*

*tomorrow? Will you care after the sun comes up?* I don't get to ask
any of my questions. I haven't even formed them all when he
pulls his hand back.

"Those things don't matter. I'm not sure they ever did. The
truth is, you scare me, Lexie." His eyes burrow into my soul as
he says words I don't really understand.

"I'm not sure what you mean."

He brushes a thread off the sheet. "I grew up in a fucked-up
house. Lost my mother when I was eight. My father and
brother were monsters—the worst kind of monsters. You know
the story." He sighs. "If Antonio hadn't pulled me out of there, I
wouldn't have survived."

I do know the story, and my heart weeps whenever I think
about the little boy stuck in hell, tormented by people who
were supposed to love him.

This time, I'm the one who takes care of him. I reach for his
hand and lace my fingers through his. There's no pity because
he'd hate that from me. I squeeze my hand so he knows I'm
here for him.

"It doesn't matter what kind of balm you use," he says softly,
"those scars never fully heal. I cope by surrounding myself with
people I trust implicitly—or that I can control. No one gets
close to me who I don't fully trust. *No one.* I keep everyone else
at arm's length."

He's not talking about physical proximity. He's talking about
the people he lets into his inner orbit—and his heart.

The pieces start to come together, and the picture that
emerges is not a bucolic scene, but rather a stormy canvas with
black clouds and torrential rain. "You don't trust me."

He runs the back of his free hand along the contours of his
chin, like he's buying time. I find that when one needs this kind
of time, it's to create a word-salad cushion to blunt a blow.

I steel myself, erecting a hasty wall, because the blow he's preparing to levy will be directed at me, and it's likely to nick an organ inside my chest if I'm caught off guard. Although I'm not sure even a carefully constructed steel wall would help—not now.

"You're unpredictable. Impulsive. Reckless. You went clubbing with sex traffickers—even though you sensed there was a problem. And you still haven't been completely honest with me about why you're in Porto."

*And now I'm less likely to tell you. It'll confirm everything you believe about me.*

"You were going to let me fuck you against the shower wall like an animal," he says, anger and exasperation in his voice. "It was your first time. Do you know what kind of damage I could have done if I'd missed the pain in your face? If I hadn't had your head tipped back, I wouldn't have seen it."

"I would have survived," I reply churlishly, letting go of his hand, but he doesn't let me pull it away.

"My goal for sex isn't that my partner merely survives. But thanks for that."

I lower my eyes, because he's right about the sex, and I'm embarrassed. I didn't see it as much of a risk. But even if I had, I would have taken it, because I believed it was the only way he'd go through with it—and because I didn't want him to think I was an inexperienced little girl. We've already discussed this. I'm not apologizing again.

"I'm not talking about tears and bruising that eventually heal. I'm talking about up here." Rafael points at my temple. "Those scars can dog you for a long time," he murmurs. "Sometimes forever. I don't want that for you."

I don't want it for me, either, but this conversation has veered off into places that have no answers. At least not the answer to my question.

"Where do we go now, Rafa? Is this it?" The words don't emerge whiny or needy. My voice is low, but strong, like a woman who can manage the response—whatever it might be. Still, I hold my breath, waiting for an answer.

He doesn't say anything for a long moment. His gaze is probing, and eventually the silence becomes so loud and uncomfortable that I begin to backpedal. "I don't care if this is it." I flash him a fake smile. "I mean, the road test was amazing, but you should see my vibrator. It works like a demon, and it doesn't require awkward conversations."

There's no sarcastic retort. No smirk. Only more of the tortured silence that slices into my self-confidence.

"I wouldn't have laid a finger on you after the shower if I thought there wasn't at least a short future for us. And I don't believe for one second that fucking vibrator has anything on my cock. And neither do you." He pinches my nipple and jumps out of bed before I can return the favor.

*A short future* is more than I expected him to say. *Much more.* But even more than a sliver of hope, it's an answer. I'm strong enough to deal with almost anything that comes my way—if I can understand it. What I don't do well with is a man who runs, even when I know he wants to stay.

"They're expecting me at Sirena," he says, pulling on his shorts, "but let's have something to eat, first, and you can tell me what's going on with your father."

*The conversation every woman wants to have after sex.*

Rafael's gaze lingers on my exposed breasts, and despite the mention of my father, my pussy flutters like a cheeky bitch.

"Why don't you get dressed, while I heat up dinner."

I don't want to be stuck here alone. Giana and Sabio are nice, but I hardly know them.

"Can I come to Sirena with you? It's starting to get a bit claustrophobic here. I'll hang out in your office. I won't be any trouble."

He sits on the bed beside me, and I already know the answer is *no* before he utters a word.

"I'd like nothing more than to stay here tonight with you, take a nap, then drag you into the shower where you're better prepared, now, to do what we started earlier. You can't come to Sirena. A Molotov cocktail was thrown at the building today, and it caused significant damage."

My heart stops. A Molotov cocktail. Simple to make, but they can cause unimaginable destruction.

"Did anyone get hurt?"

He shakes his head. "We got lucky."

"You think it was the traffickers?" *The ones I brought to Sirena?*

"I don't know. We've taken some major precautions tonight to keep the club and the surrounding area safe so we could open. But I'm not taking any chances with you."

*This is just like my father. You'll take no chances with me but barrel into the danger headfirst. Who's reckless now?*

"What about you?"

"Don't worry about me."

*That's impossible.*

"I'll be back after the club closes, and I'll be wide awake. I suggest you get some rest while I'm gone."

## 27

### RAFAEL

I PUT the saffron rice in the microwave and text Zé.

Rafael: *Anything new?*

Zé: *Nothing.*

I feel the anxiety slide off my shoulders.

Rafael: *I'll see you in an hour.*

By the time I carry the food into the living room and uncork a bottle of wine, Lexie is dressed. It's the same dress she had on earlier—when she undressed for me. I'm never getting to Sirena tonight if I don't stop thinking about her naked.

"I'll get plates and utensils," she says, eyeing the flimsy plastic cutlery that came with the food.

I decide not to press her about why she's in Porto. The Judite Furtado interview? I still don't buy it—not with Valentina out of the country. But it's likely to be a contentious conversation that doesn't need to happen tonight. There have already been enough fireworks. Besides, there are other things I want to know too.

Lexie hands me a plate and helps herself, while I pour wine.

"Tell me what's going on between you and your father that

has you pushing back against him like a heavyweight champ."
This could shed some light on why she's here, although I'm not
hopeful.

She spoons rice onto a plate, her lips pressed into a thin
line. "I'm not sure it matters anymore."

*Like hell it doesn't matter. If anything, it matters more now that
those three traffickers are dead. I need to tell her what happened.
Maybe it'll put the fear of God into her.*

"I'll tell you why it matters. Someone like you, or even me,
running around the globe without security is a recipe for
disaster—and I'm a trained soldier."

"I know, but—"

I hold up my hand to stop her. She's going to hear me out
before she starts with bullshit excuses.

"The traffickers, the two Czech guys and Misha, were killed
while in custody."

The color is gone from her cheeks before the last word is
out of my mouth, and for a moment I regret relaying the information so callously.

"Was it an inside job?"

"I don't know—I don't know how much anyone knows
about what happened." I fill my plate and sit beside her on the
sofa. "At least not yet. But our best guess is that whoever they
were working for put out the order, and people from inside—
inmates, and maybe guards too—carried it out." *I can't protect
you from people with that kind of power—not without your coop-
eration.*

She gets up and goes to the window with her arms wrapped
around her.

"Have you alerted Francesca's father?" asks the woman who
knows better than most what it's like to live in a criminal world.
The men in power are alerted when their women are at risk. It's
a custom that even bad men follow.

"Immediately. He's on it. Her safety is at risk, but so is yours."

"Did you tell my father?" she asks cautiously.

"Antonio spoke to him." It saved me from making the call. I would have done it, but I don't want to have any conversations with Will until Lexie has a chance to make her case. I didn't promise her my discretion, but I want her to trust me—especially now.

"Great," she mutters.

She's too far away, too deep into her own head. I don't want that—not for her, and not for me. "Come back here, and have dinner with me. I need you to tell me what happened with your dad."

Lexie adds a few stalks of asparagus to her plate before she sits down.

"It's a long story."

"It can't be that long. Even if it is, I've got time." Not really, but I'm not leaving until I understand why she ditched her guards and didn't contact her father when she ran into trouble —serious trouble.

Her expression is pinched as she dips bread in olive oil. "My father was diagnosed with prostate cancer. Very early stage and not aggressive."

*Valentina had the story right.*

"I'm sorry," I murmur. "Cancer is a bitch. Even if it's not aggressive."

She nods. "After the diagnosis, he started acting—not himself. I take that back. He started acting like himself on steroids. I was really worried about him and about my mother, who started making excuses for his irrational behavior. She never does that, or at least she hadn't—not really.

"I began to wonder if maybe things were more dire than they were letting on. I did some research and went to see a urologist who specializes in prostate cancer. He confirmed what my

parents had told me. Slow growing, *blah, blah, blah.*" She shrugs
—not like the cancer's not important, but like she's at a loss.

"What does that mean, acting like himself on steroids?"

"He's been impossible. He was always over-the-top
protective—"

"He has a lot of enemies. Powerful ones. He loves you—it's
hard for me to fault him for being protective."

"Protective? *Yes.* Crazy? *No.* But given how ridiculous you are
about Valentina's safety, I wouldn't expect you to understand."

It's a snarky thing to say, even if it's true, but I don't want to
fight about it. "I'm on your side, Lexie." I squeeze her leg. "You
think this is just about the cancer diagnosis? That doesn't
sound like your father. He's ruthlessly practical."

"It's not the cancer. There's more of a chance that I'll die
from his smothering than that he will from prostate cancer."

I refill her wineglass, and then mine. "So what is it?"

She gazes at me, her expression somber. "You know what
happened to his family."

"What I know is that when he was eleven, someone broke
into his childhood home and brutally murdered his parents
and younger siblings. And he walked in on the carnage." I'm no
stranger to carnage or death, but the thought of walking in on
people I love, vacant expressions, blood everywhere—I don't
know how he got through it.

"It was a revenge killing. My mother says that my father
swore he would get the bastards who did it before he took his
last breath. Most of them have met justice, but he's never found
the person who ordered the hit."

"And he's worried he's going to die before he finds him."

She nods. "My mother thinks the diagnosis isn't what's
gotten under his skin, but it reminded him that he's running
out of time. And it also reminded him that once he's gone, he
won't be able to protect us. She believes his irrational behavior
is a response to it."

"What do you believe?"

"I believe that she knows him better than anyone. She's an expert at deciphering his moods."

"Have you talked to him?"

"Not about the connection to his family—he'd just scoff and wave me away—but my mother has brought it up with him. He refuses to see a connection. At least, that's what he says. You never know with him. But I've talked to him about the over-the-top security until I'm blue in the face."

Her body tenses, and I want to lay her over my lap and work out the kinks. *That's not going to provide answers.*

"It's a bad situation," I say gently, "but I don't see how you can expect to get him to change, by fighting back the way you are. You ditched your security and walked right into the arms of the very kinds of people he's worried about getting to you. There has to be another way, Lexie."

She pushes her food around the plate, seemingly lost, and my heart clenches.

"I've tried everything. Including moving home." Her speech is slow and her words measured. This is costing her to admit. "It didn't get better. If anything, as my life became more of an open book, it became worse. I don't know what to do anymore." She shakes her head.

"But I'll tell you what I won't do," she continues. "I won't sit in a gilded cage, letting my life slip away until he comes to his senses. If he ever does."

There's great sorrow in her voice, and I'd like to shake Will until he wakes up and gets with the program.

"I love my dad, and the truth is, if it helped ease his burden at all, I might give that gilded cage another shot. At least for a little while. But it's not the answer."

No. It's never the answer, and it's the worst possible way to go about protecting someone like Lexie. It's a recipe for disaster. "Would he hold you against your will?" It's a tough question but I want to know how far she believes he'd go. Whether or not her belief is accurate isn't important. It's enough if she's concerned about it.

"My mother would never allow it. She'd leave. She's threatened. My father's not dying on that hill. He can't live without her."

This is actually good news. Samantha is the gatekeeper. We all need them, but men like Will need it more than most.

"She can't intervene on this?"

"I won't ask her to. And don't get any ideas about talking to her—I won't allow her to get involved. It's too hard on their marriage. It's not fair to ask my mother to take sides."

Maybe not. But this is beyond taking sides.

"You know, Rafael," she says softly, a twinge of wistfulness wrapped around the words. "I'm not as impulsive or as much of a risk-taker as people like to believe. I would dive off a ship's starboard into the middle of the ocean, because I'm an excellent swimmer, but I would never jump on a feisty stallion, because I'm not much of a horsewoman."

Our conversation clearly hit a nerve with her. It was honest, and I'm not sorry it happened. Although I am sorry if it hurt her. I never wanted that to happen.

She swirls the cabernet around the crystal goblet until the wine reflects the light. "I'll admit, I'm likely to be the one who orders a round of shots, or laughs too loud, or tells you what I really think. I'm not reserved, and I have some beliefs that I hold so dear that I'd be willing to lay down my life for them. I suppose from the outside it appears reckless."

I wrap an arm around her shoulders and pull her close, the blood pounding in my ears. I forced her hand on this. I made her feel like she was *trouble*. Plain and simple. I'm not the first person who's made her feel that way, but I'm a bastard for it. The worst part about it is, I don't know how to smooth things over. I can't just say, *I didn't mean what I said earlier.* I meant it. Every word.

"You don't need to justify yourself to me." Although in many ways, that's exactly what I've asked her to do.

She rests her head on my shoulder. "I know the reality isn't as much fun as the fantasies that people have concocted about me, but the truth is, I'm more likely to help a friend in trouble than I am to lead her there.

"But back to my father," she says, before I can figure out a response that has some semblance of truth. "Valentina's coming home tomorrow, and she said I can stay here for as long as I'd like."

*Good—on both accounts.*

"That should placate him. He knows security here is tight."

"For now, maybe. But I suspect it's a matter of time before he marches in here, or sends someone to kidnap me and drag me home. Especially given what happened at Sirena, and then the traffickers being killed."

*That is not happening.* She's safe here, and he knows it. I don't give a shit who he is or how strong our family ties are. This is a hill I'm willing to die on. "Do you believe that?"

"I do."

There's a lot I want to say about how the risk she took with the traffickers would worry any parent, but even a prick like me knows when to keep his mouth shut. Under the best of circumstances, Will is an unreasonable motherfucker, and I can't even begin to understand what's going on with him. *Or maybe I can.*

When my mother disappeared, I promised myself that I would find her. I've renewed that promise often throughout my life, and despite how much I've searched, I've never even come close to knowing what happened to her. The overwhelming evidence points to my father, and my uncle, Antonio's father. But mostly it's the word of monsters that I've been relying on— my father and my brother's words. There's nothing definitive.

It's my greatest failing in life. And if I go to my grave without bringing her home for a peaceful eternal rest, I'll die a broken man. *Like Will.*

What I won't allow is my mother's fate to be Lexie's. I'm not an eight-year-old. I'm a man with great resources and plenty of power and connections of my own.

I pull Lexie onto my lap and hold her against me. To my surprise, she doesn't balk. Not a single peep.

"I know you've exhausted all your ideas, but maybe I can help. I know your dad, and if nothing else, I bring a fresh perspective. Give me a few days to think about it. I'll come up with something." Although I'm not sure what, if anything, would satisfy them both.

She nods, and we sit quietly for several minutes, my lips finding the top of her head.

"When I was nineteen," she says so softly I have to strain to hear, "Valentina and I were outside by the pool sunbathing. You came out for a swim and hung out with us until dinner. I had always believed that you hung the stars, but that day—that day you went from being like a big brother to someone I wanted to do dirty things with."

The ground shifted for me that day too. It was the first time I saw Lexie as a woman, and I couldn't stop thinking about doing dirty things with her either. But she was nineteen, and I was about to turn twenty-seven and had already gone through a lot of partners. There was no way I was spoiling her.

"When you looked at me, it was as if you were stroking my skin. It tingled—everywhere. Then I went back to school and back to the boys I knew. They seemed like babies compared to you. I tried to move past my crush—but no matter how much I dated, no one came close to you." She sighs, her lips curling into a soft smile.

"Then at the wedding—I don't have to tell you what happened. Until you decided to be a prick who wouldn't even glance in my direction, you took such good care of me. After that, I knew there'd never be anyone who made me feel that way. I didn't even bother to try. That's why I hadn't had sex."

I tip my head back slightly and close my eyes. In the last twenty-three hours, I've had more emotion causing havoc inside me than I've ever had—certainly as an adult.

"I should have never treated you so carelessly—"

She presses two fingers to my lips. "I'm not looking for another apology. You already apologized. I just wanted to tell you why I hadn't had sex."

I can't change the past. But I will fix this problem between Lexie and her father. I'll figure out something. And soon. *Before something bad happens.*

# 28

# ALEXIS

IT'S WAY TOO EARLY, but Valentina is mixing a drink using a new product that Premier is about to launch. Over the last year, we've concocted all sorts of new cocktails, giving them names that had us doubling over laughing. This is our favorite—the Vaxie—a combination of both our names, because together we're an antidote for whatever ails you. We must have been half in the bag when we came up with that one.

Valentina arrived after two this morning, and I fell asleep waiting for her. "How was the trip to the US?"

"It was fun in the beginning. Then Marco left"—she groans —"and then as a special treat, I had a breakfast meeting with a major creep."

"I want to hear about the creep, but why did Marco leave?" I ask, taking two glasses out of the freezer. "Did something happen?"

She shakes the cocktail like it's an outlet for all her frustrations.

"He told me that he had a meeting with a dealer to procure some art for a client. But it came out of the blue. I'm not sure why he left."

This is not good. I don't want to ask the question that popped into mind first—the one about meeting a woman. "You don't have any idea at all?"

"I woke up to additional security prowling around. I hadn't noticed them the night before, but that doesn't mean Marco didn't. He hates when Rafael or my father add to the security detail without consulting him."

This has been an ongoing problem since before they were married. Despite what he claims, Rafael has a hard-on about Marco. And Antonio doesn't believe that he needs to consult anyone regarding his family's safety—not even his wife.

"They know it's an issue," she continues. "So I don't understand why Rafa couldn't have just contacted him to say that the infamous traffickers were arrested in Sirena and it might be a good idea to increase security until we know more. Is that so damn hard?"

"Only if you're a man who's used to issuing orders without consulting anyone. Although, in fairness to Rafael, he's had a lot on his plate."

"Don't defend him."

I raise both my hands. "Not me. You know how I feel about that kind of behavior. Tell me about creepy guy. I've been kept under such tight wraps for the last six months, I have no creepy guys in my life. I need to live vicariously through you."

She laughs. "Do we have any grapefruit?"

"I don't know—this is your apartment. But I doubt it. When I got here, there was nothing but crackers and more crackers, and not a meager wedge of cheese to be found. Not even a damn olive. But Giana and Sabio ordered groceries."

"Sorry," she says, seeming preoccupied. "I haven't stayed here in months."

"I don't need a garnish," I tell her, taking one of the cocktails. "Creepy guy. Spill the tea."

"I'll tell you about him, but then you need to tell me how you got caught up with the traffickers."

There's not a chance I'm telling Valentina anything the general public doesn't know. I don't want her caught up in it. She has enough going on, and doesn't need to worry about me.

Besides, Valentina and I see things differently. We both want our worlds—the ones we grew up in—to be a better place for women. Valentina has had a lot of upheaval in her life, and she's content running a Port company in an industry that has kept women out for centuries. She leads by example. I, on the other hand, want to eviscerate every motherfucker who buys and sells women like a commodity, or thinks rape is their God-given right. If Valentina saw my charts, she'd have a heart attack.

"I told you everything when we were on the phone. Besides, I'm getting tired of telling that story. Did creepy guy pull something?"

She shakes her head. "His name is Scott Bancroft. And no, he didn't pull anything. I've been around him several times, always in public, but he always seeks me out. You know, corners me outside the bathroom, that kind of thing."

*I hope you didn't mention this to Rafael, because if you did, your security team just got bigger—and meaner.* "What does he want?"

"I'm not sure." She shrugs. "I think he just wants information about our new product, but my Spidey sense is on high alert whenever he's around. Anyway, I agreed to meet with him over breakfast."

"Alone?" I ask, like I'm Rafael, or my father.

"Alone? Did I mention the extra security? I don't use a public restroom alone."

"That might be the case, but I doubt anyone from your detail was with you during a private meeting."

She doesn't deny it.

"Valentina, it's a terrible idea to meet alone with a man who gives you a bad feeling. I realize your guards would come if you screamed, but what if he drugged you?"

I sound like the men who want to control us. But while she was talking, all I could think about was the guy who slipped something in my drink and was trying to coax me into taking it. If I was less self-assured, like Francesca, I might have taken it, under the pressure. Valentina's not naive, but she's sweeter than I am. Although she wouldn't take a drink from a stranger.

"I'm sorry." She has her hands on her hips, and it's not *I'm sorry* as in *I'll do better next time*, but *I'm sorry* as in *What the hell did you just say?* "Did you just say it's not a good idea to meet alone with men who give you a bad feeling, Ms. Clarke?"

I roll my eyes. "The woman gave me a bad feeling," I huff, defensively. "I was worried about Francesca, not myself. Besides, the woman, Misha, was a skinny little thing. I could have kicked her bony ass."

I'm so animated that Valentina chokes on her drink before spraying it all over the counter where Rafael and I were naked. Something I would tell her about if it wasn't Rafael.

She pours herself another drink and tops off mine.

"So has Rafael been checking on you?" she asks nonchalantly, popping a piece of cheese into her mouth. She's fishing for information.

"I told Rafael about how crazy my father has been, and he feels bad. He's going to help me come up with a way to manage him."

"You told him?"

*Maybe I shouldn't have said that.*

"I'm glad you did, but you're normally not so open about your family."

"Rafael's not going to use the information to hurt my father. I'm at the end of my rope, holding on by a few frayed threads, girlfriend. But being here has been a relief—despite the fact that I'm stuck in the apartment until we have more information about the traffickers."

"Rafael will help. He can't resist a damsel in distress."

*Is that what I am to him?* No. He's clearly attracted to me. He said so himself, although I wouldn't be surprised if the whole damsel-in-distress thing heightens the attraction. *I hate that.*

"Lexie—I love Rafael with all my heart and soul, but he's a player—"

"I know. The worst kind of player. The one who keeps you around for a few weeks and then vanishes." *You've told me this before, and I've seen it for myself.* "Don't worry. I'd have to be comatose not to think he's hot, but I don't want to jump his bones."

"Hmm." That's all she says.

I hate lying to her, especially now that Rafael and I have had sex. It will be weird for a few minutes, but if I'm happy, I know she will be, too, even if she's a little worried. Plus, I'd love to talk to her about the relationship, but I won't until I know how Rafael feels about her knowing. He clearly didn't mention a word about it to her, and I'm sure they've spoken. They run a business together and talk almost every day.

"Let's go back to creepy guy," I say in an obvious move to change the subject. "What does Marco say about him?"

"I haven't said much to Marco about him. He's been preoccupied with work," she mutters, wiping away a tear.

When I see it, I still, my feet stuck to the floor. I like Marco, but that could change on a dime. "What's wrong?"

She begins to sob. I've never seen her like this. She's not a big crier. Neither of us are, really.

"It's going to be okay. Whatever it is, you're going to get through it, and I'm going to be right by your side." I hand her a paper cocktail napkin. "Talk to me, Valentina."

"I'm not sure we're going to make it, Lexie." She takes a big gulp of her drink.

*He left out of the blue.* I'm going to kill him. "Why do you think that?"

"Money is a huge issue. Bigger than it's ever been."

"Because of the gallery?"

"It's not just that, although it's a sore spot. I wanted him to have something of his own. But I should have never gone behind his back."

Valentina tried to dip into her trust fund for a large down payment to purchase an art gallery that Marco has been wanting since she met him. Her father stepped in to stop it, and even her mom, Daniela, who is normally the voice of reason, didn't support it. Rafael was livid.

If Valentina had been making the purchase for herself, they wouldn't have batted an eyelash, but her mother, especially, felt that the trust fund was her insurance policy in the event she ever needed it. I was surprised by Daniela's reaction at the time, although given her history, I guess it makes sense.

"You didn't go behind his back. You were trying to surprise him. Have you tried talking to your mom?"

"My mother is sympathetic—to a point. But she has strong opinions about men who are uncomfortable about their wives having more money than they do. I'm reluctant to talk to her about my marital problems. She's very protective of me in her own way—and she might hold it against Marco. I don't need more trouble."

If Marco loses Daniela's support, Valentina's situation will be more difficult. No doubt about it.

"Do you think Marco is being oversensitive about it?" *Because I do.*

"A small part of me does. But we all have things that push our buttons. My insecurities aren't the same as his, but I would expect him to respect my feelings. And I can totally see how being around my father and Rafael is intimidating."

*I can see it too.*

"Lydia would know what to do."

Valentina closes her eyes. "She would."

Lydia was Antonio's mother, Rafael's mother's sister, and while neither Valentina nor I were her biological granddaughters, she was our grandmother—the only grandmother that either of us ever knew. Lydia didn't suffer fools—especially the kind with cocks—and better than any other person I've ever met, she could see the forest through the trees. She would be able to advise Valentina—and she would know just how to get the authorities to listen about the traffickers. And if they didn't listen, she'd bring them down herself. That's how she was. *I miss her.*

"She would have told me to stand tough against all of them and follow my heart," Valentina says with a bittersweet smile. "But Lydia's not here, so I'm going to have to figure it out on my own."

I reach over and take her hand. "Not on your own. Never on your own, baby. Not while I'm still breathing."

She blows her nose and tosses the tissues in the trash.

*I need to talk to Rafael about this. I won't give too much away—nothing that Valentina told me in confidence. I have to do something. Relationships are hard enough without the people you love shitting all over them.*

"I don't think there's ice cream, but why don't we watch a movie?"

"Something funny," she replies. "I could use a good laugh."

We settle in on the sofa with a big cozy blanket and find a movie that has good reviews.

But despite the glowing reviews, it's a dud filled with the kind of humor that only appeals to teenage boys. Valentina is still jet-lagged and falls asleep twenty minutes into it.

I turn it off and watch my sweet friend sleep for a few minutes. She looks so peaceful tucked under the blanket. *But looks can be deceiving.* Her family, whom I love, is nearly as nuts as mine. Although not quite. I know they don't want to destroy her marriage, but they can't help themselves from interfering, under the guise of love. It doesn't make their behavior any less destructive.

My phone buzzes with a message reminding me of a haircut next week in London, an appointment that I scheduled months ago. *Cancel.* I don't plan on returning to London anytime soon, especially with Rafael here. *Don't get ahead of yourself. See how it goes.* I will, although it doesn't really matter. I didn't leave London because of him, and if things don't work out between us, I won't go back because of him either.

The sun is lower in the sky, casting a pall over the room. With the guards stationed outside the apartment door instead of in the kitchen, and Valentina asleep, the apartment is quiet —almost too quiet—and I'm restless.

I slide off the couch without making a noise and fetch my laptop from the bedroom. With a glance at Valentina, I pull up my file on Oslo. I need to book a flight, which I'm sure will require some serious negotiating with Rafael. He won't hold me here, but even after what I told him today, he's likely to feel obligated to let my father know I left. And if he doesn't, Antonio definitely will. *Maybe there's another way.*

I log in to an encrypted service and carefully compose an email with all the information I've garnered. I attach the graphs I created and highlight the patterns carefully. When I'm satisfied, I send it to the local authorities in Oslo, as well as to the Kripos and the Norwegian Intelligence Service. I send it to Interpol too. Not that they've acknowledged a single email I've sent in the past.

The clock is ticking. We have about twelve days before they strike again. I want to be in Oslo within a week.

# 29

## RAFAEL

VALENTINA HAS TURNED out to be the biggest cockblocker in the history of cockblockers, but Marco's coming back tonight, and she's going home to the valley. It's a good thing, too, because I have a ton of work to do, and I'm having trouble focusing on anything but those little mewls Lexie makes when I lick her pussy. *I need more of those whimpers. I need to feel her walls pulse around my cock.*

When I got back to the apartment the other night, I wasn't sure she'd be up for another round, but she was—more than ready—and for another just before Valentina arrived. Each time, the sex was better than the last.

That's why one-night stands have never been my favorite. Sure, they have their place, and they come with a rush that's hard to beat. But I've always preferred having a woman for a long weekend, where there's time to explore—and even push boundaries a bit. It has to be the right woman, of course, because otherwise a weekend can feel like a century. Although I never let it come to that. If it starts to go in a direction I don't like, I'm out.

But with Lexie, I have no desire to leave. If anything, I want to curl up around her and stay. I'm not sure how long that feeling will last, or what kind of shitshow will follow when it's time to part ways, but I don't expect it to be smooth sailing. She's been thinking about us for a long time. *Since she was nineteen.*

I've thought a lot about her since that day at the pool, and even more after the wedding. But my fantasies have been about her sassy mouth and my cock, not about playing house for a lifetime. Although, I like her, *a lot*, and I'm sure as hell not ready to let her go. *Not yet.* Certainly not before I rectify the situation with her father. That game he's playing needs to stop. It's too damn dangerous.

My phone rings, and Bruno Russo's name pops up on the screen. He gave me his personal cell phone number when I called to tell him the traffickers had been murdered. *Maybe he has more news.*

"Mr. Prime Minister. How are you?"

"Not as good as I will be when everyone involved with that ring is dead."

*He's pulling no punches. A man after my own heart.*

"I called to see if you have any additional information."

"Nothing more than I had on Friday. I was hoping you knew something."

"I don't have anything," Russo grunts, and I hear the frustration in his voice. I'm damn frustrated too.

"Do you think there's any connection between Saint Philomena's and what happened the other day?" he asks cautiously. "Both Francesca and Ms. Clarke were students there. It's the only connection my people can find between them."

"I've thought about it. We're looking into it, too, but so far, we've come up with nothing." *But Saint Phil's isn't the only connection between them.* "I'm not ready to let go of that angle, but it seems to me that there's another tie as well. Both are daughters of powerful men. Powerful men have powerful enemies." Will certainly does, and there is no way you get to be the Italian prime minister without leaving a lot of bodies in your wake.

"True. Although our businesses are quite different."

*You keep telling yourself that, Bruno, but from where I sit, there's little difference between what you do and what Will Clarke does. He just doesn't put on airs.*

Francesca was the original target, and Lexie became a target of opportunity. I didn't share this with him the first time we spoke, because I didn't know, and the last time, I decided to keep it to myself because I didn't want him pointing fingers at Lexie as though she did something wrong. In many ways, it doesn't matter. If they believe that either woman knows anything that might implicate them, they're equally in danger.

"I'll let you know if I hear anything," I assure him. "Please do the same. Until then, we have to be patient." It's almost comical that I'm the one advising patience.

"Patient," he scoffs. "Do you have teenage daughters running all over the globe chasing boys and begging to go to Taylor Swift concerts, Rafael?"

*No. Thank fucking God.* "I do not."

"I have three."

There's anger and despair in his voice, and I change my mind about sending him the tape I've been sitting on of Francesca shaking her ass on the dance floor. *Three daughters.* The guy needs a break.

After we hang up, I try to pull up this week's calendar, to see what I can rearrange, before setting up a meeting that's long overdue. But it's blank—although it's unlikely that I have nothing scheduled. I call Noelia, which I don't normally do on the weekend.

"Sorry to bother you on a Sunday afternoon, but I need to

talk to you about this week's schedule. My copy is blank. Is that possible?"

"In your dreams." She laughs. "I'm waiting to hear back from the US marketing team about launch activities, so I've kept most of the week penciled in. I should know more by the end of today. Let me pull up my draft so I can have it in front of me."

Noelia is a saint. Organized, discreet, loyal, even-tempered, and she puts up with my shit without complaining.

"Did something come up?" she asks.

"A couple things. I need to block off a morning this week, preferably Wednesday or Thursday. Also, I won't be in the office until after ten tomorrow." *I plan on keeping a sultry blonde up all night.*

"Okay," she murmurs. "Henry Fausto wants to see you. He's scheduled at nine. He has some important findings to discuss."

"Put a bright red line through that appointment." I don't care about eight thousand missing euros. I. Do. Not. Care. "Find out more before you reschedule."

"I asked for more information, because I didn't think you'd want to meet with him again so soon. But he wouldn't tell me anything. Said that he would prefer to speak to you about it himself. He also said it couldn't wait."

"It's going to have to wait. His urgency is not my emergency." Or however that saying goes. "What else do you have?"

We go through the list and make some decisions. "If we block off Wednesday morning, will you be available to take calls?"

"I have a very early meeting. After that, I'll be on a plane and I can take calls. Schedule it like a regular workday. Do me a favor—it can wait until tomorrow. I need the plane to be ready at six a.m. Wednesday. Arrange it, please."

"Where are you traveling?"

"Heathrow."

Before I can give her any more details, there's a knock at my door and Zé sticks his head in. "Henry Fausto was in the building, and he stopped by to see if you were here by chance."

*You have got to be fucking kidding me.*

Zé comes in and approaches the desk. "The guy is beside himself. He started sweating when I asked him some questions. You might want to talk to him."

"Don't get soft on me, Zé."

He chuckles. "Not in this lifetime."

By now Henry has spent so many hours on this audit that I'm out much more than eight thousand euros. *What a waste.* I need to stop the bleeding today.

"Tell him he can have five minutes. That's it."

# 30

## RAFAEL

"I'm so relieved you're here," are the first words out of Henry's mouth when he steps into my office. His face is red, and the man who prizes correctness and accuracy is disheveled. I've never seen him so out of sorts.

I point to a chair in front of my desk but forgo shaking his sweaty hand. "You're not normally in on Sundays," I observe calmly. "This must be important."

He nods from the edge of the chair. "I traced the missing funds."

His expression is somber, but he's been much more concerned about the money than I've been, so I don't read too much into it. "And?"

"They lead to an offshore account."

"One of ours?" It could be a simple mistake. Although we're especially careful with those accounts, because they're more vulnerable than the ones we have in-country.

He shrugs. "Not one that belongs to Premier."

*I've had enough of twenty questions.*

"Henry, I'm a busy man with so much on my plate that I'm sitting in my office on a gorgeous Sunday afternoon. Spit it out so I can get back to work." I manage to keep the worst of the harshness out of my voice, but not the impatience.

He nods, twiddling his fingers in his lap. "The account is in Valentina Cruz's name."

Premier is Valentina's company too. She's entitled to any legal share of the profits, and she can certainly set up whatever accounts she wants, wherever she wants. But this isn't like her. Besides, eight thousand euros? She probably spent more than that on shoes last month. It doesn't make sense.

"Did you ask her about it?"

"I asked her about it after we last met. She said that she didn't make any withdrawals. So I kept looking, and then I found the account."

"Any other name on the account?"

He shakes his head. "No. But from what I was able to garner, her husband is the beneficiary."

*Her husband is the beneficiary.* I would expect Marco to be the beneficiary of any account in Valentina's name that was set up *after* they were married. But still, it sets my teeth on edge.

"It's all the information I could get without involving the authorities," he continues. "I didn't want to do that without consulting you first."

*Jesus Christ.* The last fucking thing I need is the tax authorities with their noses in our business. "I appreciate it. Don't contact anyone, and don't say a word about it to anyone— including Valentina. If she says she didn't withdraw the money, she didn't. I don't want to worry her needlessly until we know more about it."

"I agree," he replies. "I don't want to speak out of school, but money doesn't seem to be an issue for her. She's very generous. A significant portion of her monthly salary goes to the women's shelter, in her grandmother's name. Apparently she matches a contribution made by her friend, Ms. Clarke. It's supposed to be confidential, but under the circumstances I think you should know. She's a lovely young woman, and I haven't ever known her to be anything but honest."

*You don't need to defend her to me.*

A warmth sets in my chest. Lexie and Valentina. Frick and Frack, carrying the torch of the previous generations. *Thankfully they're only donating money and not ferrying women to safety in the dead of night.*

I don't care about the money, but I do care about an account in Valentina's name that she didn't create. "I'm going to get in touch with Tamar Sorin. You know Tamar, right?"

"Yes. Of course. The head of IT."

"I want you to turn over everything you have to her regarding the withdrawal and the account. Tell her everything you know. She'll take it from there."

He nods.

"She's just upstairs. Can you stick around until she arrives?"

"I've been here all night, checking and rechecking. Staying a little while longer is not a problem." He stands to leave. "I want you to know that you can count on my complete discretion in this matter."

"I've never had any concerns about your honor or loyalty, Henry. I consider myself fortunate that you're on the team." *Even when your exactness makes me crazy.*

After he's gone, I call Tamar. "I hope you weren't planning a romantic evening. We have a problem that needs to be addressed immediately."

"What is it?"

"A relatively small withdrawal was made from a Premier account. The money was traced to an offshore account in Valentina's name. Marco is the beneficiary." The words leave a sour taste in my mouth.

She's quiet for a moment. I hired her, but technically she works for Valentina too. And they're friends. But Tamar is a professional. I wouldn't involve her if I didn't have complete confidence that she'll do whatever needs to be done, however unpleasant.

"Have you spoken to Valentina about the money?"

"She didn't make the withdrawal. And she will not know about the investigation until I'm ready to tell her. Do we understand each other?"

"I follow orders, Rafael."

"Henry Fausto has the details. He's waiting for you in his office."

"I'll be right down."

"I need you to dig deep and follow the tunnel wherever it leads. Wherever, Tamar. It could get messy." With any luck, it won't. But who would open an account in Valentina's name? There's only one person I can think of. *Too early to be pointing fingers at Marco, Rafael. Way too early.*

"I was Mossad," she replies. "It doesn't get messier than that."

Ordinarily I would agree. But this has the potential to destroy my relationship with Valentina. Just the thought of it sickens me.

*Marco, your paw prints better not be anywhere near this, because I'll gut you. Not for being a thief, but for breaking Valentina's heart. I made myself clear before you married her. Don't say I didn't warn you.*

Before I leave for Sirena, I send the text that's been weighing heavily on me.

Rafael: *I'll be in London on Wednesday morning. We need to talk.*

Will: *Bring my daughter.*
*That is not happening.*

# 31

## ALEXIS

RAFAEL: *I'm on my way up.*

Lexie: *Don't be shy.*

Rafael: *Me?*

I send him a little devil emoji, turn on the shower, and take off my clothes.

Rafael promised we'd finish what we started that day in the shower, but while we christened half the surfaces in the apartment before Valentina arrived, we never got back to the shower.

It was like old times, hanging out in our pajamas until noon, but I'm worried about Valentina. She's not someone who's prone to drama—if anything, she downplays things. I wouldn't be surprised if her relationship with Marco is on even shakier grounds than she let on.

When I hear the door, I step into the warm spray and reach for the handheld shower attachment. I try to remember exactly how I was positioned the day he walked in on me, but all I can remember is Rafael, naked, his hard cock jutting straight out from tight abs and bobbing as he joined me in the shower. He was in a frenzy. And I was startled, but happy, *so happy*, to see him.

I close my eyes and wait for him to join me, the warm water caressing my pussy and sending small zings of pleasure through my body.

The showerhead is on the floor, and I'm backed against the wall before his face even registers. His hands and mouth skate over my skin, searing blissful paths.

"If you think anything's going to stop me from fucking you in this shower tonight, Angel, you're mistaken. I wouldn't stop if the building was engulfed in flames."

His voice is laced with a delicious threat, and my body arches into him, seeking more of his sun-kissed skin against mine.

"How was your day, honey?" I tease, and it earns me a sharp slap on the ass that escalates the throb between my legs to another level.

"That mouth, sweetheart. It's going to get you into trouble."

*Bring it on.*

He inches me into the same corner as last time, tweaking my nipples and rubbing his palms over my skin. "Turn around," he demands, "and put your hands on the wall."

I face the wall as he asks and lay my palms on the cool stone. His cock was hard when he got into the shower, but against my ass it feels like a steel rod.

He holds me still against him so I can't wiggle against his cock, and dips his fingers into my pussy. "Such a good girl," he coos. "Always ready for me."

A flood of warmth cascades over me at the sound of his voice. The words. The praise. It makes me want to be the good girl he covets. *His* good girl.

"Always," I whisper into the steam.

"I'm going to fuck that sweet pussy. Would you like that?"

I nod, because I can't find my voice.

He takes a small step back but is still close enough that I can almost feel him. I hear the distinct crinkling of the condom wrapper, right before he kicks my feet apart and plunges into me from behind. It's brutal. *Deliciously brutal.*

I cling to the wall as a moan twists from me, along with all my breath. It's loud and lusty, and it belongs to a woman who's far more sexy and experienced than I am. The kind of woman capable of bringing Rafael Huntsman to his knees.

"You're so tight, Angel. So damn tight."

Even with my hands braced on the marble wall, his thrusts are so savage I can barely stay upright.

"Come here," he murmurs when my body hits the unforgiving stone. "I don't want you to get hurt. You have me so worked up, I don't trust myself to protect you."

He pulls out of me, and I whine like a child who's been denied a treat she desperately wants.

Rafael tugs me backward to the long bench that extends the entire shower wall. He sits and lowers me onto his lap, sliding me against his cock until it's nestled in the crack of my ass. It feels shamefully good until a sliver of doubt pings against my brain. *Is he going to want anal?* But I'm so aroused it becomes a fleeting concern. All I can think about is my warm, wet skin against his.

He hooks his long legs around mine, coaxing me open. "Stay just like this for me, Angel. You won't bruise your beautiful face, and I can have all the access I need to make you feel good."

*Yes, please. Make me feel good.*

His thumb rubs light circles around my clit, and each time it grazes the hood, I grind my backside into him. "I need you inside me again." *As much as I need my next breath. Maybe more.*

"Soon," he whispers into my wet hair. "You feel so goddamn good, I want to slow this down so I can enjoy you longer."

I whimper.

"Look at me."

I tip my head back. His eyes are black, and droplets of water cling to his eyelashes. He's so beautiful it takes my breath away.

"Have you ever done any kind of ass play?" he asks, putting a hand on my belly with enough pressure to wedge me firmly between his palm and his cock.

I shake my head, acutely aware of his thick cock between my cheeks. "No."

"Are you even a little bit curious?" he asks, his hot mouth grazing my temple.

*Yes. But I'm a little nervous about trying it. And a little embarrassed too.* "I don't know. Maybe."

"Not today—because I don't have the patience for it. But I want your little rosebud. We'll go nice and slow. I'll use my fingers, and then a plug, until you're begging me to dip my cock inside your ass and own it, like I own the rest of you."

I shiver at the lewd words, the tone, and the bite of shame that comes not with him owning my ass, but reveling in the idea. I'm so aroused that if he asks, I might just let him do it.

His fingers are more insistent now, playing with my pussy until I'm wiggling all over his lap, making him curse. He's still cursing when he lifts my hips with both hands.

"You're going to get on my cock and ride me, Angel," he demands, lowering me onto the thick shaft like I weigh nothing. "Hold on tight, and ride me hard."

The sensations and the emotions are twirling together until they're one, and it takes me a minute to find my stride. But once I do, once I list forward and dig my fingers into his thighs for leverage, I ride him with abandon, bouncing on his fat cock while he plays with my pussy, rushing me toward the orgasm I crave.

He guides me, grunting and panting as I roll my hips, pulling his cock deeper. "Angel," he pants. "You feel so goddamn good."

As the orgasm washes over me, it pulls me below the

surface, where there's no air. My body jerks in uncontrolled movements until he grasps my hips and steadies me.

"I've got you, sweetheart. Ride out the wave."

When I'm spent, I collapse on his chest, my cheek resting near the crook of his neck. The emotion untangles itself from the sensation as it worms its way into my chest.

"You're so beautiful when you come," Rafael whispers, rubbing his fingers gently on my sensitive clit while I mewl. "I can't get enough of you." He tips my head forward and sinks his teeth into the nape of my neck, hard enough to rouse me from my dreamy trance. That's when I realize that he's still rock hard inside me.

"You didn't come." I don't know why I say it, but it sounds so silly to my ears.

"Not yet. But I need to. When you're ready." His voice is tight, and when I hear the raw need in every syllable, I cant my hips. He gasps and reaches for the hose attached to the shower handle.

I know exactly what he's going to do, but even still, I scream when the first stream of water hits my pussy.

"Shh," he whispers into my hair as the sting turns to plea-sure, and I spiral tighter and higher, until I'm soaring again—my body nothing more than a bundle of exposed nerves swaying for him. *Always for him.*

"Hold this, and don't you dare let go," he commands, handing me the showerhead and easing us closer to the edge of the bench.

I'm shaking as I take it, holding it with both hands—one hand wouldn't be enough. I teeter, feeling less steady now that I can't cling to him, but I trust him not to let me fall.

With his feet planted firmly on the tile, he moves me like I'm a rag doll who exists only for his pleasure.

"Hold the spray closer to your pussy. Let it beat on your pretty pink flesh."

My womb tightens, as the orgasm gathers with such steam that I'm afraid to let go. "I can't."

"Do it," he commands, wrapping an arm around my waist.

It's steadying, and somewhere I find it in me to obey. With trembling hands, I bring the showerhead closer, edging myself toward the cliff. *I'm coiled too tight. I can't. I can't.*

His hips jerk, before my anguished scream, and I let the shower handle drop as the orgasm twists, almost painfully, from my body.

He curses loudly, before the primal sound of a wild animal fills the steamy enclosure as he finds his own release.

# 32

## RAFAEL

I GRAB my phone from the nightstand to see if there's anything from Tamar, but no such luck. I'm confident she's working on it, so that means the information is difficult to trace.

"Put your phone down," the woman lying next to me with a serious case of bedhead and bruised lips orders, like the fucking queen she is.

We've been at each other since the shower late last night like two horny teenagers. My body is sore, and I'm sure hers is worse. Otherwise I'd give her a lesson about who issues orders and who follows them.

"I'll be away Wednesday morning on business," I tell her, continuing to scroll, because there's only one person I take orders from, and it isn't her. "If it's still quiet tomorrow night, let's have dinner at Sirena."

"That sounds fabulous. I need a break from this place. I also need to go to Oslo later this week."

She drops the grenade like it's no big deal, but her twitchy eye gives her away.

"What's in Oslo?"

"The fjords."

I slap her ass, and she yelps. "Let's try it again. What's in Oslo?"

"You notice I didn't ask you where you were going on business or what you'd be doing. You're a great lay, but don't get clingy on me, Huntsman."

*Oh, Angel, you are not doing this. Before we're done, I'm going to fuck that piss-poor coping mechanism right out of you.*

I roll on top of her and rock my hips into her pelvis. "The only thing getting clingy is your pussy around my cock." I dip my head and kiss her roughly until she's gasping for air.

"What's in Oslo?" I ask for the third time, because while she's in my bed, I'll be as *clingy* as I fucking want. Besides, she's not going anywhere that I don't sanction until we have a better handle on the danger. And I won't sanction anything until I have all the details.

"I need to write an article about Anne Nilson, another up-and-coming designer like Judite Furtado."

*I don't believe Judite is why you came to Porto, and I'm not inclined to believe this either.* Although I did read the draft of her article on Judite's shop, and I know she submitted it. *Maybe I'm too suspicious.* "Can it wait?"

"Not really. It's part of a series the magazine is doing on young female entrepreneurs who are shaking things up. Kind of like you re-envisioning Port."

I've never gotten the impression that freelance writing is her passion. It's just a placeholder that allows her to travel until she finds her calling. But even so, I don't want to make it impossible for her to do her job. Although there's no way she's going unless I'm certain she'll be safe. Job or no job.

I slide off her. "We'll talk about it tomorrow night."

"Rafael?" She rolls to her side and traces a finger over my jaw, peering into my face. Her expression is warm and soft, but her eyes have the spark of defiance. "We can talk about it, but I'm going. I won't be a prisoner here, even with the sexy perks. I'm done with captivity. My father's or yours."

"We'll figure it out," I grumble. There's nothing I hate more than being compared to her father, who's out of control. Before either of us can say another word, the sheet falls to her waist, exposing her gorgeous tits, and I'm done talking. Soreness be damned.

I nudge Lexie onto her back and climb between her legs. "Sexy perk time, Angel."

"Don't think you're going to get me to relent by wooing me with orgasms."

*I would never think that.* I'm more concerned that her orgasms will change my mind, and I'll agree to whatever she wants, just to feel her tremble in my arms.

After I'm sure she's ready for me, I push her knees to her chest and make the long, vicious slide home—as her gasps and whimpers flood my soul.

If I needed any more reason to make the trip to London, this is it.

# 33

## RAFAEL

I ARRIVE at Clarke Enterprises shortly after nine. The building is heavily fortified, but you wouldn't know it by the sleek, modern lines that grace the high-rise. All sorts of things happen here—legal, illegal, and morally gray—but it all hides in plain sight, just outside central London.

After clearing security, I take the elevator to the top floor. Shortly after I sent Will the text Sunday evening, his assistant called to arrange a meeting time. I'm not surprised he agreed. I have his daughter.

I don't know exactly what to expect from him, or if he'll be amenable to my help. The one thing I'm sure about is that he won't be welcoming me with open arms. Although, in the end, it won't matter whether or not I persuade him to let me manage Lexie's security. When I leave London, if I'm still breathing, I'll be taking over her protection. But it'll be easier if he agrees.

"Good morning," a young, much-too-eager receptionist chirps. The redhead is so perky she practically bounces while she talks.

"Rafael Huntsman. Mr. Clarke is expecting me."

"Please have a seat. I'll let his assistant know you're here."

I nod.

"Can I get you something while you wait?"

"No, thank you."

Before I find a seat, an impeccably dressed man, about forty, appears at the door.

"Mr. Huntsman, right this way, please."

It's a long, lonely path to the executive suite, which is flanked with guards for my benefit, I'm sure. Much to Zé's horror, I came alone, as a sign of trust and a show of strength. For someone like Will, the latter is as important as the former. Maybe more.

The man who hasn't said a damn word to me since the reception area knocks on the door, opens it, and steps aside so I can enter.

Will is perched at the front of his desk, arms crossed. Even on a good day, he's a scary motherfucker. Not his appearance— he looks like any other top executive. But unlike most CEOs, he wouldn't hesitate to slit a throat even if it meant getting blood on his custom Tom Ford suit.

"Can I get either of you gentlemen something?" the assistant asks, as though his boss is not glowering at me like I'm not long for this world.

"No," Will replies tersely.

I'm tempted to say, *I'll take an espresso, black, please.* But he's pissed, and I don't think it's wise to poke the bear more than necessary.

The office is spacious and airy, comfortable, with a long conference table piled with folders. It looks like someone does actual work here.

Will doesn't invite me to sit, and I don't. I want to be at eye level with him or at least have a running start when he pulls a gun, because I'm unarmed. It's not how I normally roll, but I wouldn't have gotten through security otherwise.

"Nice to see you, Will. How's Samantha?"

"Cut the bullshit. You have some fucking nerve demanding an audience with me. How's my daughter?"

*So much for the pleasantries.*

*How's my daughter?* Well, when I last saw her, she looked like she'd been well fucked.

"Alexis is fine. She's safe for now."

"No thanks to you."

I've known Will since I was nine or ten, and he's always treated me well. I'm willing to show him some respect, but I'm not here to be his punching bag. Besides, if he's going to trust me to protect his daughter, he needs to know I'm up to the job.

I decide to sit. Standing like a scared kid ready to bolt at the first sign of trouble isn't going to help my cause. After unbuttoning my suit jacket, I take a seat across from him and lean back in the chair, looking more relaxed than I feel.

"Comfy?" he snarls.

Sometimes it's prudent to soften the target before lowering the boom. This isn't one of those times.

"I want Alexis under my protection, if she agrees to it." Or even if she doesn't agree, but I'm not planning to let it get to that.

Will is deathly calm. The kind of calm that pings frenetically off the walls.

I'm bigger than him. Stronger. A lot younger. And I could probably take him mano a mano. But we're in his house, and aside from the weapons on his person, I'm sure the guards outside would love to do some real damage. But it had to be said. This isn't a carnival. No reason to play hide the ball.

"You fucker," he hisses, sliding off the desk. He doesn't lunge for me, like I expect. Instead, he moves behind the desk, takes a gun from the top drawer, and lays it in front of him.

My pulse ticks up, not enough so he can notice, but enough to make me hyperaware of the distance between his hand and the gun.

"I suppose under your protection includes warming your bed."

It's his daughter. Fair question. *Sex has nothing to do with my plan. If anything, it only complicates things.* "It does not."

"I'm supposed to believe that?"

"Believe what you want, but I give you my word that her safety does not hinge on an intimate relationship." *Hinge on me fucking her* was on the tip of my tongue, but I'm not that stupid. "Nor would I ever suggest anything like that to her."

"I can protect my daughter just fine," he says through gritted teeth. "I've been doing it all her life. And until she walked into *your* club, her safety has never been at issue."

*Bullshit.* I'm tired of looking up at him. It's only making him feel more powerful. I stand and walk over to the window, bracing my back against the casing.

"You've protected Alexis from your formidable enemies all her life. I'm not here to argue that point. But with all due respect, sir, she's a woman now, with a mind of her own, and she doesn't want your protection."

While I'm tempted to glance at how close his hand is to the gun, my eyes don't leave his.

"She doesn't want to live in a cage," I continue, "not even a gilded one. So she slips her security and traipses across the Continent, doing whatever the hell she wants—with no protection. She was in danger in Porto, and she came to Sirena because she believed I could keep her safe. And I did." Although I took a risk by going forward with the operation even after I knew she was part of the group. That still weighs heavily on my conscience.

Long seconds pass, and I'm still alive. But his menacing glower tells me he's thinking about changing that.

"I don't need some punk coming in here to tell me about my daughter. I know Alexis. She came out of the womb rebelling. The minute you try to clip her wings, she'll ditch your security without chipping a nail. And you won't have a fucking clue how to deal with her."

Maybe not, but it couldn't be more dangerous than it is now.

"And you do?"

His fingers inch toward the gun, but I've come this far, and I don't shrink.

"What exactly is your plan?" he barks.

"My plan is to keep her well guarded with soldiers who she doesn't feel the need to slip, because they're not a pipeline of information to you." *Foolish, maybe, but again, it had to be said.*

"But they will be to you."

I shake my head. "They will not report to me unless there's a major problem. She's an adult and deserves some privacy and a right to make her own decisions. It's a new world, Will, and Alexis isn't having any of the old bullshit. You're going to lose her," I add softly.

He blanches, because he knows I'm right. He's stubborn and tough, but he loves Lexie, and he knows she's playing with fire. *And I haven't even shared everything.*

This is hard on him. It's a matter of honor and pride. None of that's lost on me.

He shoots daggers at me while the wheels turn. "Has Alexis agreed to this?"

"Not yet. She doesn't know anything about it. I came here first, out of respect for you. Not all the old ways should be discarded."

He eyes me shrewdly.

"But this is merely a courtesy. I'm concerned for her safety, and if she agrees, she'll be under my protection with or without your blessing."

He twirls the gun on the desk, and I watch carefully, but he's not going to shoot me. Will isn't a fool. He understands more about his own behavior and Lexie's reaction to it than he's letting on. Whatever he's dealing with from his past is bigger than him.

I won't allow him to destroy his daughter, but that doesn't mean I don't have great empathy for the man. I wrestle with demons that look an awful lot like his.

"The authorities want to interview Alexis. I think we'd both agree that it's enough for her to give them a written statement. They have our video footage and we turned over the suspects. She doesn't have anything useful to tell them. I've already informed the Porto police, and we can manage the Portuguese Intelligence Service, but I could use some help with Interpol." I can handle Interpol, but he's cornered, and I hand him an olive branch. "Is that something you'd be willing to do?"

He doesn't hesitate. "No interviews. By the time you leave the building, it'll be handled."

I nod.

"Where will she be staying while she's under your protection?"

It's more of a snarl than a question. This isn't the crime boss talking. This is Daddy.

"Huntsman Lodge. She won't be a prisoner, of course, but she'll have to negotiate with her guards or with me before she goes out and about." *Or to Oslo, which I still haven't agreed to.*

He glances at me like I'm a young fool, and snickers.

"I'm well aware that it will take her some time to get used to the system."

"You might be a young buck, but there's not enough time left in your life for you to live to see the day she bows to the system."

*This is pretty rich coming from him, considering he's made a fortune not bowing to the system but by having it bow to him.*

"I'm not asking her to bow to my system. I'm asking her to create her own—within reason." *Something you should have been encouraging since she was a kid, like Antonio did with me, and like we tried to do with Valentina.*

"You live in an apartment at Huntsman Lodge."

It's not a question, but I reply. "I do. Although Valentina's apartment is available, and that's where Alexis has been staying."

"And where have you been staying?" He's still angry, but his questions are now more in line with what any concerned father might ask.

"My apartment and the club." I leave out Valentina's apartment. I don't have a death wish.

"Sneaking around—"

I hold up my hand to stop him. "Alexis is an adult," I remind him for the third time since arriving. "Where she sleeps is neither your decision, nor mine."

He leans back in his chair and taps his index finger against his chin. "I want to speak to my daughter before I sanction anything. I'm not taking your word that there's no coercion involved."

I can live with that, and although Lexie might not like it, she can live with it, too, because in the end, he'll agree to my plan.

"I'm going directly to Porto when I leave here. I'll let you know what she says, after I've spoken with her. If she doesn't agree to my protection, you won't need to make the trip."

I weigh my next words. A smart man would run with the concessions he's gotten, but I don't like to have my word or my honor questioned.

"You know, Will, you might not like what I came to tell you, and you might not like me. But my word is gold. And you've known me long enough to know it."

He sizes me up, but I don't flinch under the scrutiny.

"What I know," he says, "and what I know when it comes to my family, are two separate things. But I'll give you one thing, Rafa. You could have lied to me—at least tried—or pulled some other crap from the safety of Porto, where your family has all the power. But you didn't. You showed up like a man."

For Will, this is as close to gushing as it gets. He'd still put a bullet in me, but he wouldn't call me a sniveling pussy while he fired the shot.

"It wasn't as difficult as you might think. She's taken some big risks that jeopardized her safety. I know that's not what you want for her. And neither do I."

When I start to leave, he doesn't stand or put out his hand. Pride won't allow for it. I don't take it personally.

I've given him a lot to chew on. Most of it I suspect he's been chewing on for a long time. But I've also offered him a solution. He might not see it as perfect, but it's the best he's got—and he knows it.

"If you'd like to speak to Alexis in person, you're always welcome in Porto." I nod and turn toward the door.

"Rafael."

I have my hand on the knob when he calls my name. When I turn around, Will has a cocked gun pointed at my head. I draw a breath. He's across the room, but I have no illusions. He won't miss if he pulls the trigger. But he won't pull the trigger. Not today.

"If you fuck this up, they'll never find your body."

*If anything happens to her because I fuck this up, you might as well kill me, because I won't be able to live with myself.*

## 34

# RAFAEL

AFTER I LEAVE WILL, I go directly to the plane. The man's certifiable. No wonder Lexie's at the end of her rope with him.

There's no question he has a soft spot for his wife and daughter—that's always been apparent—but he's a difficult son of a bitch. I'm sure Lexie's backbone was built from going up against him over the years.

My job is only half-done. Now I have to convince Lexie that her lot is better tied to mine than her father's. It won't be easy, because she's not easy, but at least she won't be waving a gun at me. *Just her cute little ass.*

I have a sip of lime seltzer and a handful of salted almonds, savoring my victory with Will, before I need to get down to work. While I'm chuckling about how the arrogant bastard aimed a gun at my head, I get a message from Tamar: *Call me ASAP.*

Nothing good comes after a message like that.

She answers on the first ring, and I brace myself for what's coming.

"Sorin," she says, her tone not giving anything away.

"What did you find?"

"Nothing definitive. But another deposit was made into the account. A big one. I watched it happen in real time."

"How much?"

"One hundred and five million euros."

*What the fuck?*

"From one of our accounts?"

"Yes. Although there appears to be some type of delay—because Henry can't see it on his end. I was only able to trace it because I watched it happen—but even then, I had to go through a back channel."

"If Henry can't see it, is it possible it didn't come from one of our accounts?"

"He confirmed it through the institutions. It actually came from several accounts. Including an operating account and the pension plan."

"Are you any closer to finding out who opened the offshore account?"

She pauses. "I have nothing definitive yet. But so far everything points to Marco Cruz."

"Son of a bitch." *I'm going to disembowel that asshole.* How could Valentina be so head over heels in love with that guy? *Valentina.* My first priority has to be to protect Valentina—her life, and also her heart. "Tamar, we can't afford to be wrong about this."

"Like I said, we have nothing definitive. Certainly not enough to accuse Valentina's husband."

*Valentina's husband. This is where it gets messy.*

"Get Lucas involved. Don't tell him we suspect Marco. See if he draws the same conclusion on his own. I want a definitive answer by the time the sun sets. And if it's Marco, I'll need to see the evidence."

I'd be happy to string him up any damn day of the week without the evidence, but I can't do that to Valentina. She'll be crushed—and angry, mostly at me. I have broad shoulders, but

I don't want our relationship destroyed because I acted impulsively. It's too important to me.

*Could there be a worse time to be on a goddamn plane?*

That bastard. Fucking thief. *And maybe much worse.* I gulp down what's left of my drink and call Zé. "Do you know where Valentina is?"

"I saw her in the building earlier. Let me text her guards."

There's no way anyone could get to her in the building. It would be *almost* impossible. Even Marco wouldn't be stupid enough to pull something inside Huntsman Lodge. I feel the tension in my shoulders unfurl a bit.

"Has Tamar talked to you about the missing money?"

"No. We stay in our own lanes."

I never warned either of them not to mix business and pleasure, but it doesn't surprise me that they came to it on their own.

"Ask her about it. Tell her I said to tell you everything."

"Valentina's in a meeting in her office."

"Good. Before you talk to Tamar, put someone we trust on Valentina. She's not to leave the building, Zé, until I get back. Not for any reason. And those guards that answer to her husband? Consider them suspect."

"What's going on?"

"Talk to Tamar. I need to get off and call Antonio. Talk to Tamar," I repeat, more for my benefit than Zé's.

I motion for the flight attendant. "Get me a bourbon, straight up. Don't be stingy with the booze."

She smiles sympathetically, like she knows that a midday bourbon means the day sucks balls.

I stare at Antonio's number before I place the call. Normally I wouldn't burden him until we had more facts, but this is his daughter, and he needs to know.

"Rafael." Antonio whistles. "Heard you were in London. I

would not have advised that." He's clearly amused, but I'm about to change his mood.

"That was yesterday's problem. We have something new to worry about."

He pauses, and I feel the energy shift. "I'm listening."

I tell him everything I know, and he reacts predictably. I'm not entirely sure Marco will still be alive when I deplane in Porto.

"We can't sit on our hands," I grumble. "The deposit was enormous, and whoever authorized it will know that we'll find out about it in short order. Marco is named the beneficiary. If I were him, I'd want Valentina dead as soon as possible, empty that account, and disappear."

"He's mine," Antonio growls.

"We need to proceed cautiously." It's a very bad day when I'm the voice of reason in a situation that involves Valentina's safety—or Lexie's. "The stakes are high, but he's her husband." I don't say he's family, because I've never thought of him that way.

"You're sure she's in the building?"

"I'm sure, and I'm also sure she isn't going anywhere."

"I'm going to find her and insist she come home with me for dinner to surprise her mother," Antonio says, like it's a done deal. "I'll tell her Daniela's not well and I'm worried—or some other bullshit. I'll keep Valentina at the house until we know where this is headed."

Not having to worry about her whereabouts would certainly make things less stressful.

I don't ask how he's going to keep Valentina at the house, because he's Antonio and he'll figure it out, even if it means blowing up the bridge in the center of town so she's stranded.

"If Lucas reaches the same conclusion as Tamar, I'll have Zé pick up Marco while she's with you, and I'll question him. Zé, Tamar, Cristiano, and Lucas can watch the live feed so that there are no mistakes." Cristiano and Lucas are Antonio's top lieutenants, but they're at my disposal when needed.

"You can question him. But I want to be on the feed, watching with the others."

*Antonio, stay out of this. She needs a hero, not another villain.*

"Let me be the bad guy. She's your daughter, and if you don't participate, you'll have plausible deniability. If Marco's behind this, she's going to need you."

"Do you think I give a fuck about plausible deniability, Rafael? Whether he did it or not, I'm her father, and I will be involved. Let the chips fall where they may."

*The chips are going to fall on your head along with the heavy glass bowl they're sitting in if we're wrong and your wife learns about it.*

"Daniela—" I begin, but he finishes my thought before I can get it out.

"Will be so pissed at me, if we're mistaken, that hell will freeze over. I'm well aware." He sighs heavily. "But Valentina's safety is a hill I'm willing to die on. And my wife knows it."

I don't push him, because in his shoes, I'd feel the same way. "I'll be in touch when I know more."

"Rafael?"

"Yeah."

"This will not be without serious implications for your relationship with Valentina either. Nobody would blame you if you let someone else take the lead."

*Not a fucking chance.*

"She's had more than her fair share of pain and loss—there's nothing I can do to change the past. But if that bastard adds to her pain, he'll answer to me."

# 35

## ALEXIS

I'm researching my trip to Oslo when Rafael walks in at four thirty in the afternoon. When the lock snicks, I expect Giana or Sabio, who are now permanently stationed outside the door instead of in the kitchen. Although they normally knock before entering. *He probably should too.*

"This is a nice surprise." I close the window on the screen without being too obvious. If he sees me looking at clubs in Oslo, it's going to be more difficult to convince him I'll be safe there.

"A nice surprise," he says, kissing me until my panties practically melt, "would be catching you in the shower."

*If only I had a little notice.* "That can be arranged. All you need to do is stand outside the door and chat up Giana or Sabio or whoever's out there, for ten minutes, and then come back. I'll make all your fantasies come true."

"As tempting as that is," he says, pouring himself a glass of water, "we need to talk."

There's nothing about his tone or posture that should alarm me, but still, the butterflies in my belly take flight.

"I went to see your father this morning."

*He went behind my back.* I still, my feet stuck to the wood floor as the butterflies swirl faster. I hope I misunderstood, but I know I didn't. "What did you just say?"

Rafael takes a seat at the island, across from where I'm standing. "I went to see your father this morning."

It lands like a dagger in my back. Even hearing it for the second time, I'm speechless for a long moment.

"Clearly you knew about the trip in advance. You didn't think to check with me last night or this morning, when your dick wasn't inside my pussy?"

I realize it's an overreaction, but this feels like a betrayal. *He went to my father behind my back to talk about me—and my life—like I'm a child.* It's enraging.

"I would have invited you to come along, but I didn't think you'd be interested in going. Besides, the conversation needed to be man-to-man."

*Man-to-man? You've got to be fucking kidding me.* "Stop right there with your misogynist bullshit."

"I'm not a misogynist. But I am a realist, and the only way I was going to get your father to listen to me was to put him on familiar footing, where he'd be comfortable. Now sit your cute little ass in that seat, and let's talk."

I stare at the high-backed stool for what feels like an eternity, unsure of whether to sit or stand in protest. All I can think about is him threatening to call my father at the club, as though I wasn't a twenty-three-year-old woman.

The thought of him conspiring with my father is too much. *Maybe that's not what he was doing. Maybe he was in London for a different reason and stopped in to see Dad. A different reason? Like he wanted a proper cup of tea and a decent scone? I don't think so.*

His motivation might be suspect, but I decide to rein in my emotions, because I sound like a shrew, or worse, the kind of *emotional* woman that men dismiss easily.

I slide onto the stool, carefully, my heart still pumping hard.

"*Sit your cute little ass in that seat and let's talk* might not be the best way to convince someone you're not a misogynist. Just saying."

The corner of his mouth curls, and I know he's taken my little quip as the apology it's meant to be. He's not off the hook for cavorting with my father behind my back, but I need to pull myself together if I'm going to hold my own with him.

"What did you and my father discuss?" The first thing that pops into my mind is that he's had enough and is shipping me back. It's not as suave as disappearing on me, but it would be highly effective. And after the last few days with him, it would sting more than falling face-first into a nettle bush.

"I told him that I want you under my protection if, and only if, you agreed to it."

I'm not sure if I should be annoyed or pleased or flying around in a murderous rage. *He went to my father about assuming my protection.* I'm dumbfounded. It's the equivalent of walking into a lion's den and demanding to share dinner. And not just any lion, but the king of the jungle.

"No cute comebacks?" He drums his fingers on the creamy stone countertop, like he's unsure of how I might respond. It's endearing from a man who always seems confident about the outcome. "What are you thinking, Lexie?"

I take a sip of tea, buying a little more time to grapple with my thoughts. "I'm thinking that going to my father like that was more reckless than anything I've ever done. I'm surprised you're still alive."

His eyes are that irresistible startling blue as he snickers. "There might have been once or twice when I thought the end was near."

*I don't doubt it.* As the shock wanes, I remember what it was he proposed to my father.

"You and my father deciding *my* fate, without a drop of input from me. How nice. I get to move from my father's stifling protection to yours." *I don't buy for one second that either of them is actually going to leave the final decision to me.* Murderous rage is edging out annoyed, and pleased is at least a lap behind. "Lovely."

He finishes the water and slams the glass on the counter with such force I'm surprised it didn't shatter. I've tried his patience. *You've tried mine, too, darling.*

"Why don't you actually listen for a minute? I have no intention of smothering you. You'll have the same kind of freedom that I had."

"I noticed you said had, not have." I doubt it was a mistake.

"Very few people have the kind of freedom I have, Lexie. You know that," he adds quietly, the impatience lessening a drop.

*It's true.* He has the kind of freedom enjoyed only by powerful men. It's been that way since the beginning of time, and regardless of how much we pretend to have evolved, it's no less true today. But I'm not powerless, either, and I won't bow to his wishes so easily. I deserve to have a life—one that I live according to *my* wishes and desires.

"You clearly didn't go to my father without a cogent plan. You're not a fool. I want all the ugly details before I make a decision." I square my shoulders. "Tell me everything."

His expression softens. He thinks he's won. *Maybe he has.*

"You'll be assigned guards, and you will negotiate directly with them. You're free to come and go as you please, as long as you and your guards come to an understanding."

*Guards provide security, but they're also babysitters who tattle. At least mine have always been.*

"And if we can't agree?"

"Then you'll come to me. Or they will."

His expression is earnest and sober. I have no reason not to trust him—about this.

"You'll have privacy. They won't be reporting every hiccup.

The guards who work for me are trained professionals, and they'll respect your autonomy." He pauses, his gaze sharpening. "But if you slip them, Lexie, I will find you, and I will put your ass on a plane and personally deliver you to your father. If you think he's been smothering in the past, wait until that happens."

*Prick.*

"So, to quote my American friends, the buck stops with you. You'll be the one to restrict my movement." *Not a big change from the way my father operates.*

"I hope not. But you need to be reasonable. Everyone named Huntsman, as well as your parents and the Russos, will be taking fewer risks until we know more about the traffickers. It's not a personal attack on you or your freedom. It's common sense." He takes a breath. "But yes, I'll have the final word on anything that involves your safety."

Anyone listening to this conversation would be surprised I haven't told him to take his proposal and stick it. But I'm not anyone. I'm the daughter of a notorious Brit with the power to make almost anything happen. This puts me at substantial risk. I've lived with security all my life, and I'll live with it until the day I die. It's a given.

What I'm weighing is whether Rafael's protection will be less onerous than my father's. I'm not even considering what we did on this very island the other day. Not yet. That would make things even more difficult to sort through. *Although it is the elephant in the room, and someone needs to address it before it pisses on the furniture.*

"Why are you doing this?"

# 36

## ALEXIS

HE GAZES at me for a long moment. "Because you deserve to live the life you want, and I believe you can do that safely. I won't pretend it'll be easy, but the alternative is untenable. You're far too precious to lose. That's something your father and I easily agreed on."

*You're far too precious to lose.* If I think about it too long, my resolve will melt, and I don't intend on negotiating for my freedom with a soft heart. I can think about his words later, after this is settled.

"If I want to visit friends or my mother?"

"Negotiate with your guards."

"Oslo?"

"Negotiate with your guards."

*This feels too easy.* "These aren't just empty promises to mollify me, are they?"

He shakes his head. "Not my style."

"Is there anything else I should know?"

"A couple more things." He reaches for my hand and rubs circles with his thumb, on the palm, until my pussy flutters, like the damn distraction it is. "You'll be required to have a tracking device, on your person, that must be enabled at all times. It's not negotiable."

I've worn tracking devices my entire life. My mother has them too. At Saint Phil's, sometime between Latin class and water polo, I learned how to disable them from the older students. Rich girls with overprotective daddies stick together when it comes to evading security measures.

But Rafael isn't going to track me like I'm an inmate on home confinement. I won't agree to it.

"Because I'm an unreliable prisoner?"

He squeezes my hand hard and doesn't let go. "No. Because you're too goddamn important not to have a way to find you, if you're missing."

He says it with such *oomph*, such heart, that I have to swallow the emotion lodged in my throat.

"Will you be monitoring my every move?" I ask softly, praying he'll say no, because I want to choose his protection. *I want to choose him.*

"I will not do that."

"Give me your word."

His phone vibrates, and the temperature of the room cools as he glances at the message.

"You know what, Lexie, your father will be in Porto in a couple of days. If you can't trust me without a multitude of assurances, go home with him, because it'll never work between us."

*My father is coming to Porto? Don't get distracted, Lexie.*

"I trust you, Rafael, but imagine if the shoe was on the other foot. This is my life we're talking about. I deserve some assurances." I pull my hand away from his. "Why is my father coming to Porto?"

"He wants assurances too. He wants you to look him in the eye and tell him that you're not being held hostage in my bed."

I throw my head back and laugh until there are tears rolling down my cheeks. Not that it's so funny, although it is, but the emotion that's been building inside needs somewhere to go.

Rafael grins, and he looks young and carefree, and I vow to bring out more of this side of him. *Every day, even if it's just for a few minutes,* I silently promise him, *I will make you forget the burdens that sit on your shoulders.*

"That must have been quite a conversation with my father."

"Oh, it was."

"Did you mention anything about what we've been doing? You know." A small part of me hopes he did tell my father—not about the sex—but about us. Telling my father would be the equivalent of taking a step toward a committed relationship.

"Did I tell Will Clarke that I've been banging his daughter? Nooo. Do I look like an idiot?"

I snicker. *It's probably for the best he kept his mouth shut.*

"All kidding aside," he says soberly. "I didn't feel it was my place to tell your father. I'm not in the habit of discussing my sex life with anyone, Lexie. I don't like to sneak around, either, but I'm willing to take my cues from you in that regard. You tell whoever you'd like—your parents, Valentina, write an article about how amazing my dick is. I don't care."

"Your dick's nice enough. But I'm not sure it's the kind of amazing that warrants an entire article."

"Pfft."

"I haven't said anything to Valentina, because I didn't want to betray you in any way. But I hate keeping secrets from her. Besides, she has that sixth sense, and she always knows when something's up."

"I don't care what you tell her. But given that she's like my little sister, I don't think she'll appreciate the dirty details—at least I hope not." He wrinkles his nose.

"I'm not sharing the dirty details with anyone, Huntsman. Those belong to you and me."

Rafael leans across the island and pulls me toward him,

finding my mouth with the kind of fervor that makes my knees wobble. *Don't get off track, Lexie. First business, then pleasure.*

I force myself back and try to find some poise and right my breathing.

Before I can ask anything, Rafael's phone rings. His expression hardens when he answers, and the temperature of the room plummets several degrees. "Yeah," he barks, getting up and walking into the living room.

I don't have a moment to contemplate his reaction to the call before my phone rings. *Valentina.* It's like she knew we were talking about her.

"Hi," she chirps when I answer. "It's last minute, but I'm having dinner at my parents' house tonight. Do you want to come?"

*I'm with Rafael negotiating my future. It's a bad time.* "I would love it, but I'm not dressed to go out and I have work to do. Can I take a raincheck?"

"Of course. "My father's walking toward me," she groans. "He's in a big hurry to leave. I'll call you on my way home from my parents'."

"Say hello to them for me, and give the kids big hugs."

When I hang up, Rafael's still on the phone.

I listen, but catch only bits and pieces of his side of the conversation. He mentions Marco, but it's cryptic. All I know is he's not happy.

*Hopefully this has nothing to do with why Valentina's so stressed lately. Rafael getting involved in her relationship with Marco is a bad idea—for Valentina and for him. If he causes any more trouble for her marriage, I'm afraid she won't forgive him.*

# 37

## ALEXIS

"Everything okay?" I ask when he comes back to the kitchen. He doesn't look okay. He's tense, and his jaw is ticcing.

"Fine. Who were you on the phone with?"

"Valentina."

He nods, his expression grim. But he doesn't ask about the conversation, which surprises me.

"What about you? Who were you on the phone with?"

He shrugs me off. "Business."

I don't press because I want to finish our conversation from earlier, and it's clear he's not going to say a word about the call. "Before the phone rang, you mentioned that there are a couple more things I should know."

Rafael gazes at me. "Your security is not, in any way, tied to sex. It's not a quid pro quo. I will continue to offer you protection, even if you decide you don't want to be in my bed."

*Or if I decide I don't want you in my bed.* He doesn't say it, but the sentiment hangs in the room like a musty smell in a dank basement.

"I appreciate it. But, technically, you've been sleeping in my bed."

"Technically, we haven't done much sleeping." He smirks, and his mood lightens. "And that's the last piece. I want you to stay at my apartment while you're in Porto. At least until we know more about the traffickers," he adds. "It's ridiculous for you to stay here when I have a place down the hall. I'm too old to be running back and forth like a college kid."

My heart is beating so hard I can almost hear it. *I want you to stay in my apartment. Don't read too much into it, Lexie. He's not asking you to play house. It's a matter of convenience, nothing more.*

"I can do that. But if you expect me to share an apartment with you, you best have ample closet space."

"Not an apartment, Angel—share a bed."

*A bed, of course.*

His phone vibrates, and he glances at the screen, his expression unreadable.

"Something's come up. I have to go in a minute, and dinner at Sirena is off tonight. I'm sorry. But if you decide to move into my place, we'll have a midnight snack. What do you think?"

"I'd like that." *What I don't like is seeing you so agitated.* But I know better than to press for details. I just pray, whatever it is, that it doesn't cause more of a rift between Valentina and her husband. I remember how happy she was when she first met Marco—how idyllic their relationship had been until the whole thing with the art gallery.

"I'm going to put Giana in charge of your security team," Rafael says, pulling me out of my head.

"Giana?"

"Is there a problem?"

"No. I really like her. I've never had a woman in charge of my security, and it surprised me. In a good way," I add, sorting through my feelings.

"It's either her or Sabio. They're both excellent soldiers. But she has seniority."

I smile, a smile that begins in my soul. *I can work with Rafael on security.* It won't be ideal, but his ideas are so much more modern than my father's, and less draconian. We can make it work. *I know it.*

"One more thing before I go." He pulls a velvet pouch from his pocket and hands it to me. "Your tracking device."

I unloosen the drawstring, while he watches, and take out the jewelry.

"It's an anklet," he explains. "We can get you something else if you prefer."

I hold the white gold anklet. It's simple enough not to call too much attention to it, but lovely. "No. It's perfect," I assure him, fingering the charm—angel wings. *My angel.*

The emotion rattles me—and I try not to cry by reminding myself that it's a tracker, nothing more.

"When you don't want to wear the anklet, the angel wings clip off easily, and you can attach the charm to a bracelet or a necklace, or slip it in your wallet—the sky's the limit. It has a separate tracking system from the anklet."

"The angel wings are a nice touch." I'm not talking about how they have their own tracking system.

"You're an angel who needs to spread her wings. It seemed right."

Not right. *Perfect.* It seems perfect. The kind of perfect that scares me.

"When did you have time to get this?"

"I commissioned it about five minutes after I had the idea to go talk to your father. It's not a complicated piece—it didn't take the jeweler long to create."

*Maybe not, but it has me feeling all complicated.*

"Pretty sure of yourself, Huntsman." I smirk.

"I'd say more determined than sure."

"Go," I tell Rafael, from tiptoe, as I reach for a kiss, "so you can come back. I'm already craving that midnight snack."

# 38

## RAFAEL

WHEN I GET to the caves, Marco is seated in a comfortable chair at a table in the center of the well-lit room, looking every bit the aristocratic pretty boy. Hard to tell from his appearance that his family was shunned by high society almost a century ago. *His great-grandfather was a thief too.*

The bastard has a water bottle in front of him, and he isn't cuffed, which rankles me, even though I ordered it this way. It's more than he deserves. He has his wife to thank for our hospitality.

"Rafael," he says grimly, "what's this about?"

I nod at the guard who's standing watch, and he exits as I take the seat across from Marco.

"Does Valentina know you had me dragged here against my wishes?"

*Against my wishes.* What a fucking pussy.

"She didn't hear it from me. I don't burden her with the business of men."

He rolls his eyes like a teenage girl. "What the hell is going on?"

I don't respond immediately, because I want him to sweat.

Neither Lucas nor Tamar could come up with anything conclu-
sive. There's no question all roads lead to him, but they didn't
have enough time to travel each of those roads, picking up
rocks to see what was underneath. But we couldn't give them
any more time. With Valentina's life potentially at risk, the
stakes were too high to wait until we were certain about him.

"So it's all true. This is where you bring people to interrogate them."

*You're getting the royal treatment, asshole.* "This is a cave
where we age Port. It's not where we bring prisoners. And this
isn't an interrogation. If you were being interrogated, you'd be
chained to the chair or strung up from the rafters while my
knife and I peppered you with questions. You're here for a
conversation."

He snickers. "A conversation. Right."

Despite the fact that his great-grandfather was a war criminal, Marco has always lived a soft, sheltered life. I once heard
Valentina refer to him as a gentle soul. But I never bought that
line. Marco is an opportunist. It might be an unpopular opinion, but he's never given me any reason to believe otherwise.

Because he's been so sheltered from my world, he'll be
questioned a bit differently. We always look for tells during an
interrogation, and often they're more honest than the words we
elicit. But the types of men we question have usually learned to
control and manipulate their emotion and their reactions—at
least until the torture begins. Marco has not.

I want to see his expression when he learns about the
account. That will tell me a lot.

I pull out a copy of the application and place it on the table
in front of him.

"What's this?" he asks, squinting at the paper.

"It's a bank account opened in Valentina's name." I take the
account statement and set it right next to the application.
"Someone withdrew money from Premier accounts to fund this

account." I point to his name on the application. "You're the beneficiary."

The moment the pieces fall in place, the anxiety slides off him in large sheets.

He looks me straight in the eye, cool as a cucumber. "I had nothing to do with that account or the withdrawal of Premier funds. Nothing."

*He's telling the truth.*

*Fuck. Fuck. Fuck.*

"Have you asked Valentina about it?" *What a disloyal little prick.*

"Do you actually think Valentina would embezzle money from Premier?"

"Not any more than I would," he replies with great disdain. *Like I give a fuck that he doesn't like me.*

I tap my finger over the number on the statement. "Fair chunk of change. Bet it would buy an awfully nice art gallery."

"You haven't gotten over that yet? Fuck you. I don't need Valentina's money. I earn a good salary, and I have a substantial trust—it's more than enough for us to live on. I never asked her to buy that gallery," he sneers.

He has a trust, although *substantial* is a relative term. I won't rub it in his face, because I'm done here. Anything I say now will only make the fallout with Valentina worse.

"This is exactly why she chose to marry a cultured man instead of a brute like you and her father, always swinging your dicks around like they're something special."

*You might be cultured, but you're not much of a man.*

"You know, Marco, you've had a lot to say since I walked in. But you know the one thing you haven't mentioned? Huh?"

"What?" he snarls like a churlish teenager.

"Does that account mean trouble for Valentina? Or, Is Valentina in any danger? Or, Should I increase Valentina's security?"

"You haven't asked about her well-being at all." Antonio's deep voice booms through the speaker. "At least not that I or my swinging dick heard."

Marco pales, and I try hard not to smirk. He doesn't have to see my ugly face except at family functions, but Antonio is Valentina's father, and he's not an easy man to ignore. Especially if you're on his bad side.

My phone pings with a text from Tamar: *It's not him. We're in the interior conference room.*

*Not exactly news.* The second Marco saw the account, he knew he was in the clear. And I'm sure everyone watching did too.

"We're through," I tell him, standing. "I'll have one of the guards drive you home. They can stop for a binky so you'll have something to suck on until you can cry to your wife."

Most men would take this as a challenge not to blab to their wives, so as not to look like a coward. I doubt it'll be enough to keep his mouth shut, but I can't threaten to murder him if he talks. If Valentina hears that, there's no hope she'll forgive me. *Not that I have much hope as things stand now.*

"You're a dick," he sneers.

I put my hands flat on the table and lean across until I'm six inches from his face. "And you're a pussy. It's a shame," I taunt. "We could be such good friends, if only we got along."

———

WHEN I GET to the conference room, the whole crew is there, aside from Antonio, who I spoke with on my way up. He agreed that Marco looked too damn relieved when he saw the account to have had anything to do with setting it up.

"While you were with Marco, the money was put back into the Premier accounts," Zé explains.

*Someone's fucking with us, but it's not Marco.*

"You saw the feed. He's not involved. But the money could have been scheduled, at any time, to be returned."

"Could have been," Lucas says, "but look." He turns his computer screen so I can see it.

"What exactly am I looking at?"

"It appears the request for the account originated with someone from Walsh Holdings."

"Bancroft Spirits is a subsidiary of Walsh Holdings. Elizabeth Walsh is Bancroft's wife. He didn't earn his wealth. He married it," Zé adds with contempt.

*Bancroft Spirits.* The company that will be taking a big hit when we launch our new Port. Valentina met with that slime-ball Scott Bancroft when she was in the US.

"What do they have to gain by doing something like this?" I need more specifics, because it doesn't make sense that they'd take this kind of risk.

"It's disruptive at this stage, right before the launch. Could cause a rift in your relationship with Valentina, who is a princi-pal. I'm sure there are dozens of other things we haven't thought about yet," Cristiano replies.

"All we have is a preliminary finding," Tamar cautions. "We need some more time to do due diligence."

"Agreed," Lucas adds.

It would have been nice to know this before I stuck my foot up Marco's ass. But I don't say a word, because Tamar's tech skills are mind-blowing, and Lucas's are even stronger. I put them under an impossible deadline. *There was no damn choice.*

"I'm going up to my apartment." To lick my wounds from this colossal fuckup. And to lose myself in the woman I depend on for comfort, more than I'd like—certainly more than I'd ever admit to anyone. *I can barely admit it to myself.*

"If you find anything more tonight, let me know."

## 39

# ALEXIS

"Where are you?" Valentina asks, breathless, before I say hello.

"I'm in the building," I reply, buying myself some time to think. Rafael doesn't care if I tell her about us, and as much as I want to tell her, a small part of me is worried about coming clean. Once she knows, it could get weird. The last thing I want is for my relationship with her to change. "How was dinner?" I ask, hoping to distract her.

"It was a hoot. My sisters called out my father, left and right, all evening. Politely, of course. It was a beautiful thing."

I laugh, imagining the three little girls, with *big* personalities, bossing around Antonio.

"My mother sends her love and said to tell you that she expects you to come to dinner next time."

"I'm in." By then everyone will know about Rafa and me, and I won't have to lie.

"I was just at the apartment to grab my laptop so I can work from home in the morning," she says matter-of-factly. "I didn't see you or your laptop. Are you working in the coffee shop?"

I should have known Valentina wouldn't let it drop. She isn't easily distracted.

*No.* I take a deep breath. "I'm at Rafa's apartment."

She sounds in a hurry, and I might have been able to ward off more questions if I'd used a casual tone. But the words emerged in a voice that sounded guilty as sin.

There's a long silence that makes my mouth dry.

"Is that where your laptop is too?"

"Yes."

"What about your makeup?"

"It's here," I admit, the blood rushing in my ears.

"What's going on, Lexie?" she asks softly, concern woven around every word.

*Just tell her. Spit it out and be done.* "I'm staying at Rafael's while I'm in Porto."

"With him?"

I blow out a breath. "Yes."

"Tell me everything."

*You don't want to hear everything. Trust me.* "We got together the night of your wedding."

"You had sex with Rafael the night of my wedding and I'm just hearing about it?"

"No sex. Just other stuff."

"*Ew,*" she says like a seagull shit on her. "I don't need the details. Maybe just the broad strokes."

"There's really nothing more to tell."

"You moved in with him and there's nothing to tell?"

"Don't make too much of it. I'm not." *Liar.* "I know how you feel about Rafael and me—together. I love you, and I hope this doesn't change anything between us."

"Oh, Lexie. Nothing will change."

I know it's easy for her to say right now, but I hold on tight, because it's just what I need to hear.

"You and Rafael," she continues, "I love you both with all

my heart. There's nothing that would make me happier than seeing you happy together. But whatever happens, I'm on your side—always. Count on it."

Valentina doesn't say it, but she doesn't see a happy ending for me—not with him. Maybe she's right. I don't know. But I have no doubt if it ends—*when it ends*—she'll be there for me with a bottle of cabernet and a box of tissues, and she won't leave my side until she's convinced I'm okay.

"Let's finish this conversation tomorrow," she says, seeming a bit preoccupied. "I haven't been able to reach Marco all evening. I want to let him know I'm on my home so he doesn't worry."

When we hang up, I pour myself a glass of wine. Telling Valentina about Rafael wasn't as difficult as I anticipated. Still, I'm relieved it's behind me.

Now to prepare for my late-night snack.

## 40

---

## RAFAEL

AFTER BEING WAYLAID BY NOELIA, who was waiting for me when I left the conference room, I'm finally on my way up to find my angel. Today has been a brutal motherfucker. *I need her in the worst way.*

I haven't heard a word from Lexie all evening, but the guard, stationed at the elevator upstairs, texted Zé after they finished moving her into my apartment. Zé didn't utter a negative peep when he relayed the message to me, but I'm sure he's not happy about my new roommate. *Too fucking bad.*

When I enter the foyer, soft jazz filters through the apartment. Lexie is nowhere to be seen, but dozens of lit votives flank a path to the bedroom.

Someone gave her a heads-up that I was on my way. I should be annoyed, but as I follow the flickering light into the bedroom, I want to give them a nice fat bonus, instead.

"I see you've made yourself at home," I say to the beautiful woman whose back is propped against the headboard of my bed. Her hair's down, and she's wearing a flimsy nightgown with thin straps that's not long for her body.

She smiles. It's a seductive smile that goes straight to my cock. "A girl's got to do something to stay out of trouble."

Her eyes skim my body brazenly while I tug off my clothes. She's a handful, but tonight I'm not in the mood to cut her any slack. If she starts, she's going to get more than she bargained for.

"It's been a hell of a day," I mutter, straddling her thighs. "I'm impatient and edgy, and I need you, Angel. Need you in a way that you've never experienced." I kiss her and nip her bottom lip before pulling back. "If it gets to be too much, you have to stop me."

With demons clawing at my chest, I tear the nightgown from her body and latch onto her nipple before she can form a single word.

"Rafa," she whispers. "What's wrong?" Her voice is wobbly, and her apprehension makes my cock harder and thicker.

"Are you afraid?" I taunt.

She shakes her head. "No. Not really."

Despite what she claims, I think she is a little afraid, and because I'm not a good man, it sends a jolt of adrenaline surging through me.

"It's just that this is different. You're different," she adds, her brow furrowed, as she searches my face for answers.

"I've been careful with you, up until now. I wanted to ease you in, not scare you away from sex. I don't have it in me tonight to be careful. You should stop me if that's what you want."

She gazes pointedly at me. "And you'll stop?"

"I will." Somehow, somewhere, I'll find it in me to stop. I've never taken anything that a woman didn't give freely, and I'm not going to start with her. That's for damn sure. "You have my word."

My cock throbs, as if challenging me, and for a long moment I wonder if I can stop.

"That's good enough for me," she murmurs, twining her arms and legs around me, pressing her body to mine. "Show me your worst."

*Show me your worst.* A groan twists in my chest as my cock leaks.

*Oh, Angel, I don't think you're ready for my worst. But there won't be a single heart or flower tonight. By the time I'm done with you, you'll be begging me to stop.* My imagination is going places it shouldn't—not if I actually expect to stop.

I disentangle myself from her arms and pull back, still straddling her. "I think it's about time you got on your knees for me, Angel."

There's a flicker of mischief in her eyes, and I should warn her that tonight is not the night to push me, but I don't. I want her sass. Her insolence. I want something to push back against. An excuse to take and take, because I'm not in the mood to give. *Not even to you, Angel.*

I roll onto my side, beside her, my face hovering near hers. She's sucked my cock, but never from her knees. I want that tonight. I want her full submission. *I need it.*

"Get on your knees. I'm not going to tell you again."

She sits up, taking the sheet with her, but like the little vixen she is, she lets it fall to her waist, baring her gorgeous tits to me. "I'm Alexis Clarke," she says haughtily, tossing her head. "I bow to no one. Nor do I kneel."

Her voice is a sultry vise around my cock. When she licks her lips, the vise tightens, slowly, painfully. If it were any other night, I'd be the one on my knees—begging for it. *But not tonight.*

"You will kneel *for me,* pretty girl."

Her eyes darken with a reckless glimmer. "Not even for you."

*Oh, baby. You are* everything *I need right now.* "Is that so?"

She nods, a ghost of a smile crossing those pouty lips that *will* be wrapped around my cock before the night's over.

I lean over until my face is inches from hers. "How long do you think you'll last before you need to come so bad that you'll not only lick my cock from your knees, but you'll swallow it into your throat and lap up every drop of cum off your lips when I'm finished?"

"Never." The sparks flicker in her eyes as she throws the gauntlet, daring me to pick it up.

*I will not be the man to disappoint her.*

"Oh, Angel. A challenge. You can't imagine how much I'm going to enjoy owning you."

I inch closer and take her mouth with mine, and the wench grinds her cunt into my cock, forcing a rumble from somewhere deep inside me.

"You up for a little play?" I grunt when I come up for air.

"Kink?" she asks, like she's been hanging out in sex clubs for years.

I ordered a few toys the other day. Nothing she can't handle. I had planned on introducing them slowly, but that's out the window. I want to overwhelm her senses. I want her in a puddle of fucking need when I sink my cock into her.

"Would you like a little kink?" I ask, holding her tits and flicking the nipples until her mouth opens into a sweet little O.

She nods, and there's not a single misgiving in her expression. She's trusting. Too trusting. More trusting than I deserve considering how hard I want to use her. "I hope you have something extra special in mind."

*Oh, I do.*

*Don't be reckless, Rafael. She talks a good game, but she's relatively inexperienced.*

I push the warnings away. I need this. And I need it with her.

"Be careful what you ask for, Angel. I'm in a mood." It's a warning, and there's menace in my tone.

She shivers under my fingertips, and her eyes dance with sin as she lures me further along a path we shouldn't travel tonight. *She's not ready—but I'm too far gone to change course.*

"Stop me," I mutter, the words emerging as a gruff plea.

She shakes her head. "No. I want this. I want you. Use me, Rafa. Whatever you need to calm your soul, take it."

*Use me, Rafa.* The words reverberate in my head, in my chest, in every fucking corner of my being. I lower my mouth to hers, exploring every crevice, every nook, drowning myself in her essence, until my demons demand more.

# 41

## RAFAEL

LEXIE'S quiet as she watches me open the nightstand drawer. She doesn't blink when I drop the toys on the bed. There's not a single nervous comeback masquerading as bravado. Her gaze is steady when I flip on the fireplace and cover the leather bench at the foot of the bed with a soft towel.

"Lie on your back, Angel." I glide two fingers over her flushed cheek. "I'm going to give you everything you asked for."

Her throat ripples, but Lexie doesn't hesitate as she moves her gorgeous body onto the bench.

I lower myself to my haunches beside the bench, dangling a toy so she can see. "Do you know what this is, Angel?"

She doesn't flinch. She made the decision to let me have her as I want, and she's not going back on it.

*That means you need to watch her carefully for any sign she's in trouble.* The warning registers as a blip, but it evaporates as quickly as it appeared.

"A butt plug," she replies. It's part question, part answer. She's reasonably sure, but not certain.

"A narrow, *very* narrow, butt plug." I brush the hair off her face, enjoying the feel of the silky strands on my fingers. "I'm not going to hurt you," I promise, as much to myself as to her. "It's going to be intense, and there are times when it might feel like torture, but there won't be any pain."

"I'm nervous," she admits. "But I'm not afraid. I know you'll take care of me."

*I know you'll take care of me.* It's a steel plate dropped on my chest, because right now I'm mostly concerned with taking care of myself. *Do not let her down.*

I stand and ease her knees to her chest. "I want you to hold them just like that," I murmur, stroking her clit. She's soaking wet, and I want to end this now and fuck her until she screams. But I won't. Because I want more than her screams. I want her submission, and I want it from her knees.

She whimpers and closes her eyes. I take the lube and spread it between her crack, massaging the area near her back hole. She squirms, just a bit. But when I slide my finger inside the virgin passage and breach the first ring of muscle, she gasps, and her eyes fly open.

"Relax, Lexie. It's just my finger. The more relaxed you are, the better it will feel."

After I've worked her a bit and she's less tense, I remove my finger from her ass and lube the plug well, while increasing the pressure on her clit. When I seat the plug at the entrance, she tightens again.

"Open your eyes, Angel, and listen to me."

She opens her eyes, and there's still no fear, no apprehension, only that goddamn trust that feels like the weight of the world on my back.

"What's your dog's name?" I ask.

"Wimbledon."

"Wimbledon. That's your safe word."

"That's a terrible safe word."

The woman's insufferable, and it takes everything I have not to shove the plug into her ass and twist it until she can't form words. But despite the line I'm teetering on, I want her to enjoy this. I want her to love it so much that she wants to do it again and again.

"It'll be easy for you to remember. Say it."

"Wimbledon," she replies, a twinge of impatience in her voice.

"I'm going to guide you while I slide the plug in."

She nods.

"Push out, Lexie, while I push in. Go ahead. That's it." I find a thimbleful of patience—*I find it for her*—and push the plug in slowly until it's fully seated.

She's breathing through her nose, nice big breaths as her body adjusts to the intrusion.

"Good girl." I stroke her pussy, keeping my fingers well away from her clit. "How does it feel?"

"I'm not sure," she whispers, her cheeks pinkening. "It feels good. It doesn't hurt."

*I don't want to hurt you, but I'm having a hell of a time holding back.*

"It's not supposed to hurt, baby. It's supposed to feel great. And it will—just give it a little time."

"I'm going to cuff you to the bench," I explain, securing her ankle to the bench leg, while my cock bobs painfully. Her breathing is normal now, and she doesn't react as I bind her.

"You okay?"

She nods, her mouth curling softly. I bind the other leg until she's spread nice and wide, so I can enjoy her glistening cunt.

I gaze into her eyes, dilated pools edged in brown and green. When I take her wrists, her pulse is beating at a good clip, and my cock gets thicker and heavier.

Without a word, I cuff her arms above her head, leaving enough slack to be moderately comfortable but not enough to allow her to roll off the bench and hurt herself.

She's tempting, trussed and helpless, and open to me. *So fucking tempting.*

"I hope you have the keys," she murmurs.

*Bravado.*

I don't tell her that those cuffs release without a key. "Most women ask that question *before* the cuffs are on."

She rolls her eyes, but I don't say a word about it. Her insolence is on short time.

I take a cherry-red wand off the bed. It's powerful but small enough not to be intimidating.

"I have that vibrator," she says, her eyes lit with lust. "At my apartment in London."

I graze her clit with the wand, which I haven't turned on. "Does yours have a little stand like this?" I show her the sling.

She shakes her head. "What's that for?"

"It'll come in handy when I get hungry, or if my hand gets tired of holding the wand against your pussy. I'll rest the toy here and turn it on *real* low so it can torture you slowly."

"Torture me?" She smirks much too defiantly for a woman securely bound. "I hardly call that torture."

I turn it on full throttle and press it to her clit without a second of warm-up.

"Ahh," she cries, trying to writhe away from the powerful vibration, but she's bound too securely. My cock weeps as she struggles with the restraints.

"There's nowhere to go, Angel. You need to embrace the sensations." I pull it away after a few seconds, and she gasps. Then I do it again. And again. And again. And again. I do it until there's no more sass. No more huffy replies. Just those sweet whimpers and pleas that make my balls ache.

"Rafa," she whines, her flesh covered in a damp sheen. "Please let me come."

I want her to come. I want her to squeeze my cock and take me with her as she tumbles off the edge—but not yet.

"Are you ready to get on your knees?" *Say yes. End this torment for both of us.*

"That's not fair," she whimpers.

"You can give up anytime, Angel. After you get on your knees and swallow my cum, you can have as many orgasms as you'd like. You'll tell me if you want my mouth, my hands, or my cock to drive you over the cliff. Be a good girl, and you can have anything you want. You can have it all."

The flush staining her creamy skin is no longer a subtle pink but a deep crimson. She's in a frenzy, but I'm out of my mind too. It won't be long before I blow my load spontaneously, like a fucking teenager.

I lay the wand in the sling and move it until it's just grazing her pussy. She struggles to get closer, pulling on the bindings, but it only leads to more frustration for her. I've kept the wand, like her orgasm, just out of reach. Watching her frustrated escalates my own need, until I can't wait another fucking second to come.

My body is coiled tight when I straddle the bench and gaze at my angel. Her hair is matted to her cheeks, and her eyes are dark pools of lust that reflect my wanton disregard. She's aroused beyond anything I ever imagined. *And so am I.*

With a palm full of lube, I take my cock in hand and tug on it from root to tip, sucking in breath after breath as my arousal spirals higher and tighter.

Her eyes are wide, and she pants and struggles with the bindings as I tug and pull. Harder and faster. I yank ruthlessly, showing myself as little mercy as I've shown her.

"I surrender," she gasps. "Untie me so I can kneel."

My movements slow, but they don't stop. It takes a moment for the words to register. "Is that what you want, Angel? Are you sure?"

"Do it now," she demands, desperation punctuating each word.

I should give her a lesson in saying please, but I need her on her knees.

With shaky hands, I unbind her arms first, and then her legs. "Slowly," I caution, helping her into a sitting position. But she's having none of it.

She slides from the bench to her knees and doesn't waste a single second with preliminaries before she takes my cock into her warm mouth.

*It's heaven. Fucking heaven.*

Digging her fingers into my ass, she swallows me, and my knees buckle from the force.

My spine begins the telltale tingle much too soon. *Fuck.* I finger her hair, struggling with control.

When I can't hold back, I push her away. "What do you want, Angel?" I ask gruffly, pulling her to her feet.

"I want to come," she cries, saliva pooling around her bruised lips. "Fuck me."

*Yes. Now.*

I lead her to the bench and kiss her until I'm shaking with need. "Turn around and hold on tight."

The moment her palms hit the leather, I plunge deep, her cunt wedged between my hand and my cock. In seconds, I feel her tighten, her walls squeezing around me. *She's almost there.* I sink my teeth into the back of her neck and work her harder. *Rougher.*

When the orgasm consumes her, I pull out the plug.

I'm not gentle. I yank it out in one long pull. She screams as her body jerks and trembles uncontrollably. The sound thrums in my veins until my vision is hazy, my mind blank, and all I know is surrender.

## 42

# ALEXIS

I'm in Rafael's closet, searching for something to wear, still a little shaky after that intense sex. Not just the physical part, although that was something else, but the emotions were raw and primal—and not just mine.

The man who craves my power, who needs to lead, barely had control over himself. Something had him teetering between restraint and madness. He struggled not to tip too far, but I could see the conflict in his face.

Something happened tonight. It started with the call before he left, and then when he got back—

When he held up the butt plug, there was something unhinged in his eyes. I almost bailed, but he needed me. I was sure of it. I still am.

I acquiesced to his wishes, even when he begged me to stop him. Not because I'm weak, or because I wanted to please him, although I did, and not because he might have turned around and left. *Although he might have.* I agreed because I'd fantasized about *this* very thing, *with him.*

*Kink.* Not the kind of kink that involves whips and pain, but the kind that steps well over the vanilla threshold to a glorious place where there are secure bindings and just enough forbidden pleasures to make the experience otherworldly.

He offered an opportunity to explore a fantasy, something I dreamed about, while holding a vibrator against my throbbing pussy. But he didn't promise a safe exploration—sure, he said there would be no pain, but nothing about him felt safe tonight. I must be the craziest woman on earth, because I enjoyed that side of him—enjoyed the thrill more than I care to admit. *Maybe I am reckless. Maybe risk turns me on in some godforsaken way.*

The closet smells like him, costly sandalwood wrapped around spicy musk, against the cedar backdrop.

I glance at a rack lined with shoes. Above it is a shelf with sweaters and a small car enclosed in a glass case. The case isn't much different from the ones that hold my childhood trophies, except it's smaller.

I reach up and take it, looking to see if there's some kind of plaque. *Maybe he's started racing cars, like Antonio.* But there's nothing to indicate that he has a new hobby.

It's a child's toy, a red hot rod with orange and yellow flames.

"Lexie, I have to—" The words die in his throat when he sees what's in my hands.

I know then that it has something to do with his mother, and my chest tightens.

"It's sweet," I coo, a second before he takes it out of my hands gingerly and puts it up on a high shelf that I can't reach without a step stool.

"I'm sorry. I didn't mean to—"

The muscles in his back are taut as he quietly rearranges a few things on the built-in dresser.

This is my fault. I should have never touched the car. I'm the one always squawking about privacy, but I invaded his—in the worst possible way. I want to comfort him. *I'm not sure how.*

After a few more moments of uneasy silence, I can't stand it anymore and I do what I would want a lover to do for me. I wrap my arms around him and press my cheek to his back.

He's twitchy again, almost like he was before we had sex.

"Does the car remind you of your mother?"

He doesn't reply. We just stand quietly, his heart hammering, while I imagine a blue-eyed boy whose mother vanished when he was eight.

Eventually, he nods. "I struggled to read when I was a kid. My father didn't want to get a tutor, so my mother would work with me every night. She always gave me a small treat when we were done. Sometimes a small car. I collected them. She gave me that car the night before she disappeared."

The emotion inside me is nearing a crescendo, but I keep it in check. He doesn't need my pity. It would be just another thing to burden him.

"Do you have any idea what happened?"

"Not enough to lead me to her."

His phone rings. It's shrill in the quiet space, and he pulls away to answer it.

"Yeah." His face is serious, with a twinge of sorrow, but as he listens, anger creeps into his expression.

"Have they identified her?"

Terror seizes me, its tentacles foraging deep into my soul. *The traffickers struck again.* I know it. *How could that be? How? It's too soon.*

"I'll be there in thirty minutes." It's all he says before ending the call.

"What happened?" I'm not sure he'll tell me, although he's been forthcoming about anything to do with the ring. At least I think he has been.

"A woman was abducted in Oslo."

*A woman was abducted in Oslo.* I expected this. But still I'm not prepared for it. I can't move for several seconds. It's like I'm rooted to the ground as the pain twists inside. There's a wail from somewhere—maybe from me—and I crumple to the floor.

"Lexie. Are you okay?" His words are muffled, and I can barely make them out, but I don't care about what he's saying. *A woman was abducted in Oslo. Before I got there. Another woman taken.* I tried to warn them. I sent emails. I did. But they never listen. *Because you send them anonymous emails, and they think you're just another unstable person following the case.*

Rafael is on the floor beside me, and he pulls me onto his lap. "Shh," he murmurs. "I'm right here. It's okay."

It doesn't feel like it's ever going to be okay. It's been two years. *Two fucking years.* They're never going to catch them. Some days I'm not even sure they're trying. "When is it going to end?"

"I don't know," he responds gently. "But it will. Eventually they'll be caught."

*I once thought so too, But I'm not sure, anymore.*

We sit like this for a long time. He rubs my back, my neck and shoulders, petting me like I'm an anxious kitten, while I soak his T-shirt with my tears.

"I was too late."

"Too late for what, sweetheart?"

I stiffen when I realize I said it out loud, trying to quell the rising panic inside. *You're unpredictable. Impulsive. Reckless.*

If he thinks I'm tracking the ring, he'll blow an aneurysm before he locks me up and throws away the key. *Who am I kidding?* He told me exactly how he feels about trust. How vital it is to him.

*"I cope by surrounding myself with people I trust implicitly—or that I can control. No one gets close to me who I don't fully trust. No one."*

He won't lock me away. He'll wash his hands of me completely, and there won't be any second chances.

I shake my head, my heart pounding in my ears. "That's not what I mean. It's a good thing I planned to get to Oslo later. What if they recognized me?"

He runs his mouth over my hair. It's a tender caress that gives nothing away.

Rafael has run a successful company since he was in his early twenties, and he's poised to take over all of the Huntsman empire. He's shrewd and he reads people well.

I'm not sure he believes me.

# 43

## RAFAEL

I peek in on Lexie, who's sound asleep after a meltdown in the closet, which I still don't fully understand. Despite my best attempt at aftercare, she might have still been out of sorts about the play earlier. It was a lot for a beginner, and although I didn't edge her for hours, I still pushed too damn hard.

That might explain the overreaction to the news. But what I can't get past is that she was headed to Oslo, to yet *another* location where the flesh traders struck. It's not a coincidence, just like it wasn't a coincidence she was in Porto.

*I was too late.* She didn't misspeak. She was distraught and let it slip.

*What the hell are you up to, Lexie?*

She was in no condition to answer questions tonight, but it wouldn't have mattered. She would have just told me more lies. *Lies that will end any relationship we have before it plays itself out naturally.*

I could get the truth from her. She wouldn't be hard to break, but I'm not prepared to interrogate her in that way.

*I have to get to the club.* I'm late. It's become a regular occurrence—always the same. I'd rather stay with her—even with all the lies—than go to the club.

Before Lexie, Sirena was how I spent my nights, and it had been enough. I love Sirena, but it's a different siren who calls to me now.

She stirs but thankfully doesn't wake. Even wrapped in my arms, she whimpered when she first fell asleep. Not whimpers of pleasure, but of pain—emotional heartache. It took her a long time to slip into a peaceful sleep.

I leave a note beside the bed, letting her know that Giana is in the kitchen. She likes Giana, and I don't want her to be alone while I'm gone. Ordinarily I might text Valentina and ask her to call and check on Lexie, but Marco went home hours ago, and I suspect by now she's livid.

I'm surprised she hasn't called to rip me a new one. Valentina won't—

*"It's Lexie. I'm surprised she didn't try to capture the bastards herself."* That's what Valentina said when I told her Lexie got caught up with the traffickers.

My blood runs cold.

She couldn't possibly—*no.* But I can't let go of the thought. Lexie's just the kind of woman who would take that kind of risk —like my mother and *Tia* Lydia.

*"I have some beliefs that I hold so dear that I'd be willing to lay down my life for."*

She's just like them. *Son of a bitch.*

I nod at Giana and call Tamar on my way out.

"Sorin," she says, like it's not two a.m.

"I need you to do something."

"Name it."

"We still have a copy of Alexis Clarke's passport?"

"A few copies."

"Make a list of everywhere she's traveled in the last two years, with dates, and then make a list of every city where a woman has been abducted—only abductions where we think the traffickers have been involved. I need those dates as well. Send me the lists as soon as possible."

"Depending on the country, Alexis might not have been subject to the same standards that someone flying commercially would have had to adhere to."

"I don't know how often she flies commercially." *The answer would be never, if she wasn't sneaking around behind her father's back.* "But unless she's with her father, I doubt she's able to skirt immigration control. It's not so easy."

"Is there anything else I should know?"

"No. Just get me the information as soon as possible."

I hope to hell I'm wrong, but either way, I need to know. Not just because she's under my protection now, but because I'm not spending another night with a woman who has no regard for her safety.

*I'm going to string you up by your fingernails, Lexie. An hour for every match I find.* And it won't end in an orgasm.

## 44
---

# ALEXIS

MY FATHER'S assistant contacted me this morning to let me know Dad was on his way to Porto to take me to Sunday lunch. I've been giving myself *stand your ground* pep talks since then.

I'm not going back to London with him, but I love my father and don't want this to turn into something we can't walk back from. The whole thing has me jittery.

His visit isn't exactly a surprise. Rafael told me he was coming. I should be annoyed that he didn't bother to ask if I was free to meet him today, but I've been too busy being anxious that this is just a ruse to get me home.

Rafael wouldn't conspire with him against me—not at this point. And he'd tell me if there was any hint that my father was up to something. Well, maybe he wouldn't tell me, but he wouldn't lie.

I glance at my outfit in the mirror and grimace. I've already changed my clothes three times to have lunch with a man who doesn't care what I wear as long as my ass and breasts are covered.

As the moment gets closer, I'm practically jumping out of my skin. I wish Rafael was here, but he's been stealing time here and there to spend with me, and today he's paying the piper. Still, I need some assurance from him, and I don't care if it seems needy.

Lexie: *I want your word that my father isn't here to take me back to London.*

Rafael: *I don't think your father is coming to take you to London.*

Not very assuring, Rafa.

Lexie: *You don't* think?! *You're going to have to do better than that, Huntsman.*

Rafael: *I can only give you my word about things I control. I don't control your father.*

Still not reassuring.

Lexie: *I'm worried.*

Could I be any more pathetic? Although, Rafael knows my father. Almost anyone who meets with him is either anxious, terrified, or a fool.

Rafael: *Do you want me to come along?*

*Yes, I want you to come and protect me from the Big Bad Wolf!* That's what I'd like to say. But I'm a grown woman, and my father loves me. He's not here to hurt me. I can handle him. I repeat this over and over to make sure the universe understands the kind of intervention I might need.

If worse comes to worst, I'll make a huge scene. He'd love that. This isn't the UK, where he's feared. No one's going to ignore it here. He could drug me, but if his plan is that nefarious, no one will be able to help. They'd just be courting danger. Before I let my wild imaginings scare the bejesus out of me, I reply to Rafael.

Lexie: *I don't need you to come. I was just having a minor anxiety attack.*

Rafael: *I know a good antidote for anxiety.*

I smile, imagining the possibilities.

Lexie: *I wish. But he'll be here any minute.*

Rafael: *Contact me at the first sign of trouble.*

One of the things I appreciate most about Rafael is that he doesn't bullshit by telling me it's going to be okay. He knows it's somewhat precarious—not as precarious as my imagination has made it out to be—but with men like Will Clarke, there are no guarantees.

There's a knock on the door, and I know it's Giana, who's stationed outside the apartment. My stomach churns like it thinks lunch is a bad idea.

"Your father has arrived," she says sympathetically, as though she can see the worry on my face. "I'll escort you downstairs."

I nod and grab my purse. The one Rafael asked Judite Furtado to bring. *Somehow it feels like a lifeline to him.*

"Sabio and I will be following in case you need anything," she explains. "Rafael asked me to remind you that while he's not expecting your call, he's prepared for it."

Unlike Rafael's, her assurances are comforting. I'm an only child, and other than Valentina, who would drop everything to help me, anytime, anywhere, there's really no one else besides Rafael whom I would trust enough to call—not in a situation like this. No one who would be willing to stand up against Will Clarke.

My father's driver is waiting in the lobby to escort me to the car. He's exceedingly polite, but always a bit standoffish.

Giana follows us, and when we get outside, she waits near a black SUV parked behind my father. The windows are tinted, but I'm sure Sabio is driving. I'm not sure exactly how they'd help me, but I'm happy to have them on my side.

I don't get into the car immediately. While Giana watches, I go around to where my father is seated. He puts down the window.

"What is it, sweetheart?" he asks, even before I can say hello.

My heart clenches at the endearment, but I don't let it soften too much. I glance at Giana before saying my piece.

"Promise me you're not here to take me back to London."

His expression is unreadable, even for me, who's been studying his tells for years.

"It's not my intention—but things could change."

*Not good enough.*

"I want to have lunch with you, but I won't get in the car unless I have your word."

He cocks his brow. "If I wanted to force you onto a plane, I would have done it yesterday or last week. Or I would have my security shove you into the car now. But those are extreme measures. Nothing I know right now concerns me enough to go that route. If it makes you feel any better, I promised your mother that I would act judiciously, and I intend to honor that promise."

My father is a man who very rarely reneges on his word, but a promise he makes to my mother is sacrosanct.

I nod at Giana so she knows I'm okay, and my father opens the door so I can slide in beside him.

Not one uncomfortable moment passes before he wraps his arm around my shoulder and pulls me close, pressing a kiss to the top of my head. I rest my head on his shoulder as myriad emotions conspire to turn me into a huge mess.

"Your mum says hello," he murmurs.

"She didn't want to make the trip with you?"

"She did, but I wanted to speak with you alone. If your mother were here, she would ease the strain, filling in the icy silences with sweet chatter. When lunch was over, you and I would still be at an impasse."

He's not wrong. Anytime there's tension between my father and me, she intervenes, redirecting the negative energy instead of forcing us to hash out our differences.

"Where are we going?" I'm confident in his promise to my

mother, but his behavior of late has been off, and I can't help but be a bit wary still.

"To a small restaurant nearby."

I'm sure he's arranged for it to be empty, or maybe for a private room.

The car pulls into a port lodge not far from Huntsman Lodge. Three SUVs pull in behind us—security, mine and his. The army of guards doesn't entirely surprise me, although two vehicles with armed guards is unusual. He's normally more relaxed in Porto.

"I've missed you," he says, while we wait for the guards to check the premises. "No one to argue politics with. My debate skills are getting rusty."

While we rarely agree, political debate has always been our thing. "I miss it too. Maybe we can argue on the way back to Valentina's. I would hate for you to get rusty." I feel the edge of his mouth curl against my head.

As we sit here, I remember how much I love my dad. I would do almost anything to rewind the clock a year or two. He was difficult then, too, but it was the kind of difficult that I could live with. I sigh.

A guard opens the car door while I'm still trying to figure out how to get back to something less toxic with him. Maybe an hour or two over lunch will be just what we need.

"All good inside," the guard says to my father.

*I hope he's right.*

# 45

## ALEXIS

WE'RE SETTLED around a small table in a private room that overlooks the Douro River, with wine and olives, and tasty croquettes, courtesy of the chef.

"I'm sorry I missed that meeting between you and Rafael. It must have been interesting," I say, popping an olive into my mouth. *Must have been quite the pissing match.* I keep that part to myself.

"He's not a boy. That's for sure. Almost ready to take over from Antonio. Even with the arrogant veneer, I could sense the power behind him." He pauses. "That's largely why I'm here."

I gaze at his face while he struggles to configure words into sentences. His hair is beginning to gray around the temples, but that fuck-with-me-and-you-die vibe doesn't show any signs of age. I felt it as soon as we left the car to enter the restaurant.

"Did he blackmail you or threaten you in any way to get you to agree to his little plan?"

Verbalizing emotion, aside from anger, is not something my father does particularly well. But somewhere in there is an *I love you, and I would never allow you to be party to any arrange-*

*ment with a man that didn't have your full consent.* It's hard to find, unless you know what to look for.

I shake my head. "No. He got me to agree by making promises that I could live with."

"What kind of promises?" he asks, not bothering to hide his displeasure.

"The kind that will allow me the freedom to live my life and still be safe."

His hands curl into tight fists on the white tablecloth. "It's tough to accomplish that. Impossible. And I want to forbid it."

I *want* to forbid it, not *I forbid it*. It's small, but significant.

"But you won't," I say softly. "And I thank you for that."

He doesn't respond for what seems like forever, but I watch his expression tighten, not with anger, but with sorrow. "I won't lose you, Lexie." His voice is gruff with uncharacteristic emotion, and every word lands in my soul.

The threats he worries about are real. I can't quarrel with that part. *I need to make Rafael's plan work, not just for me but for my father too.*

"Dad." I reach over and squeeze his fingers.

"I've given Huntsman more control over your safety than I've ever given anyone else. *Anyone.*"

It costs him to admit this, or maybe what costs him is relinquishing to another man what he feels is his fatherly duty. *A younger man.* One who is poised to take power, unlike my father, who comes closer, each day, to the end of his reign.

"It kills me to put your life in someone else's hands."

*What about putting it in my hands? Is that such a foreign concept?*

"Rafael is going to give me some measure of control over my own security. Did you ever consider doing that?" I ask the question gently. It's not meant to be an accusation. I want to know, and I think he'll be honest with me about it.

"I can't. I've tried. Your mother has pleaded with me to do it. I just can't. It's not in my nature."

*It's not in my nature—and that's it.* I'm not convinced he's tried very hard.

"Because I'm a woman."

He shakes his head. "Don't be ridiculous. It has nothing to do with you being a woman. You're clever and tough, but you're not trained. You haven't been groomed, from the knee, to understand the ins and outs of security—and the enemies who threaten us. That was my fault. It was too late by the time I realized the world had changed."

"It's never too late to right the ship."

"I'm afraid it is."

The words are spoken with finality, but he's being candid with me, and I'm not quite ready to let it go. I doubt I'll change his mind, but maybe I can get some answers that will help the relationship.

"That's so cynical. Even for you. You raised me to believe that nothing was impossible."

"My entire nuclear family was wiped out as an act of revenge. Gone, in the blink of an eye. It changed my life. Made me the man I am today." He stares out the window as though there are answers in the river. His face is drawn, and in this moment, I would do anything to give him the solace he seeks.

"My enemies are powerful," he continues. "I couldn't go on living if something happened to you. It's easier to live with the unhappiness and anger in your face than the pain in your mother's, if something happened to you. I couldn't bear it, Lexie."

It's almost incongruous, that a man like my father could love a woman the way he loves my mother. She's his everything. He loves me dearly, but they have something special. Something that transcends all the blood on his hands, and the hate in his heart.

"I'm not going to change, Lexie. My demons are entrenched. They're not going anywhere. But I can do better," he mutters under his breath.

There's anguish in his face—a grief that cuts deep. I take a sip of wine swallowing the rising emotion.

He rarely mentions his family. But he's made a connection between his recent behavior toward me and what happened to them. My mother might have helped him see the tie, but it's no small feat for Will Clarke to admit he's scared.

"Dad, I'm an adult. I'm smart and capable. I'm your daughter, and we're probably more alike than you think. I wish you had been more up front with me. If we had this conversation six months ago, it would have saved us both a lot of heartache." I pause to let the words sink in. "I can do better too."

The last part was hard to choke out. Mainly because I don't feel like I was in the wrong. Although I did go about things in the wrong way. It was the only way I knew, but it was still wrong.

It's become my hallmark. Good intentions, always, but I often choose a path that's rocky and sometimes more perilous than need be.

"I don't suppose *doing better* means you're coming back to London?"

"Was this all just a manipulation?" I ask pointedly, even though I know it wasn't.

"To tell you the truth, I didn't consider manipulating you. I take definitive action and issue orders. The kind of manipulation you're referring to is not a man's game." His expression is harder, and Dad recedes for a moment, while the powerful leader emerges.

*I won't be cowed by him.*

"I'm not going back to London," I say respectfully but firmly. "I'm going to stay here and see if I can learn some life skills. Like how to negotiate with my guards to create a safety plan that allows me to live my life." *In the words of Rafael Huntsman.*

He scowls at my pronouncement. I'm not even sure he knows he's doing it. "That's all well and good, but change isn't easy."

"You don't believe I can learn to work with the system rather than around it?"

"You're not a woman who falls in line easily. It's not in *your* nature." He peers at me. "And you're damn proud of it." The corner of his mouth twitches. "When your independent attitude isn't being a thorn in my side, I'm proud of it too.

"But I'm not convinced you want to change, Lexie. If that's the case, no one, not even a prince with too damn much swagger, can keep you safe."

"A prince?" I say, tongue in cheek, ignoring his concerns, even though he's not wrong about all of it. "Rafael would be chuffed to hear you say it. He thinks he's a damn king."

"Not yet he isn't. Almost. But not yet." My father takes a sip of his gin and tonic. "A king wouldn't be sitting in the back of an SUV in the parking lot. Or at least he wouldn't allow himself to be spotted."

*Wait a second.* "Rafael's outside?"

My father nods. "My guys caught his reflection in the window when the female guard opened the SUV door."

For a moment, I'm annoyed he didn't trust I could handle this problem. But my father isn't an ordinary problem. *He's the mother of all problems.*

If Rafael wanted to control the situation, he could have just told me that it was too big a risk to meet my father, and I probably wouldn't have come, or he could have insisted on joining us, adding a measure of safety that I could touch. But he let me negotiate the land mine, staying far enough back that I have to do the heavy lifting, but close enough that if my father decides to force me back to London, he can intervene. There's actually something empowering about it. I try not to smile, but I can't help myself.

"You're not going to press me any further about whether he's holding me against my wishes?"

He narrows his eyes. "Is he?"

I shake my head.

"I didn't think so. I might be out of my league when it comes to spirited daughters, but I know the measure of a man. I also know you well-enough to know that you'd cut off his balls if he tried something like that."

"You can count on it. I am your daughter, after all."

My father's phone rings while we're laughing. He excuses himself to take the call, and I send my king a message.

Lexie: *It's all good here. But you've been made.*

Rafael: *I was never trying to hide my presence from your father. You're not being forced back to London on my watch.*

*Oh, Rafael. I'm liking this thing with you, whatever it is, too much—way too much.*

Lexie: *I hope you've had a good rest, because the thank-you I have in mind requires a lot of stamina.*

Rafael: *I told you I'd always be there for you, Angel. They weren't just words.*

Rafael: *I hope that thank-you involves you getting on your knees without too much back talk. On second thought . . .*

# 46

## RAFAEL

WILL DIDN'T TRY to take Lexie back to London on Sunday, which not only made my night sweeter, but also makes my life a hell of a lot easier. Going to war with him is not something I relish. I didn't think he'd actually force her onto a plane, but I won't gamble on anything when it comes to her.

Other than that, not a damn thing has gone my way. Dead traffickers, homemade incendiary devices tossed at the club, and Scott Bancroft pulling shit that he's going to regret, and the icing on the cake? Accusing Marco of being a thief.

I'm still not sure what to do about that, but it's been eating at me for days. Every time I see Valentina, I brace myself for an earful, but so far nothing.

"Do we have absolute confirmation that Scott Bancroft is behind the offshore account?" I ask Tamar and Lucas.

"We have absolute confirmation that it initiated with someone at the highest levels of the company," Tamar replies. "It's impossible to know who exactly."

"That's good enough for me. I want you to walk me through how they did it, step by step. I want to understand it cold before I meet with him tomorrow."

"Tomorrow?" Zé's eyes are trained on mine. "In the US?"

I nod. "Tomorrow. In the US. Noelia arranged the meeting. I want to put him on notice before he pulls any other shit." Before this is over, he's going to rue the day he fucked with me.

"What time do we leave?" Zé asks, pulling out his phone.

"*We* don't leave. You're not much more tech savvy than I am." I glance at my head of IT. "I'm taking Tamar."

Zé's expression is stony. He likes to be where I am. Not because he craves power, but because he believes that he's the best person to protect me—especially if I decide to go rogue. He's not wrong, but the last word on my safety is mine.

"Bancroft took a big risk," he says, prevailing to my good sense, which is in short supply these days. "Only desperate men take that kind of risk. You need backup."

"Find me some guards you trust. I need you here. There's too much happening for us both to be out of the country."

"Zé's right," Lucas adds, because he can never mind his own damn business.

This is exactly why I'm often reluctant to get Antonio's team involved.

"What part of *I'm former Mossad* don't you two understand?" Tamar demands, staring down Lucas and then Zé. She has them by the balls.

It's something to watch, and I bite the inside of my cheek to stop a grin.

"You were a tech specialist," Zé replies, and from the look she just gave him, I'd say it's going to be a cold day in hell before he gets laid again.

"And you know so much about Mossad training that you're certain I can't protect an asset?"

With her focus off him, Lucas is almost as entertained by this as I am.

I turn to Tamar, dialing up the heat on the hot water Zé's in. "I know nothing about Mossad training, but I have no doubt you can protect me should it come to that. But it's not going to come to that," I say pointedly at Zé, "because I know how to protect myself."

He doesn't say a word, but he's steaming.

"When we're through here, take the rest of the day off," I tell Tamar. "Our flight leaves at five a.m. We meet with Bancroft first thing in the morning. Noelia is trying to set up meetings with a couple distributers later in the morning or early afternoon. We'll leave the US by midafternoon. It'll be a quick trip."

# 47

## ALEXIS

I'M FINISHING breakfast when my phone vibrates with a message. I turn it over, hoping it's Rafael telling me he's on his way up and wants me naked when he gets here.

It's not him, but it's Valentina. I smile. Maybe I was foolish to worry that my relationship with Rafael would change things between us.

Valentina: *I need to talk to you. Can you meet me at my apartment?*

*I need to talk to you.* She sounded less stressed when I last spoke with her, but it was a quick call, and we spent most of the time discussing Rafael.

Lexie: *Sure. What time?*

Valentina: *ASAP. Please don't tell Rafael.*

*Don't tell Rafael? Are we going to start this so soon?* It's bad enough I'm hiding the stuff about the trafficking ring from him. I don't want to keep any other secrets. *This isn't some huge secret, Lexie. He doesn't need to know everything you do.*

Lexie: *On my way.*

I tell Sabio on my way out that I'm going to Valentina's. I don't ask him not to tell Rafael, because I don't expect him to go blabbing. He can see the doorway from here, and there's a guard stationed outside Valentina's apartment too.

As soon as I knock, Valentina opens the door and pulls me inside. Her eyes and nose are red, and her cheeks tear-stained. *This is not good.* "What happened, sweetheart?"

She begins to sob, and I pull her into a hug. "Tell me. Maybe I can help."

"Marco left." She sniffles.

I pull back so I can see her face. There are dark circles under her eyes that I didn't notice when I came in. Even through the tears, I can see she hasn't slept.

*This better not have anything to do with Marco leaving her in the US and going off unexpectedly.*

"He moved out?"

"He took a large suitcase with him, mostly filled with clothes and electronics. He's leaving tonight on business, and then he's going to spend a few days in France before coming back to Porto. He told me that while he's gone, I need to decide between him and my family."

My blood is boiling, and I take a breath before I say something about Marco that she might not easily forgive. Asking Valentina to give up her family for him is like driving a stake through her heart. He knows it. *What a huge asshole.* "Did something happen?"

"I don't know. He won't talk to me about it. When I got home from having dinner with my parents last week, Marco wasn't there. He came in shortly after, and he was in a mood—preoccupied and gruff. Which isn't like him."

My heart falls into my stomach. "What night was that, again?" I ask, even though I know the answer.

"Wednesday."

*Shit.* "He didn't say anything at all?"

She shakes her head.

"Do you know where he was before he came home?"

"Meeting a client." She begins to pace the kitchen, reordering items on the counter. "How can we possibly work things out if he won't talk to me?"

My insides are shaking, and I pull out a stool from the island and sit down. I know this has something to do with Rafael. I just know it, but I can't tell her. Maybe someone else knows. Someone who's not afraid of the truth. *Daniela.* "Have you asked your mother about it?"

"No. I can't talk to her about this."

"You can," I say gently. "You might not want to, but you can."

"I can't, Lexie. I'm still a newlywed. I feel like a damn failure."

*Exactly how I'm going to feel if I tell you what I know, and Rafael kicks me out on my ass. Because he will.* I glance at her anguished face. *This isn't about me.*

"Stop it right now. You are not a failure. You're running a very successful Port company that's about to become even more successful."

She takes a bottle of spray cleaner and a rag from under the sink and begins to scrub the spotless counters. Some people collapse in a heap, but Valentina is a whirlwind when she's anxious.

"I get why you don't want to talk to your parents about this, but there isn't a chance in hell that they would ever think of you as a failure."

She doesn't respond.

"Did your father let on, over dinner, that he had some kind of problem with Marco?"

I don't know if Rafael was on the phone with Antonio, when he mentioned Marco's name the other day, but I'm hoping I can lead her to the information she needs without betraying Rafael or lying to her. It's an untenable predicament, and I'm starting to worry that I'm going to be forced to choose between my best friend, *my sister*, whom I love, and the man I've wanted—*and yes, loved*—for so long.

She thinks for a moment. "No. His name never came up until I left. My father told me to send him his best."

With Antonio, it could go either way. Maybe he wasn't involved, or maybe *send him my best* was the equivalent of sending Marco a huge middle finger.

*Have you asked Rafael?* I don't say it because it feels wrong to encourage it, but it's only a matter of time before she brings it up.

"Has Rafael said anything to you?" she asks, and my stomach rebels.

I can't lie to her, but I can't betray him either. I need to walk the line between two bad choices, but that prospect doesn't feel very good either. *You have no choice.*

"He hasn't said anything to me. Why don't you talk to him?"

Valentina stands by the island, across from me, with both hands on the quartz top. "You know something, don't you?"

*Oh God.*

I shake my head. "I don't know anything that could help you." My conscience twitches as soon as the words are out.

She shakes her head, and a different kind of sadness and maybe disappointment envelops her. "I thought we were friends, Lexie. Sisters." She pounds her index finger on the counter. "This is my marriage I'm fighting for. What do you know?"

I stand and clutch the counter, wondering what the women I love and admire would do in this situation. My mother would attempt a balancing act. Grandma Lydia would tell Valentina. But what eventually sways me is that if the shoe were on the other foot, I don't have to guess what Valentina would do. She would tell me.

I would want to know, and she has a right to know. Her

family—Rafael, especially—has no right to destroy her marriage.

"Do you love Marco?" Her answer could save me from stabbing Rafael in the back—because that's how he'll see it.

"Of course I love him. What kind of question is that?"

Maybe the other day had nothing to do with Marco. Maybe I'm drawing inferences that are ridiculous. *Maybe. Maybe. Maybe.* But in my heart, I know the conversation he had before he left the apartment was connected to this, and I know his mood when he returned was connected as well. As much as I want it to be different, I'm certain it's all linked.

"What do you know, Lexie?" Her tone is desperate now, and it tears at my heart.

I sigh, thinking about the possible ramifications for Valentina's relationship with Rafael. She's going to be furious with him, especially after the way he behaved about the art gallery. I'm worried about my relationship with him too. I don't think he'll forgive this easily—maybe not at all. I know this isn't about me, or it shouldn't be, but it's painful just the same. *So painful.*

*She has the right to know. She would tell you.* It's true. She would tell me.

I glance at her swollen eyes. She deserves better from her family. And she sure as hell deserves better from me.

"I really don't know anything. But on Wednesday, Rafael got a call, and he mentioned Marco's name. I don't know who he was talking to."

"What did he say?"

"I couldn't hear. He took the call in the other room, and then you called to invite me to your parents' house for dinner and we talked for a few minutes. When he came back to the kitchen, he was—tense." *And his jaw was ticcing.*

"Tense?"

I shrug. "Edgy."

"Lexie, I never thought that you would compromise our relationship, compromise me, for a man. Especially one who isn't in it for the long haul." *Ouch.*

She's hurt and confused, and angry. Her words, every single one, are daggers to my soul. They're especially painful coming from her—she's sweet and kind, and I doubt she's ever even squished a bug, let alone hurt someone she loves.

"I'm trying to remember, Valentina, and I'll tell you everything I know, but don't act like this should be easy for me."

I'm choosing Valentina over Rafael. My relationship with her over my relationship with him. It's the hardest thing I've ever had to do.

I start to cry. "I realize my relationship with him is new. But I've loved him for a long time."

"I'm sorry," she coos, coming around the island and wrapping her arms around me. "I love you, Lexie, but I'm trying to save my marriage. We just got started, and it's already slipping away."

"I've told you everything I know about the call. Everything. He left the apartment shortly after."

"Do you know where he went?"

"I don't. I assumed he was downstairs in his office. I don't even know why I assumed that, but I did."

"There must be some reason. Think back, Lexie. Think."

I do think back. But there really is nothing. "I don't remember, Valentina. Maybe he told me he was going downstairs. I just don't remember."

"What about when he got back? Did he say anything?"

"He was wound tight and—"

"And?"

*And he tore off my nightgown like a man possessed and cuffed me to the bench. Then edged me until I agreed to get on my knees for him.*

"He was in a mood. Like something happened."

She flings a book from the counter across the room, knocking a glass pitcher onto the floor, where it shatters spectacularly. "That bastard."

I've known her more than a decade, and I've never seen her like this. She's not going to forgive him, or maybe she will, but she won't forget. Their relationship will be forever changed— because of me.

"I know you're angry. But we don't have any idea what, if anything, happened between Rafael and Marco. There could have been any number of things that upset Rafael. I'm sure the same is true for Marco."

"You're right. But this isn't my first go-round with Rafael. His dirty fingerprints are all over it. I knew it from the start. I just didn't want to believe it."

I need to be the one who tells Rafael. It's the only hope I have for our relationship. It has to come from me. "I need a favor."

"Anything," she says. "Just don't ask me to go easy on him. I won't do that."

"Don't tell him I told you. Let me tell him. It'll seem like less of a betrayal."

"Of course. But, Lexie, you can't say anything until after I talk to him. First, I want to talk to Marco. He's meeting with a client at eleven. I'm going to try to catch him before then. Once he knows I'm onto Rafael, maybe he'll be more forthcoming."

I'm not sure how it's going to work. My brain is like mush.

"Listen," she says, gently taking my hand. "I asked a lot of you. I know how you feel about Rafael, and I'm sorry if this causes a rift between you. I really am."

I know she's sorry about all of it, and I'm sorry too. Rafael was right—our family ties are intertwined in a way that makes this sort of thing inevitable. I just thought we'd have a stronger foundation before we were tested.

"I'll keep your confidence," she continues. "I won't tell Rafael, or anyone."

"Valentina, please think about this long and hard before you go for the jugular. You don't actually know anything. You're grasping at straws because you need to have something to hold on to. I understand that. But don't blow up your relationship with Rafael over a few sketchy details. He loves you so much. You're the one link he has to his mother, and he's the one link you have to that part of your family."

She draws a breath.

"That kind of love is toxic," she says finally. "You know this. The reason men behave like your father, and mine, and Rafael, is because they're allowed to."

I don't say anything as we embrace, because she's right. There's no denying it.

Rafael did this to her. I'm sure it was under some guise of protection. I'm also sure that one day he'll do the same thing to me under that same guise of protection.

It almost doesn't matter if he hates me for telling Valentina. *I can't live like that.*

# 48

## RAFAEL

FIVE HEADS POP UP, at once, as Valentina storms into the villa. We gave her access because she's a partner, and it was a show of trust, but she never comes down here.

Her hair is uncombed, and her eyes are rimmed in red like she's been crying. My gut starts to burn the moment I lay eyes on her.

"Get out!" she shouts at Zé, Cristiano, and Lucas, who aren't quite sure what to do. "No. Stay. I want you fuckers to hear this, too, because I'm sure you were in on it."

Neither Antonio nor I ask what's wrong, because we both know. I'm sure the other three know too. She's a woman now, but all I see is the twelve-year-old girl who wormed her way into my heart before I even met her.

"How dare you?" she shrieks at me. "You don't think you've already caused enough trouble in my marriage?"

She marches closer, and as pissed as she is, I prefer it to seeing hurt in her face.

"You dragged my husband into the caves and accused him of stealing money?"

"He was not dragged anywhere, and he wasn't treated like a

prisoner. No one, not me or anyone else, accused him of a fucking thing. I asked him some questions. That's all."

"That's all? I would have expected this from him"—she points to Antonio, who doesn't flinch—"but not from you. Why didn't you come to me first? How am I ever supposed to trust you as my big brother, or a business partner? How?"

The pain is all over her face now, and in her voice. I feel it in my bones.

"Every shred of evidence pointed at him," I explain, going to my desk to retrieve the copies of the account I showed Marco. I hand her the application and the account statements. "Take a look for yourself." It's all there in black and white, but I'm not sure she's in any frame of mind to give us the benefit of reason.

"Someone went to a lot of trouble to make it seem like him," I continue. "That account was set up in your name, and he was the beneficiary. It was funded with a million and a half euros from Premier accounts, Valentina. A million and a half euros. That's a lot of reasons to want you dead." I'm livid just saying the words.

Her eyes haven't left the statements as she struggles to make sense of it.

"We go where the facts take us," I say softly, "even if it's in a direction we can't bear."

"Can't bear?" she repeats, scowling. "Bullshit." She tosses the papers in my direction, and they land at my feet.

"You never wanted me to marry him. He doesn't have enough money. Or enough power. It never mattered to you, to either of you," she says, looking from me to her father, "that I loved him or that he loved me."

"That's not true, *menina*," Antonio says quietly. "You're angry, and I can appreciate that, but you damn well know that I never interfered in your relationship with Marco."

Valentina glowers at him in a way that most people would never dare to do. "You didn't interfere because"—she points to me—"he had his nose so far up my business, and was reporting every detail back to you."

She's not wrong. But I won't apologize for thoroughly vetting her future husband, and I'll be surprised if Antonio apologizes. She was a kid when Marco came sniffing around, and we didn't know much about him except that his great-grandfather was involved with stealing art and funneling it to the Nazis. Not much of a calling card.

"Let me tell you both something. I'm a grown woman, not the teenage girl who put up with your nonsense because she didn't know any better. If you manage to break up my marriage, not only will I never forgive you, but I'll find another man if it takes me all my life. I'll fuck everyone with a dick from here to hell and even a few people without—"

"Get out," Antonio yells in the direction of Cristiano, Zé, and Lucas, who flee the room without looking back.

"You crossed the line, Valentina," he chides, sternly, once they're gone.

*Not what I would have said first.*

"I crossed a line?" She puts a hand on her hip. "Really? Does my mother know about this?"

"I don't share every business decision with your mother."

*That would be no.*

"I'm not surprised you didn't have the courage to tell her." She's pushing her father more than is wise. Antonio is giving her some leeway to vent, but it won't last forever.

"This wasn't meant to embarrass either you or Marco." I pick up the papers and wave them under her nose. "We took great pains to avoid it. But we needed to get to the bottom of it. Don't tell me it's not mighty suspicious."

"Have you gotten to the bottom of it?" she asks, the sugar dripping from her voice like arsenic. "Or should we prepare for another chapter of the Inquisition?"

"I'm never apologizing for protecting you, *menina,*"

Antonio says with his unique ring of finality that signals to sane people the conversation is done. "I love you too much for that."

"That's not love, Dad. I'm tired of you both trying to pass off your despicable behavior as love."

She's not going to stop until he explodes. *I don't want that for either of them.*

"If Marco wants to clear the air with us," I tell her, hoping to deflect some of the ire away from her father, "he's welcome anytime." It would kill me to see her relationship with Antonio destroyed. *It would kill him too.* "But you know what? A man fights his own battles. He doesn't send his wife."

"Marco didn't send me," she hisses. "He waved me off when I asked why he was upset when he got home the other day. So shove your damn misogynist slogan up your ass."

Without another word to either of us, she turns and storms out, like she came in, hair flying behind her.

"That went well." I plop on a chair across from Antonio at the table where we'd been working and blow out a loud whoosh of air.

"She's just like her mother," Antonio mutters. "Carbon copy."

*Given how many times you've pissed off Daniela, maybe you know how to fix this.* "Any ideas about how we can smooth this over?"

He grunts. "She's got a soft heart. She'll eventually come around, but it might require me to have a heart attack or step in front of a bus before it happens."

*That's helpful.*

Antonio's phone rings. He glances at the screen and ignores it.

I'm sorry she's hurt, and I'm sick that my relationship with her might have suffered irreparable damage, but given the circumstances, I would question Marco again. Better to have her furious than dead. You can come back from furious, but you can never come back from dead.

When Antonio's phone rings for the third time, he throws it across the room so hard it bounces several times before it falls silent.

"Who is it?"

"My wife."

It doesn't surprise me that the first phone call Valentina made when she left was to her mother. I'm sure the second was to Lexie. Neither of whom will have an ounce of sympathy for me or Antonio.

"If Marco didn't open his mouth, who did?" Antonio asks, leaning back in the chair.

I think back at who knew we were hauling Marco in for questioning. Zé, Tamar, Cristiano, and Lucas are the only people, aside from Antonio and me, who knew everything. There's no way they breathed a word. Zé picked him up, and there were a couple of guards who saw him here, but he wasn't restrained or in a location that would have sent up any red flags.

When I got the call about Marco, I was in Valentina's apartment, upstairs. There are no surveillance devices in any of the apartments, and they're swept regularly, as are our cars and offices.

Lexie was with me. But I stepped out of the room to take the call. My stomach begins to roil. *Did she eavesdrop?* That's the only way she could have known a damn thing.

*It was her. It has to be.*

I'd like to put my fist through a wall to defuse some of the rage building inside. She betrayed me. She fucking betrayed me. The woman is not only a liar, she's disloyal. Untrustworthy. Not the kind of person I need, or want, in my life.

"I know who told Valentina," I mutter to Antonio on my way out to find the traitor.

# 49

## ALEXIS

I'M in the kitchen when the apartment door slams so hard it rattles the photographs on the wall—and what little hope for us I have left.

"You betrayed me," Rafael snarls, rage vibrating off every syllable.

His eyes are weapons shooting daggers that pierce my skin. Regret seeps from the gaping wounds, but I made my choice this morning, and there's nothing I can do now.

I don't need to ask why he's angry, and I won't feign ignorance. Valentina called me after she spoke with Marco, and then again after she confronted Rafael and Antonio.

She swore she didn't mention my name once. I believe her. But neither Rafael nor Antonio are fools. I'll accept responsibility for what I did.

"I'm so sorry. So very sorry, Rafael." I mean it sincerely. I am sorry. For Valentina. For him. And for me. But as sorry as I am, if I had it to do over, I would tell her again. "I wanted to tell you myself."

"Sorry?" he taunts. "I don't believe you're sorry."

"Her marriage is in trouble. Marco left, and she was beside

herself in a way that I'd never seen her. I didn't want to tell her. I was worried about what it would mean for your relationship with her." Vomit tickles my throat. "And what it would mean for our relationship."

His nostrils flare as he glowers at me, and the sliver of hope I held on to all day evaporates in the charged air.

"Relationship? We have no relationship. Whatever we had is finished." He leans across the island until his face is inches from mine. "We have nothing." His voice sends shivers down my spine. "You squandered my trust, and you'll never get it back."

He might as well have stuck a knife in my stomach and twisted until I bled out. It would have been less painful.

"It wasn't an easy decision," I say softly, "but there was no other choice under the circumstances. She would have done the same for me."

"No choice?" he roars. "You could have come to me. You could have said that you didn't know anything."

*You weren't here to see how distressed she was this morning. You got her anger, which I doubt was anywhere near as heart-wrenching as her tears.*

"I couldn't lie, or put her off. She was distraught. They're newlyweds. There's been so much pressure on them since the beginning. She's the one from the powerful family. The one with the money. Now with the new product that the two of you are launching—it's been so successful and garnered so much attention. It's just made things more difficult for them." The words emerge, but it's all blather. Yes, they're true, but he won't see it the way I do.

"Listen to yourself," he says, flinging his keys on the island with such force they slide off the other side. "What you're saying is that he's jealous of his wife. Jealous of her success."

"That's not what I'm saying." *Not exactly.* "Men care a lot about the size of their dicks, and money and power are the measurements they use. I hear what you're saying, and maybe it's true. Maybe he's a petty son of a bitch. But he's her petty son of a bitch, and she loves him. Until she says something different, we all need to respect that."

When he came in, all I felt was sorry, but the anger is rising. He hasn't taken any responsibility for his part. Instead, he dumped all the blame on me.

"Don't tell me who or what I need to respect," he hisses. "I respect those who deserve my respect."

Rafael stalks around the island and grabs me by the arms. There's such rage in his expression that I'm almost frightened. "You eavesdropped on my conversation. That's the only way you could have known a fucking thing."

I don't deny eavesdropping. I tried to listen, although I didn't hear anything of substance.

"When Antonio retires, I'll be taking over Huntsman Industries with a responsibility not just to the company, but to the Port industry and the entire region. Can you imagine what it would be like if your father couldn't take a phone call or confide in your mother about anything without her betraying him at the drop of a hat? Can you imagine?" he sneers.

No. I can't imagine. But I don't utter a word.

"You're not only reckless, you're a liar and a traitor."

*Traitor.* My blood runs cold.

Maybe in some corners of the universe, the word *traitor* is just an insult people toss around in anger. Where I come from —and where Rafael comes from—it's the most serious accusation one can level against another. It's a grave charge, more serious than murder, and punishable by death. There are no second chances for traitors.

"Let go of me," I snarl, the fury twisting in my chest. He clenches my arms tighter before he finally lets go.

I lift my chin. "You're calling me a traitor?"

He doesn't even have the good graces to flinch.

"That's exactly what you are."

"Should I be afraid to close my eyes tonight?" I ask not with fear, but with contempt.

He doesn't answer. His expression is stony, and there's an ugliness to him that I saw leveled at the traffickers in Sirena. I should be unnerved, but this asshole isn't getting my fear, and he's not getting another damn apology from me.

"Here," I say, holding out my wrists to him. "Cuff me, and toss me in a cell to await torture and execution."

He doesn't utter a word or make a move.

"Imprison me, or shut your fucking mouth, because I won't stand here and be accused of treason by the likes of you."

His jaw is ticcing, madly, and his gaze is scathing. I've had enough of being the scapegoat.

"Do you know what betrayal is, Rafael? It's when you go behind someone's back and haul their husband in for questioning. It's when you storm in and hurl accusations at a woman who's been sharing your bed before asking a single question."

"Don't you dare lecture me about betrayal. You've done nothing but lie to me since you arrived at Sirena."

"Oh yes, I forgot. I'm not allowed to have opinions because I'm reckless. Have you looked in a mirror recently?"

"Don't push me, Lexie. You won't like what you get."

*Don't you dare boss me, Rafael Huntsman. You have lost that privilege.*

"You know what's funny?" I ask, ignoring his warning, because he's going to hear everything I have to say. "The other night, after you fucked with Valentina's marriage, you came to me like a man possessed. Yet, despite your mood, you expected me to play with you—or rather, to let you play with me, however you chose. You wanted my trust. You needed it, and I gave it to you, without hesitation, even though I knew it could get out of hand because you seemed so on edge." I draw a breath to calm my pounding heart.

"Not one time," I continue, "not once, before, during, or after, did you accuse me of being reckless with my safety. You never mentioned it. Not once. Do you know why? Because the risk I took benefited you. It made your dick hard and your balls tight. And that's all you cared about."

"You have no idea what I care about," he spews, like venom. "You're selfish and untrustworthy, and I knew I'd come to rue the day I let you into my life."

The poison lands so deep, and it hurts so much, I can barely stand. But I will not give him a single damn tear. He moves away from me with the ease of a man with too much power.

"You might have some modern ideas," I say calmly, "but when push comes to shove, you lean on the old ways. You're no different from my father. Maybe worse. At least he knows exactly what he is, and he doesn't pretend otherwise."

I'm done. *Done.* There's nothing left to say. I gather my things off the counter.

"I'm leaving for the US tonight." His voice has a dangerous calm to it that puts me on alert. "With the time changes, I'll be gone a couple days."

"I won't be here when you get back."

Rafael takes a step toward me, and I see a flicker of regret in his face. It lasts just a second before the fury is back, swirling in his eyes. He puts a firm hand on my arm and starts to say something, but he stops and drops his arm.

"Where are you going?" he asks.

"London."

"It's for the best," he mutters under his breath. "You can take the small plane, and Giana and Sabio can travel with you."

He's all business now. The big fucking boss.

"I promised that I would provide security regardless of our relationship, and I will. Zé can work it out. He'll be your connection going forward."

*Not a fucking chance.* "My family has planes and security. I don't need yours." I'm not above spewing a little venom either.

"Whatever you decide," he replies, striding toward the bedroom.

The kitchen reeks of rage and love lost. *My love for him.* I'm not sure he ever got beyond liking my pussy.

I wander into the living room to get away from the stench, pretending to look at something on my laptop, while he rustles around the bedroom. The anger is beginning to retreat, and I'm left with a gaping hole in my heart. A hole that I'm not sure will ever heal. *Not this time.*

A few minutes later, he walks by with a leather duffel slung over his shoulder. He doesn't spare me a glance. When the apartment door shuts, I start to cry.

I always knew it would end badly for me. But I never expected this.

# 50

## ALEXIS

AFTER RAFAEL LEAVES, and I have a giant pity party for myself, I fall asleep on the couch wrapped in a soft quilt. It's not exactly comfortable, but I can't bear to sleep in his bed and I'm too exhausted to make up the one in the guestroom.

I sleep in fits and spurts. Every noise startles me awake, and I lie there wondering if it's him coming back to apologize. *I'm a foolish, foolish woman. He's not coming back, and I know in my heart that it's for the best. But still, it hurts.*

When I finally decide I've had enough, I get up and take a shower, before puttering around and accomplishing nothing until early afternoon. I need to call my father so that he can send a plane, but I've been dragging my feet. Not because I plan on staying, but because I haven't figured out how to approach him.

When I can't stand being in the apartment any longer, I open the door to face a guard who surely overheard us arguing yesterday.

"I'm going down to the executive offices to see Antonio," I inform Sabio.

I've been thinking about Antonio off and on all day. I'm sure Valentina's anger yesterday just added to his sorrow.

"Antonio?" he repeats, like I'm insane. "You have an appointment?"

"I don't need one. I checked with his office, and Cecelia said I could drop by whenever I wanted."

She also told me that Rafael's out of the country. *Good.* I won't have to worry about running into him. Not that it's any of his business if I visit Antonio.

Sabio gives me a wary nod and follows me to the elevator.

I have to figure out how to get my father to buy into the same security arrangement I have—*had*—with Rafael. Antonio and my father aren't exactly the same, but they know each other well, and more importantly, they understand one another. While it's not my main reason for wanting to see him today, he can help me think it through.

While we wait for the elevator, Zé appears. It's not exactly out of nowhere. He and Tamar share an apartment on this floor. Although he's the next-to-last person I want to bump into.

"Where are you going?" he asks Sabio, totally ignoring me. Zé's never cared much for me, not as Valentina's friend and certainly not as Rafael's *friend*.

"Alexis is going to see Antonio."

"Antonio?" He raises his brow.

*What is it with these guys?*

"Yes," I reply curtly. "And yes, he's expecting me."

"I'll escort her down," Zé mutters as the elevators open.

*Great. Like I haven't dealt with enough surliness in the last twenty-four hours.*

He doesn't say a word, but he knows what happened. I have no doubt. There isn't anything that goes on with Rafael that he doesn't know. They've been best buddies since they were kids, even before Rafael's mother disappeared. *Rafael's mother. Lydia's sister. Too many family connections.*

I side-eye Zé. "Do you know anything about the search for Rafael's mother?" I've been wanting to ask him about it since I found the little toy car in the closet. But I don't know why I think he'll tell me anything—or what made me ask about it now. Maybe because I'm leaving and there won't be another opportunity. Or maybe it's because I've been thinking about Lydia since I woke up this morning—about how hard it must have been to lose her sister, *her baby sister*, without a trace.

Zé flips a switch to stop the elevator, and the alarm blares.

"What are you doing?" I ask, while he enters a code on the keypad. The noise stops, but he doesn't answer my question.

"Rafael's mother is not your concern," he snarls. "Don't bring it up again."

I've had enough of high-handed men to last me a lifetime. "I appreciate your concern, but don't tell me what I can talk about."

We're face-to-face, and he has nearly a foot on me, and maybe a hundred pounds. But he won't hurt me. He wouldn't dare—although I'm sure he'd love to wring my neck.

"I was there when she disappeared." His voice, like his expression, is stony. "I saw him. I know the hell he went through. Leave. It. Alone. I won't warn you again."

It's an empty threat. But I do respect him for having Rafael's back.

I flip the switch to activate the elevator. "Relax. I have no intention of hurting him or anyone."

It's a short ride, and we don't say another word to each other.

When I get off the elevator, Zé follows me to Antonio's office and waits until Cecelia greets me before disappearing. *Good riddance.*

"You can go right in, Ms. Clarke," Cecelia says, smiling.

I hesitate for a moment before knocking on the partially open door. It's unlikely Antonio was surprised that I told

Valentina what I knew about the situation with Marco—which really wasn't much. He won't see it as a betrayal, not the way Rafael did.

Antonio glances up and catches me loitering in his doorway. "Lexie, what are you doing out there? Come in."

He rounds the desk to greet me, with that same easy manner about him that he's had with me since I was a toddler. *He doesn't seem angry.*

"Is everything okay?" he asks, motioning toward a chair in front of his desk.

"It's her birthday, and I miss her. I thought you might be missing her too."

A pang of sorrow crosses his face as he takes the seat beside me, turning the chair until it's facing mine, and I do the same. "I've been thinking about her all day too," he murmurs. "It would have been her seventy-fifth birthday."

"We would have had a big party for her that she would have said she didn't want, but ended up loving."

She would have taken Valentina and me out dress shopping, and maybe Antonio and Daniela's young daughters, whom she never got to meet. We would have had tea after, and maybe gone to a show.

Antonio's mouth is curled, but his gaze is far away.

I'm glad I came, even though the memories are bittersweet. Valentina and I normally reminisce about Lydia and toast her with champagne every year on her birthday, even if it's via a Zoom call. But this year Valentina wasn't in the right frame of mind to think about anything besides her marriage.

"That's exactly right," he murmurs. "She loved parties, and people. Even at seventy-five, she would have been partying long after the rest of us wanted to be home. My mother was a force of nature."

She was, but not the destructive kind. "She always told me to listen to my gut, follow my dreams, and save some of my allowance so that I'd have money of my own in case of an emergency."

I didn't really understand that when I was a girl. My parents were there in case of an emergency, but she meant the kind of emergency that I might not want to share with them.

He shakes his head. "Sounds like her. She loved you. You were her first grandchild—the girl she always wanted."

"She loved you too," I say softly. "She was so proud of you— except for that whole betrothal contract thing."

He clears his throat, and I press my lips together to quell a smile.

"Too soon?"

"It will always be too soon," he replies with a pointed look.

Lydia was at Daniela and Antonio's first wedding, but she died before they were remarried. I'll never forget the day they were killed. My grandfather was on the plane too—my father's plane.

"Have you forgiven my father for what happened?"

He cocks his head. "I was angry at your father for about ten minutes. Maybe less. It could have happened on my watch, just as easily. Your father doesn't take security lightly, especially when it involves people he loves."

"Tell me about it."

He snickers, and I wonder if he has any idea how burdened with the past my father has become. But I'm not going to tell him. *I've spilled too many secrets recently.*

"Can I ask you a question?"

He raises his brow. "As long as it isn't about betrothal contracts."

I smirk and shake my head. "Do you ever worry that the life you lead—that we all lead—is harmful to your relationship with your children?"

He sits back in the chair and studies me. "Every single day."

"How do you manage it?"

"I make sure they feel my love at least as much as my protection. It also gives me great comfort knowing they have a mother who's strong enough to stand up to me and push back, when necessary. Daniela, like your mother, isn't afraid to say enough is enough."

*My mother does that less frequently these days.*

"Do you listen to her and the kids when they have concerns?"

"Complaints, you mean?" The corner of his mouth twitches. "I always listen. But I don't always do as they ask."

"Even if it causes a great rift?"

"Even then. Although it hasn't come to that yet. But we might be close."

I know he's talking about the situation with Valentina, but I'm not going there.

"Have you ever thought of leaving it all behind? Walking away and doing something else?"

"That's not an option," he says without a moment's pause. "Not for me. Not for your father. And not for Rafael, because that's who you're really wondering about."

A rush of emotion floods me, but I push it away. Rafael's not someone I need to wonder about anymore. It's a bitter pill, but I swallow it without grimacing.

"Actually, I'm wondering about my father. I'm going back to London later today, and I'd like things to go more smoothly than the last time I was there. I thought I might get some insight from talking to you."

Antonio stills, his gaze keen. "Does Rafael know you're leaving?"

I nod, and I'm grateful he doesn't press, because despite all the tears earlier, I'm feeling a little weepy again.

"Why not walk away from everything? You have enough money and a young family."

"Because as imperfect as we are, especially your father and

me, we're hardly the worst." He sighs heavily. "The day we put down the mantle of power, someone who is far, far more evil will pick it up. We have a responsibility to ensure that doesn't happen."

"Even if it means losing your family?"

"I'm not a man of great faith—of any faith, really—but I believe that when we love someone, we can repair almost any well-intentioned damage we do to the relationship. At least, that's been my experience. That's why I'm not too concerned about Valentina." He winks at me, and I smile sheepishly.

"It's when evil takes the reins that we lose everything, Lexie. *Everything.*"

He searches my face, as if looking for something. "I'll tell you the last thing my mother said to me: 'Heavy is the head that wears the crown.'"

"She was a wise woman."

"Wise and fearless, as was her sister, Rafael's mother, and Daniela's mother too. The three amigas." He shakes his head. "Have you heard the stories?"

"Some of them. They risked a lot to help other women. I've always wanted to be like them, especially your mom. I wrote an essay about her in middle school." I remember how proud I was to be her granddaughter. It never mattered that we weren't blood relatives. Not to her, and certainly not to me.

His mouth curls. It's almost a smile, but it's fraught with something bittersweet.

"There was a point when I found her antics infuriating," he admits. "Although the truth is I wasn't angry. I was afraid of losing her. Time has softened those memories. My mother and her partners in crime did what needed to be done at a time when no one was doing anything. It was a moral imperative for them. Hard to quarrel with that."

Impossible to quarrel with that. They followed their hearts, and they used their stashes of emergency money to ferry women out of the country and away from danger.

By the time I leave Antonio, I have a better sense of where I'm headed and how I'm going to manage my father. But even with that, my heart is still in tatters about Rafael.

*I believe that when we love someone, we can repair almost any well-intentioned damage we do to the relationship. At least, that's been my experience.* I think the key word here, Antonio, is *love*. Something that I'm certain wasn't part of the equation between Rafael and me.

I always hoped that one day he would love me, but it's too much of a stretch now, even for a girl who grew up believing in fairy tales. Some damage, even well-intentioned, is too great to be repaired.

# 51

## ALEXIS

"Hi, Dad."

"What's wrong, sweetheart?" My father's sharp, and he knows I wouldn't call him during the workday just to chat.

"Maybe nothing's wrong, and I just wanted to hear your voice."

He doesn't say a word while I swallow my pride. It's not actually that hard to do. My father won't revel in my failure or rub it in my face. He's not like that. *It's me.* I hate to fail—and this failure is especially painful.

"I'd like to come home. To London—but back to my place. I'm wondering if you could send a plane and some security." It's almost a relief to get the words out.

"What did he do?" His voice is low and tightly controlled, with contempt leaking from the edges.

"Nothing," I reply, mustering all the cheer I can find. "I realized pretty quickly that the grass isn't any greener in Porto." *I betrayed him, and he called me a traitor.* "Rafael's actually a lot like you." I knew this from the beginning—I've always known it. But I never expected to be the target of his cruelty. "What's that saying about sticking with the devil you know?" I stop talking because I sound ridiculous.

He doesn't respond for a long moment. There's pity in the silence. Even over the phone, I'm sure he sees through the bravado.

"Your place is safe, and I'm sure you'd like to go directly there, but why don't you come home for a couple days and let your mum spoil you? It would make her happy."

My mother would enjoy it, and I could use the TLC. But I need to wallow in grief for a few days before I pick up my chin and go back to living. There's no way I'll be able to do that at my parents' house. It'll be an endless string of questions from my mother, and my father might not ask, but he'll be watching, shrewdly deciphering every breath I take to see if he needs to end Rafael's life or if taking a few fingers will be enough. It'll be exhausting.

"I don't know." I'm not prepared to commit. I don't know much of anything right now except that I need to leave Porto.

"I won't stop you from going back to your flat provided you're willing to be responsible about security, if that's what's worrying you. You have my word."

*It crossed my mind, although my most pressing concern is still privacy to grieve, but since you brought up security, let's discuss it.*

"I want a female guard assigned to my team. Not someone who's a chaperone, but a real guard. I need a security team that's sensible and willing to help me figure out how I can go about living my life without jeopardizing my safety—in any situation."

"I'll see what I can do." The response is glib and dismissive, and I won't let it slide.

"No, Dad. I need more than a hope and a prayer. I don't want to get to London and find out that we're exactly where we were when I left." After just a short time with Giana, Sabio, and Carlos, I can't go back to the way things were.

"I get it," he grumbles.

Although I'm not entirely convinced he does.

But this is where it gets particularly thorny. I draw a breath before I drop it on him. "My guards are not to report every little thing to you. I'm twenty-three years old. I'm entitled to some privacy."

"Is there anything else you want? My testicles, perhaps?" He's annoyed and frustrated.

Normally I manage my father by going in from the edges, but today I marched right down the middle. He's unhappy, but I'm not backing down.

"Those are my requirements. The alternative is that I come home and bring the guards I've been working with here." Which I should do, because they're exactly the kind of people I want on my team, but that would mean they would have to leave their home and their families. I won't do that to them.

"You're a tough negotiator. But I have one condition of my own."

*Of course you do.*

"What's that?"

"You need to come home before you go back to your flat."

He agreed to everything I asked—at least I think he did. There's always a risk he won't let me leave without a war, but if he's going to trust me, I'll have to trust him too.

"I'll agree to that."

"When would you like to leave Porto?"

It's not lost on me that he didn't *tell* me when he'd be sending the plane, but he *asked* for my preference. Maybe we can actually make this work.

"I'd like to leave as soon as possible, although nothing's chasing me out of here. There's no real rush." I don't want him to think I'm in any danger—he'd skin Rafael.

"I'll make a phone call and let you know the timing. Unless

it's an emergency, it could be after midnight before I can get a plane there. You up for a late-night flight?"

*It's perfect. I'll be gone before he gets back.* "No emergency. I'll sleep on the plane. Thank you. I'll talk to you soon."

"Sweetheart?" he calls before I hang up.

"Yes?"

"I'm sorry things didn't work out the way you wanted. I know you've had your eye on him for years."

"Thanks." I don't say more, because there's a lump in my throat the size of a grapefruit.

*I'm sorry too.*

# 52

## RAFAEL

TAMAR and I arrive at Bancroft's office long before the place opens for business. He didn't want to take an early meeting with me, but I insisted. If that asshole can meet Valentina for breakfast, he can meet me.

"You'll wait outside his office," I instruct Tamar on the elevator up.

"Outside his office?" she asks, like it's the worst idea she's ever heard.

*She's been spending too much time with Zé.*

"I'll come get you if I have any trouble explaining how he put a remote device on Valentina's phone." One that allowed him to get the information he needed to open that account and gain access to the Premier accountants. *He's lucky we're not in Porto, where the payback would be swift and meaningful.*

"What if he gets defensive and takes a swing at you or pulls a weapon?"

*Let the bastard try. It'll give me a good excuse to beat him to a pulp.*

"Have you seen Bancroft? No need to worry about me. But I

want you outside, guarding the door to make sure no one comes in who might help him. Can you handle that?" I ask, signaling I'm done with any more questions about how we're going to proceed.

"Yes," she replies, like she's insulted.

"I won't be long," I mutter as the elevator doors open to a spacious reception area.

Bancroft is waiting for us with that smarmy smile. He's much too smug for someone who needs a tailor and a gym membership.

"Rafael," he gushes, putting out his hand, "such a pleasure to see you again."

*We'll see if you still feel that way when I'm done with you.* I take his hand firmly, and even though I'd like to break his fingers, I don't.

"Who is this lovely young lady?" he asks, his beady eyes skimming her body in a way that makes me want to poke them out. *Young lady.* Tamar looks like she's itching to cut off his dick and stuff it up his ass. Before this is over, I might let her.

"Ms. Sorin is accompanying me on the trip. She'll wait out here while we chat."

"My office is right through here," he says.

I follow him into a room that's filled with heavy wooden furniture, drenched in polish, and uninteresting artwork in dark frames. The decor is tired and outdated, like his brand.

"Asked them to set up breakfast for us, but they brought pastries." He shakes his head. "I hope you don't normally eat a big morning meal."

"I don't," I reply, glancing at the wall with photographs of Bancroft and a variety of dignitaries. I don't see a single family picture, anywhere. I'm not impressed with his priorities.

"How do you take your coffee?"

"Black." *Like my mood.*

There are no active surveillance devices in the room. We sent someone in with the cleaning company last night to sweep the place. He found an old-school recording device and disabled it.

While Bancroft's pouring coffee, I take out my knife and inch toward him. I could slice his throat and he'd never see it coming. But that's not much fun.

I hold the blade against his fleshy jowls.

He drops the cup and saucer, and coffee splashes everywhere.

"I strongly recommend you don't make a sound."

"I-I-I don't understand," he whispers. "What are you doing?"

"You don't understand," I taunt, grabbing him by the ear and shoving him into a corner.

He stumbles back, but there's nowhere to go. He can't escape my wrath.

"Let me explain, *Scottie*." I squeeze his neck with one hand, the heel pressed into his windpipe, and hold my knife in the other. "We traced a bank account in Valentina Cruz's name to you."

"I-I-I don't know what you're talking about."

*Bullshit.*

I grip his neck tighter and jostle him, letting him get a glimpse of my sharp blade. "Don't open your fucking mouth until I give you permission."

His face is beet red. He's already sweating like a pig, and I'm just getting started. If he doesn't have a stroke before this is through, it'll be a fucking miracle.

"I'm not here for an inquiry. I know you did it. You're no better a hacker than you are a businessman. You left bread-crumbs all along the way that we followed straight back to you. We have all the damning evidence. More than enough to convict you in a legal proceeding *and* in the court of public opinion."

"Can I-I-I—"

"I'm talking. Don't be rude," I tut, pushing the heel of my hand deeper into his neck.

"I'm here to inform you that if there's even a single hiccup with Premier's US launch, you will experience an unfortunate mishap. One that's long and painful, and involves knives and ropes and body parts being chopped off in tiny pieces."

He chokes on his whimpers.

"Don't worry. I'll keep you alive so you can watch. My knife work is almost as special as the new product we're introducing."

He's gurgling, and I lower my hand from his windpipe and replace it with the blade.

This wasn't supposed to go down this way. We spent hours planning how I would walk him through everything he did— step by step—let him see for himself how we tracked his digital fingerprints and how airtight our case is against him. Then I would explain that if there were *any* more problems, I would turn our evidence over to the FBI and the Portuguese Intelligence Service. Normally we'd take care of this in-house, but we have little sway in the US, and a cautious approach seemed prudent.

But I spent the entire plane ride awake, thinking about what happened with Lexie, and getting more and more worked up. I wasn't feeling particularly cautious when we landed. This son of a bitch is lucky I don't carve my initials into his chest before I remove his organs and feed them to the pigeons gathered on the window ledge.

"Don't even think about going to the authorities, because if you do, all the evidence we have goes directly to them. All of it. If that happens, your ass is going to be sitting in jail for a long time, until we send someone in with a shiv to end your misery. Trust me when I say you won't do well in prison."

He's sobbing now, and I expect him to piss himself any minute.

"Can I say something?" he pleads between gasps.

I don't give a damn what he has to say. I came to talk, not to listen. But maybe he has something worth hearing. I let him twist in the wind while I consider his request. "Go."

"I-I-I won't tell a soul. Not even my wife. You don't need to worry about me. I'm—I'm sorry. I don't know what I was thinking. The company's been in my wife's family for eighty years. I can't lose it. She'll never forgive me."

"Not my problem. But you fuck with me again, and you're going to have a much bigger problem than a bankrupt business and a pissed-off wife."

I slide the knife across his throat so he understands I'm not playing games. It's a surface cut, but it draws blood, and he pisses himself.

"You definitely won't do well in prison." I wipe my knife on his shirt and sheathe it. "I didn't kill you today because I want you to be around to watch your family business wither before it dies a slow, painful death."

He's clutching his throat like the paper cut is a gaping wound that requires pressure to stop the bleeding.

*What a pussy.*

I snatch an almond croissant off the sidebar on my way out.

"Let's go." I hand Tamar the pastry. "Not sure if it's any good. The guy has terrible taste."

"That was quick," she says on the way to the elevator. "What did he have to say for himself when you showed him the evidence?"

"I didn't go through it piece by piece. It wasn't necessary."

She side-eyes me. "Are we going to be allowed to leave the country?"

"He's alive. Don't worry. There were only a few drops of

blood shed." Not anywhere near enough to satisfy my lust for revenge, or to take the edge off from my argument with Lexie— I'm not sure a murder spree would be enough to calm my soul.

Bancroft's not going to open his mouth to anyone, but we probably shouldn't hang around too long in case I'm wrong.

# 53

## ALEXIS

MY EMOTIONS START to get the best of me after the sun sets. It won't be long before I need to leave for the airport.

Running on fumes, I take another shower, hoping it will make me feel better. Although I'm not sure anything can make me feel better.

Rafael and his spiced woodsy scent are everywhere. I can't even go over to Valentina's apartment to escape—there are as many memories there as there are here. Maybe leaving Porto, with all the reminders of him—of us—will help.

I pack my suitcase, stuffing in as much as will fit—even the things I normally keep at Valentina's. I don't see myself staying at her apartment in the future, at least not for a long time. I can always visit their house outside the city. There's certainly plenty of room there, and I won't risk running into Rafael. *If they still have a house—and a marriage.*

Marco's not Rafael. *That's why she married him.* Eventually, he'll come around. At least I hope he will.

It feels wrong not to call Valentina to say goodbye. But she'll blame herself for what happened, and that serves nothing. It's not her fault—none of it. She has enough to worry about.

Although the real reason I don't call is because I'll begin to sob again, and I'm tired of crying. I've cried more today than I have in the last year—maybe longer.

I glance at the gorgeous purse Judite Furtado brought me. *I'm not going to take it.* Every time I look at it, it'll bring back memories of how sweet and generous Rafael can be. How thoughtful. I need to remember him like the ogre he was before he left the apartment.

The last thing I do is remove the anklet with the tracking device. It's a beautiful piece, especially the charm. I unclasp the angel wings and run my finger over the intricate detail. It's delicate, yet it feels so heavy in my palm. *My angel.*

Giana knocks on the door just in time to prevent a deluge of tears and self-pity.

"Your ride is here," she says kindly.

"Just give me a second."

I admire the anklet with everything it represents, one last time, before leaving it on his nightstand. We were going to try to make it work. This was a symbol of that effort. *A promise.*

*It's all in the past now. There's nowhere to go but forward. Pull up those big-girl panties, Lexie. You've got this.*

I take one last look around the room, committing it all to memory—the bed, the leather bench, *everything.* When I'm done torturing myself, I close the door behind me with a heavy heart and tears that threaten but don't fall.

# 54

## ALEXIS

THE LIGHTS inside the plane dim as we leave Porto, making a swoop around the old city until the pilot finds his route. I stare out the window, seeing nothing, but feeling everything. A big fat tear plops on my cheek, and I wipe it away.

The guards my father sent, Ivy and Callum, are at the front of the plane. I smiled when Ivy introduced herself. My father moved quickly, in a show of good faith, which I appreciate.

I love London, and I'm looking forward to getting back to my friends and my life. The life I had before my father's behavior forced me back to my parents' house.

I'm going to reschedule my haircut and see if I can round up a group to go to that new pub in Hackney Wick that I've been dying to try. I barely left Huntsman Lodge the entire time I was in Porto. It'll feel amazing to be in the city again, surrounded by the throngs. *You promised to go home first.* I did and I will—for three days. That's it.

"Do you need anything, miss?" the flight attendant asks with a smile.

She introduced herself when I arrived, but I don't remember her name. This isn't my father's usual flight crew. My request to come home was sudden, and the regular flight crew must have been unavailable.

"I don't need anything, thank you. It's been a long day, and I'm sorry, but I missed your name."

"Anya," she replies with a hint of an Eastern European accent.

"Thank you, Anya. And the pilot? I didn't get his name either," I admit sheepishly. He'll be out to say goodbye when we arrive, and it would be nice for me to know his name when I thank him for the uneventful ride.

She cocks her head, studying me, like she's wondering why I want to know his name. *Don't worry. I have nothing bad to report to my father.*

"The pilot?"

I nod.

"Roman," she replies curtly. "If there's nothing else, I'll check to see if your escorts need anything."

*My heavily armed escorts.*

The hum of the engine is the only sound in the cabin, and thoughts of Rafael are starting to creep through the *amazing* plans I have to erase him from my memory. *What a joke.*

I close my eyes and replay the bittersweet conversation with Antonio—anything so I won't think about Rafael. *It doesn't work.* He continues to seep into my consciousness, where he's lived for years.

When I can't take it anymore, I pull out my laptop. The alphabetical list of cities pops up unprompted, like a sign from the universe. I skim through the graphs I meticulously created.

Either Rimini or Riga should be the next target of the traffickers, unless I'm wrong—again. *You weren't wrong about Oslo. The timing was off.*

*Just the timing, like it's not an integral piece of the puzzle.*

The truth is there are many European cities that begin with the letter R, although given the patterns, Rimini or Riga are the most likely to be hit next. Although I can't be absolutely certain. But Quimper will come after. *I'm sure of it.*

There are only three European cities that begin with the letter Q, and also fit the profile. A woman was already abducted in Quartu Sant'Elena, and Queluz is in Portugal. It's a small country. They won't be back so soon. Not if the pattern holds.

There's been no information in the media and no chatter on the dark web about the woman who was abducted in Oslo. Either she was poor and her kidnapping has been deemed not newsworthy, or she's from a powerful family who has the ability to quash the story. The former is much more reprehensible than the latter, although both scenarios lack any sense of morality.

*"My mother and her partners in crime did what needed to be done at a time when no one was doing anything. It was a moral imperative for them. Hard to quarrel with that."*

A moral imperative. Antonio's words speak to my soul, rousing the part of me that everyone wants to quash. My father, Rafael, even my mother would prefer if I were less interested in immersing myself in controversy.

*Is buying and selling women like cattle controversial? I think not.*

I might have been off about the timing, but the location was spot on. I wasn't wrong about that. If there was ever a moral imperative, this is it. *I'm not wrong about that either.*

With a new sense of purpose, I go to the front of the plane to speak to Ivy and Callum. We need a cogent plan before contacting my father.

# 55

## ALEXIS

"Lexie, are you on your way home?" my father asks when he answers the call. He seems more relaxed than when we last spoke.

"Yes. I'm actually in the plane's conference room with Ivy and Callum. We're on speaker."

"What's the problem?"

"No problem. But I'd like to make a stop before London." I need his permission to divert the plane.

"Where?" he asks.

I can almost see the prickliness in his expression.

"Quimper. I've talked it through with Ivy and Callum, and they believe we can make it work safely."

"What's in Quimper?" His tone is suspicious and far less relaxed than when he first answered.

"All sorts of things, but I'm interested in pottery. I owe a few people wedding gifts, and I'll pick up Mum something nice while I'm there too." It's all technically true, and I feel only a small pang of conscience for omitting the fact that the traffickers are the main reason I want to stop in Quimper. I can't think about the damage the omission could do to our new agreement—*but I have to go.*

He's quiet, too quiet, and I brace myself to do battle. One way or another, I'm going to Quimper, although maybe not on his plane. That's up to him.

"I'd like another day to get my head straight before I come home. I didn't want to stay in Porto, but . . . I really could use another day." This is mostly true too. I didn't want to remain in Porto, but neither my heart nor my head will be straight unless I go to Quimper.

"Callum and Ivy," my father says, in a voice that's deadly serious, "can you protect my daughter in Quimper?"

"Yes, sir," they reply in unison.

"It's not a bustling city, like London," Ivy adds. "And it's midweek. There are several hotels that can accommodate our security needs."

"I'll send word to the pilot to file a new flight plan," my father says after several tense moments. "Lexie," he continues in a no-nonsense tone. "I expect you home for a late dinner tomorrow evening."

*That wasn't so hard.* I blow out the breath that's been caught in my chest. "I'll be there. One day should be enough to do everything I need to do." *I hope.*

After we hang up, I leave Ivy and Callum to manage the details and go back to my seat. When I'm settled, I pull up a photo of Lydia, Valentina, and me from my thirteenth birthday. We had a spa day, and she had tickets for us to see Lady Gaga in concert. We were spending the night with her. I look so young. *And so happy. We all look happy.* It was the last picture we took together.

*Happy birthday, Grandma. I love you. I wish you were here. Valentina needs your best advice. I could use some too.*

# 56

# RAFAEL

WE'RE on the way back to Porto when Zé contacts me. *Prime Minister Russo's assistant is trying to reach you. Says it's urgent.*

Russo must have news about the traffickers, otherwise he wouldn't be trying to reach me at this hour.

*Send me the contact information.*

I call the number and a man answers immediately.

"This is Rafael Huntsman. I understand the prime minister has been trying to reach me."

"Good evening, Mr. Huntsman, although it's long past evening in Rome. My name is Gio Ardente, Prime Minister Russo's personal assistant. The prime minister asked me to inform you that his daughter was killed earlier today."

My heart stops. "Francesca?"

"Yes, Francesca. I apologize. It's been a rough evening."

More than just a little rough, from the sound of his voice.

"Do you know how it happened?"

"It's too soon to know all the details with any kind of confidence, but Francesca's sister believes she was meeting her boyfriend."

The bile begins to rise in my throat. "Paolo?"

"I believe so."

*Fuck.* "Did she have security with her?"

"She was with a seasoned guard, who was also killed."

I pound my fist against the seat beside me. They took out an experienced guard to get to her. *It's those fuckers.* It has to be.

"Did it happen in Rome?" I'm sure he doesn't have time for my questions, but I need details to understand the kind of danger Lexie's facing.

"Less than a mile from the prime minister's residence. I really don't have any more to share, but the prime minister will call you after the funeral."

"Please send him my deepest condolences. If there's anything I can do, don't hesitate to contact me."

*Lexie's in danger.* The words are pounding in my skull.

I pace while trying to reach Will. The phone rings and rings, but he doesn't pick up, and he doesn't have voice mail set up. *Of course not.* Why would he have voice mail? *Goddamn it.*

I try Lexie next, but the call goes straight to voice mail—which is full. *What the hell is wrong with these people? No one needs to receive a goddamn message?*

I send them each an urgent text. But I can't tell if either message was received. Communicating from forty-one thousand feet is a bitch. *Why am I always on a damn plane when there's a crisis?*

The prime minister's daughter killed—*murdered* is the correct word—with an armed guard protecting her. A mile from home. Lexie's next.

A chill runs down my spine. *If it hasn't already happened.*

I'm about ready to jump out of my skin when I reach Zé. "Has Lexie left?"

He told me earlier that she was gone, and I was happy to hear it. At least that's what I told myself. Now I'm hoping against hope that he was mistaken. I'm grasping at straws. But I don't know what else to do.

"She left some time ago. Probably in the air by now."

*Probably* isn't good enough. I need to know where she is with certainty. Even then it might not be enough to calm my gut.

"I can't reach her or her father. Neither are answering their phones or responding to messages. Are we sure she's on her way to London?"

"As sure as anyone can be about anything with her."

"Cut the fucking shit, Zé," I shout. "Francesca Russo was murdered tonight, and I don't have the patience for your little digs about Lexie."

"She was murdered?" he asks, just above a whisper.

"Along with an experienced guard, not far from where the Russos live. She was meeting the same boyfriend she was supposed to meet in Porto."

"It's those bastards," he replies, his voice barely controlled.

No doubt in my mind. "We need to warn Will and Lexie. She's in danger." *A fuck-ton of danger.* "Can you activate the tracker in her phone and the one in the anklet?"

"Give me a minute."

*I won't be happy unless that signal shows her safely locked in a room inside her parents' house with no way to escape.*

"I'm getting nothing from the phone."

*Goddamn it. I knew she'd find the damn thing and disable it.* "What about the jewelry?"

"The signal from the tracker in the anklet has her upstairs in your apartment. She must have left it."

"Go upstairs and look around. Maybe she's not gone."

"Giana put her in the car," he replies softly.

"Fucking humor me, Zé."

"I'm on my way up, but listen. You're a target too."

"I'm on a damn plane forty-one thousand feet over the Atlantic Ocean. If it's been sabotaged, it's a little late now to do anything about it."

Zé's quiet on the other end. *Plane disappears over the Atlantic —a plane I should have been on, but fate intervened.* He's heard this story before—it doesn't have a happy ending.

We've been friends for more than twenty-five years, like brothers, but this isn't just about me. Tamar's on this plane too.

"I won't take any risks with Tamar. You have my word."

"I know you won't," he barks. "That's why I was pissed you were taking her and not me. You can never remember that you're the protectee, Rafael. She's a soldier."

*She's a soldier. Right.* Tamar's highly trained, but she's more than just a soldier. She's his woman.

I hear a door slam through the phone. "She's not here," he says quietly. Zé's not a fan of Lexie, but there's great empathy in his voice.

*He knew how much I wanted her to be there. How much I needed her to be there.*

"The anklet is on the nightstand."

*Fuck. Fuck. Fuck. Fuck. Fuck.* It's a punch to the gut, and even though I expected it, the blow is painful.

"I know they're not picking up, but did you try to email Will or Alexis?"

"Not yet. It's the middle of the night in Europe—only people like you and me are awake. Lexie's phone is off. But I'll leave them messages when we get off."

"I'll get Sirena secured."

Thankfully, Sirena is buttoned up for the night. The worst that could happen is an empty building would blow up. *Not the worst.* "Warn the guards around the club to stay on high alert, not just for the property, for their own safety as well." I'm not ready to lose Sirena to those sons of bitches, but I don't want a single casualty.

"Let me know if you need anything else."

"Yeah."

I call Will as soon as I hang up with Zé. Now there's an

automated message: *The customer is unavailable.* The fucker blocked me.

I try Lexie again, but her phone is still off. I email her: *I have information about the traffickers. It's a matter of life and death. Contact me as soon as you get this.*

# 57

## RAFAEL

I RUSH to the conference room where Tamar is working. "Get any information you can on a flight plan filed by Clarke Enterprises. The flight originated in Porto and the destination is likely London, but we're not certain. I want to know if and when the plane took off, and where it was headed. If it's not filed under Clarke Enterprises, try William Clarke. The manifest should have Alexis Clarke as a passenger."

*She's in the air,* I keep telling myself, as though that always works out well. I wanted Will to know about Francesca so he could make sure there was extra security when Lexie lands. It'll be more difficult from here, but I can arrange extra security for her too—as soon as we know the particulars.

Tamar pounds on the keyboard relentlessly.

"Anything?" I ask, apprehension coiling in my chest.

"It looks like the flight plan was originally filed with London as the destination and Alexis is indeed listed as a passenger. But—"

"But what?" I snarl impatiently.

"It's been modified."

"In what way?"

"That's what I'm trying to figure out. I see the modification code, but that's it."

"What does the code tell us?"

"Only that the destination has been changed. It can take a while before the system updates."

*Lexie, where the hell are you going? There's danger waiting for you, and I'm on a fucking plane where I can't do a damn thing to save you.*

I'm raw, and my damn stomach is a cauldron of acid eating at the lining.

It's my fault she left Porto. I was furious—I'm still mad as hell—but she brought something to my life that no other woman ever has. She made me want to stay, even when every instinct was telling me to run. But it doesn't matter how she makes me feel. I can't live with someone like her—*I can't love someone like her. I can't.*

That doesn't excuse my behavior. I didn't need to let the fury consume me, until it erupted and drenched us both in vitriol. But it wasn't all rage. There were a myriad of emotions spinning inside—some so unfamiliar, I can't name them.

*What if those monsters are waiting for her when the plane lands? What if they already got to her? She could be dead, or they might have abducted her. I might never see her again. I might never fucking know what happened to her. No! I won't let that happen. I won't survive that hell again.*

"Anything new?" I growl at Tamar.

"No."

*She looks like an angel when she's sleeping. Curled up on her side, as peace claims her, quieting her noisy brain. My Angel. She'll always be my Angel.*

"I don't understand why they—"

*Angel. Angel wings.* Maybe she left the anklet, but took the wings. *Just another straw to grasp. Don't care.*

"Tamar, can you activate a tracking device from here?"

"Sure. What am I looking for?"

"Lexie's on a flight destined for—somewhere. It's a long shot, but she might have a tracking device on her. One of the new prototypes that can be retrofitted into a piece of jewelry."

"A tracking device on land is one thing." She glances at me warily. "But we'll need a satellite to track something on a moving plane."

*A satellite?* "Where the hell are we going to get a satellite?"

"I know where to find one, but if we're caught, it's going to cost you. Not money, but a big favor to a foreign agency. Maybe even to a foreign country."

"Whatever it takes."

I don't ask a single damn question about the satellite while Tamar sends a message. I assume it's to someone affiliated with her old agency. I don't care—to ensure Lexie's safety, I'd make a deal with the devil himself.

While we wait to hear back, I take out my phone and pull up the information about the tracker on the angel wings. *I'm the only one who has it. The wings were between me and her. Our special thing. I didn't even share it with Zé.*

"We're set," she says, "but it's going to take a little time for the stars to align."

"How much time?"

"Five or ten minutes. In the meantime, give me the tracking information."

"Here." I hold my phone while she inputs the data, my eyes glued to the clock on the computer screen. Five minutes come and go.

"It's activated," she announces exactly six minutes later. "It'll need another minute or two before it can get us the codes we need to proceed."

"Put it up on the monitor," I instruct, pointing to the large screen on the wall.

*You don't even know if she has the wings with her. Maybe she dumped them in the trash on her way out.*

While I wait, I pray the signal won't come from somewhere in my damn apartment. It's been so long since I prayed, that I've almost forgotten how. I'm not a believer, but I'd get on my goddamn knees and kiss a ring if I thought it would help me find her.

"Look," Tamar says, relief resounding in her voice. "The plane's over the Atlantic, skirting the European coast. It's definitely not on its way to London," she adds. "Or if it is, it's taking a strange route. Right now, it looks like it's headed toward northern France. But that could change."

"Northern France? What the hell?" I stare at the blip on the screen. It's so much more than a blinking point on a map. *It's everything.*

*They have her. The monsters have her.*

I can't think. My mind is racing in circles. Chasing all sorts of nightmare scenarios. *I'm never going to see her again.* I kick over a chair, and Tamar startles.

*Pull yourself together, Rafael. You're not going to be able to help her like this.*

I clasp my fingers behind my neck and dig my thumbs into the muscle until it groans. "Okay." I draw a breath. "Let's go through what we know.

"Lexie boarded a plane in Porto with a flight plan filed for London. Somewhere en route, the flight plan was modified." *I've done this myself many times.* "And a code indicates that the destination was changed."

"Maybe to northern France," Tamar adds, "but we don't know for sure. Why do you need her location?" she asks.

*Fuck. I haven't briefed her.* I was in the cabin when I spoke with Zé, and she was here.

"Do you remember Francesca Russo?"

She nods.

"She was murdered earlier today."

"You think the flesh traders are involved?"

"I do."

"Alexis has guards with her," Tamar assures me. "Giana contacted me earlier. She wondered if I needed her to do anything. She had some downtime because Ms. Clarke had her own security when she left."

*A lot of good security did the Russo girl.* "Did she say anything else?"

Tamar shakes her head. "No. But I doubt Will Clarke has fools protecting his daughter."

*Don't bet on it.*

"Francesca Russo was killed along with an experienced guard. These bastards don't fuck around."

My eyes and my heart are trained on the screen, studying the small dot as though my life depends on it. *In many ways, it does.*

*Where are you, Lexie?* Maybe it's somewhere totally innocuous, but that's not what my gut's telling me.

I go over to the screen on the wall and touch my fingertip to the lit speck, blinking on an image that represents her plane. I touch it gently, like it's Lexie herself. *I'm coming for you, Angel. I'll find you wherever you are.*

When I lift my trembling finger, the tiny dot is no longer blinking. It's gone. *Gone.*

"Tamar!"

"We lost her," she replies, the strain in her voice palpable as she bangs on the keys.

"The satellite or her tracking device?" My heart pounds ruthlessly against my chest wall while I await a response.

"The satellite is still online. It's functioning. We lost the tracking device."

"What about the plane?" I demand, eyes glued to the large monitor, searching for any sign of Lexie. "I don't see the plane." She shakes her head frantically. "It's gone."

———

THANK YOU FOR READING PRIDE! For more of Rafael and Lexie's story, find WRATH HERE

# ABOUT THE AUTHOR

Eva Charles is the *USA Today* bestselling author of steamy romantic suspense with dangerous billionaires and strong heroines.

When she's not writing, trying to squeeze information out of her tight-lipped sons, or playing with the two naughtiest dogs you've ever met, Eva's creating chapters in her own love story.

*Sign-up for my monthly newsletter for special treats and all the Eva news!*
Eva's VIP Reader Newsletter

*I'd love to hear from you!*
eva@evacharles.com

# MORE STEAMY ROMANTIC SUSPENSE...

## A SINFUL EMPIRE SERIES
### TRILOGY (COMPLETE)

Greed

Lust

Envy

### DUET

Pride

Wrath

## THE DEVIL'S DUE (SERIES COMPLETE)

Depraved

Delivered

Bound

Decadent

## *CONTEMPORARY ROMANCE*
## NEW AMERICAN ROYALS

Sheltered Heart

Noble Pursuit

Double Play

Unforgettable

Loyal Subjects

Sexy Sinner

Made in United States
Troutdale, OR
12/02/2023

15236922R00193